Death Caller

Clay Warrior Stories
Book #13

J. Clifton Slater

Death Caller is a work of fiction and part of the continuing Clay Warrior Stories series. Any resemblance to persons living or dead is purely coincidental. I am not an historian although I do extensive research. This book is about the levied, seasonal Legion of the mid-Republic and not the fulltime Imperial Legion. There are huge differences.

The large events in this tale are from history, but the dialogue and close action sequences are my inventions. Some of the elements in the story are from reverse engineering mid-Republic era techniques and procedures. No matter how many sources I consulted, history always has holes between events. Hopefully, you will see the logic in my methods of filling in the blanks.

Hollis Jones has attacked the manuscript for Death Caller multiple times. With each assault, she and her red pen have tightened and adjusted the story. Her editing notes are the reason the story makes sense and flows. For her work and, sometimes not so gentle insistence on changes, I am grateful.

Bravo! You have read a dozen books in this series and have made Alerio's adventures a success. This book is lucky #13. I hope you avoid the wrath of ancient gods while reading it or, at least, end up on the winning side.

Euge, to you!

Website: www.JCliftonSlater.com

Email: GalacticCouncilRealm@gmail.com

Death Caller

Act 1

With no separation between religion and government, priests were ubiquitous during the administration of the Republic and in daily life. They generally served in one of two capacities. Some clerics told officials how to worship the Gods and Goddesses to get the most favors from the deities. Others, called Augurs, interpreted signs from the deities and translated the meanings. Whether ceremonial sacrifice or word of God, no one in a command capacity would perform any action without consulting a priest.

Thucydides of Athens, 430 B.C. - "Whatever comes from God is impossible for a man to turn back."

Ship Captains assisted by priests sacrificed and prayed before starting a journey and prayed again at the end of the voyage. Military Commanders along with priests offered sacrifices to the deities asking for success in battle. Afterward, Legion Commanders and priests made public displays in front of the Legionaries thanking the Gods and Goddesses for victory.

However, before ships sailed or Legions marched, the Senate debated foreign affairs and treaty negotiations. For help, the Senate required guidance from a God. Who better than Jupiter, the Sky Father? And to interpret the God of Good Faith and Thunder, the Fetial-Priests from Jupiter's Temple were called to translate Jupiter's words on foreign affairs. In the process of speaking for the divine, the Fetiales gained exceptional power and prestige.

Plato of Athens, 388 B.C. – "The measure of a man is what he does with power."

As custodians of an emerging Mediterranean power, Rome's Senators found themselves dealing with a list of growing problems. One of the issues was evolving the Legions to meet the demands. Once limited to regional garrisons with the ability to create four marching Legions when threatened, the expanding foreign involvement required activation of the four marching Legions every year. Training and equipping the Legions created a burgeoning industry. Unfortunately, the Republic's military held tightly to tradition. Thus, they attempted to manage the changes without modifying their systems.

Welcome to Spring, 258 B.C.

Chapter 1 – My Good Deal

"You will keep up with the oxen and keep the line straight or I will beat every third man," a voice threatened. "Now, get back to work."

"What about noon rest and food?" an older worker inquired.

Sweat dripped off the old man's face and neck. Using a rag, he wiped his forehead while peering up at the sun. The glistening on his skin highlighted his thin frame, adding to his already starving appearance.

"Your noon repast is the seeds trampled underfoot by the laggards," the farm manager bellowed. After a moment, he bristled as of someone had called him an insulting name. Then he charged down the line. "I'll just have to make an example of you."

The overseer reached the old man and clubbed him to the dirt with a single blow. When he raised the truncheon for another bash, a youth, barely large enough to be a planter, raced to stand between the boss and the old man.

"I said I'd beat every third man," the overseer sneered at the boy. "But you'll do."

He drew his arm back, cocked his wrist, and brought the club around. Before it reached the lad, a forearm, marred with a scar from a knife blade, slammed into the manager's elbow.

His arm and the club shot up with force enough that the overseer was jerked to the side. His large gut twisted as tight as the animal sinew on a bolt thrower. And, like a ballista released, the torsion spring of his gut unwound and pulled his broad shoulders and the club back around. In every fight, the quickness of the big man surprised his victims. Unwinding, he aimed the backhanded swing at the interloper's head.

Most farm workers would stand in shock at having touched the overseer. Or they would step back trying to avoid the knob of wood at the end of the club. But the farm worker who shoved the arm stepped up.

When the manager rotated back, Alerio Sisera ducked under the club, stood, and shoved his nose into the overseer's face.

"I would stop right there, Ipsimus," Alerio warned.

"You are a dead man, cūlus," the farm boss cursed. "You will not be good for riding a mule to Tusculum after I thrash you."

3

"Ipsimus, for a swindler, you aren't very smart," Alerio suggested to the overseer.

"Teamsters get over here," Ipsimus called to the men on the seed cart and the manure wagon.

Without taking his eyes from the overseer, Alerio's arm shot out and, with an open hand, pointed towards the animal handlers.

"Life is hard enough already," he cautioned the teamsters. "Come over here and it will become unbearable."

Handlers who worked with beasts developed animal sense. Part of it was knowing the difference between an animal that would accept the lash and an alpha that would fight against the abuse. Based on the scars, muscles, and the attitude of the man facing Ipsimus, they recognized his type.

"Not our fight," the teamsters begged off.

"I don't need them to…" Ipsimus didn't finish.

In mid-sentence, he snapped his wrist and swung the club at Alerio.

The garden spade in Tribune Sisera's hand arched up, blocked, and then knocked the club off to the side.

"Don't you realize I am holding an edged tool," Alerio pointed out. "You really aren't…"

Alerio flipped the spade and positioned the handle, so it protruded from below his fist. With a single blow, he knocked Ipsimus to the ground. Sprawled on the planted soil, the overseer blinked to clear his vision and watched for his next opportunity to attack.

"When the Goddess Minerva runs her fingers through your mind," Alerio remarked to the overseer, "one should listen."

Twice Alerio had thought the farm manager was a bull and not overly intelligent. The second time Alerio had to block the man's attack with no acknowledgement of the feat or respect for his opponent, Alerio realized the significance of the notion. Ipsimus did not have the brains to back away from a losing fight or to mastermind stealing from the farm.

"What do I care if your personal deity is the Goddess of Wisdom and Defense," Ipsimus remarked.

"You are lucky it was Minerva prompting me," Alerio stated. He kicked the club from Ipsimus' grip. "Because if it was my Goddess, I would have used the sharp edge of the spade."

***

The farm manager sucked in air and stumbled. Alerio took his arm and guided Ipsimus across the field to the backdoor of the farmhouse.

"You need some conditioning," Alerio observed.

They moved through an equipment storage space before stepping into the great room.

"What are we doing here?" the overseer asked. "I have seeds to get in the soil."

"Not anymore you don't," Alerio told him.

"Who do you think you are?" Ipsimus demanded.

A woman stepped through an archway and replied from the other side of the great room, "Why overseer, that is my son, Alerio Carvilius Sisera."

"Lady Carvilius. I didn't see you," Ipsimus begged.

5

"Or shower me with honesty," Aquila accused. "My son has uncovered discrepancies coloring your management of the farm in a sickly pale light."

"I protest," Ipsimus said switching from humility to indignation. "The Maximus farm has been profitable every year I have been in charge."

"True," Alerio acknowledged, "the farm has been profitable. But the story between the lines of the ledger tells a different tale."

"There is your answer," Ipsimus pointed out. "I don't do the accounting. If there are issues with the numbers, you cannot blame me. Ask Mystacis if there are mistakes."

"The accountant is in the Capital explaining his numbers to Belen and an accountant scholar," Alerio told the manager. "You are here to tell me who is really in charge of the farm."

Aquila coughed politely into her hand.

"Lady Carvilius, please feel free to comment," Alerio urged his adopted mother.

"I don't mean to interfere in your investigation," Aquila offered. "But I had assumed Ipsimus was managing the farm."

"In person maybe, Lady Carvilius, but he is getting instructions from someone else," Alerio informed her. "How did General Maximus come to hire Ipsimus?"

"I do wish you would call him father," Aquila requested. "Or at least Spurius."

"I apologize, old habits are hard to put behind me," Alerio explained. "You were saying about the farm boss."

6

"Overseer Ipsimus came to us when our former manager left to run his brother's farm. The priest at the Temple of Jupiter recommended him," she told Alerio. "Not the one in the Capital. Jupiter's Temple here in Alban Hills. Cleric Evandrus is the priest."

"The Honorable Evandrus is not a man to cross," Ipsimus advised. "Why make a big affair of him collecting a fee for his guidance. What's the harm in that?"

From the backdoor, a voice called into the farmhouse.

"Ipsimus. Someone reported you taking a worker into the house," one of the farm guards commented. "Is everything alright?"

The farm manager, emboldened by the support of the guard, stepped close to Alerio, and puffed out his chest.

"I'll be leaving now," he said. With one hand he untied a pouch from Alerio's belt. Then he approached Aquila. Bending his face close to hers, he sniffed her perfume. "You'll excuse me, but that necklace looks valuable."

Ipsimus' hand reached for Lady Carvilius' throat. Before his dirty fingers could touch the jewelry, Alerio kicked the manager's legs out from under him. Both feet slipped on the tile and the man fell, hard.

"No, please," Aquila gasped.

The farm manager grunted before snarling, "I'm going to…"

He stopped talking in mid threat. His focus shifted from pushing off the floor to the tip of the dagger poking him between the eyes.

"Thank her," Alerio instructed.

Ipsimus assumed the 'no, please' was a delayed reaction to his attempted theft of the necklace.

"Thank her for what?" Ipsimus demanded. "Having you come around and ruin my good deal."

"The last man to threaten my adopted mother, I gutted," Alerio described to the manager. "She just spared your life."

"Who are you?"

"Tribune Sisera, Legion raider and weapon's instructor," Alerio replied.

"I have nine loyal men at the backdoor," Ipsimus warned. "You can't take us all on."

"I've faced worse odds," Alerio assured him.

From outside, the sounds of a horse trotting up to the front of the farmhouse reached the great room.

"Who is that?" Aquila inquired.

"I believe it's twenty Legionaries and a Centurion," Alerio responded. He stepped back. "You can stand Ipsimus."

The farm manager pushed off the floor and righted himself.

"I'm leaving," Ipsimus declared.

"You are correct," Alerio said. "You and your men are going to Ostia. The fleet needs rowers."

"I'm not a slave," Ipsimus bragged. "I am a citizen of the Republic."

8

"That's a good thing because the fleet cannot spare Legionaries to guard slaves," Alerio informed him. "You'll be paid and fed. But you will be among strong men. Try to raise a club to a group of oarsmen on a warship and they will hurt you."

A pair of hobnailed boots clicking on the tile floor preceded the entrance of a Centurion.

"Tribune Sisera?" a scarred, limping combat officer asked.

"I'm Sisera," Alerio replied, "and this is Lady Carvilius. Your new boss."

Chapter 2 – A Worthy Donation

"I've been told Centurion Accantus is a decorated officer and a cultivator of grapes," Alerio explained to his adopted mother.

"Unfortunately, I have a bad hip and can no longer march with the Legion," Accantus remarked. "Battle Commander Claudius had pity and allowed me to do training. But now, he's traded me for Tribune Sisera."

"Excuse me? Traded," Aquila questioned, "like horses?"

"No ma'am. It's more comparable to swapping skills," Accantus clarified for the lady. "I am an experienced manager and grower. When Colonel Claudius heard, your son would have to manage the Maximus farm, he decided there were better uses for our talents."

"If you've come to manage the farm," Aquila asked. "What is my son going to be doing?"

"The Colonel just said he needed the opinion of a staff officer he trusted," Alerio replied. "Let's assume, it is a good assignment."

The Lady Carvilius' eyes glossed over for a moment before she turned her full attention to the Centurion.

"Accantus, you are an experienced grower of grapes," she commented. "I've always wanted a vineyard. Is that possible?"

"I have to warn you, Lady Carvilius," Accantus explained. "You'll need land on a higher elevation, and it will take four or more years before you have grapes worth pressing."

"Alerio?" Aquila asked.

"I'll write and have Belen buy the hills to the east of the farm," he promised. "Then after a stop, I need to report to the Legion."

"After what stop?" Aquila questioned.

"After the Maximus family makes a donation at the Temple of Jupiter," Alerio responded.

"Are we doing that?" she inquired.

"Yes ma'am, we are," Alerio told her. "In a manner of speaking."

***

Alerio Sisera nudged the chestnut stallion and the big horse responded. Together, they trotted along the lane. Glancing to his right, Alerio studied the empty fields. Soon, crops would grow, turning the land green and golden. The Maximus farm stretched from the farmhouse to the property line five miles away. Soon, once Belen received the letter, the farm would encompass the hills beyond the border.

They reached a larger trail and Alerio reined in the horse and stopped. To his right was the community of Tusculum and the Maximus country estate. He was tempted to visit Aquila Carvilius and say goodbye. Instead, Alerio guided Phobos to the left and allowed the horse to pick his gait. They rode in the shadow of a summit for part of the morning.

At a main artery, he directed Phobos to the left. Had he gone right, they would have intercepted the Via Latina and been on a course to the Capital, some nineteen miles to the north.

Not much further south, he took the horse off the road and started up a twisting and climbing path. Nine hundred feet above the plain, the Temple of Jupiter at Alban Hills nearly touched the sky. It was fitting for the King of Gods to have a view of the surrounding landscape. And while the Temple was visible to those far away, on the trail through the forest, the walls were hidden by the trees.

***

Phobos rounded a switchback and, suddenly, the grade flattened and ran straight. At the top of the slope, the trail widened into a carriage parking lot just outside the walls of the temple.

"Welcome to the Temple of Jupiter, traveler," a young celebrant greeted Alerio. "I will rub down and feed your horse while you pay homage to the God."

"Do you do that for a lot of people?" Alerio asked while handing the youth a coin.

"For everyone who comes up that hill," the cleric in training replied. "It's a steep climb."

"He bites and kicks," Alerio warned. "But I'll pay double if you have him pampered and ready to go when I come back."

After accepting another coin, the apprentice cleric promised to have Phobos waiting. Alerio marched to the gate and into the Temple of Jupiter.

**

"What does that mean?" Cleric Evandrus demanded.

Alerio stood in front of the priest holding out both hands with the palms up. A Legion dagger spanned one hand while a single gold coin rested on the other.

"Read the inscription," Alerio urged while extending the hand holding the dagger.

The Priest of Jupiter bent and studied the letters etched on the blade.

"Memento Mori. Is that a threat?" the priest questioned.

"Not at all," Alerio assured him. "It's just a reminder that the Goddess Nenia visits everyone. Because, in the end, we all will die."

"It feels like a threat," Evandrus described. "What is your name and what do you want?"

"My name is not important," Alerio stated. "What I want is for you to take this offering of five gold coins."

"You are mistaken, sir," the priest pointed out. "There is only one coin in your hand."

"Look with your black, scoundrel's heart," Alerio instructed, "and visualize the other four. Then produce them from the coins you fleeced from the Carvilius Maximus farm."

"The Senate has voted two bills that mark further changes," Claudius explained while ignoring Alerio's question. "They voted Aquillius Florus as Proconsul of Sicilia. It's the first step in making the island a territory and a prerequisite before assigning a Governor."

"That is serious," Alerio offered. "But what does it have to do with me, sir?"

Claudius held up a finger, took a sip, and continued, "The other piece of the directive is to fund a half Legion for Sicilia."

"A fulltime Legion?" Alerio inquired. "Like the regional garrisons?"

"Fifteen hundred permanent infantrymen and officers in Sicilia. But only a half Legion," Claudius reminded Alerio. "We're not sure if it will be an addition to the Southern Legion. Or a new outfit all together. No matter what the Senate decides, Central Legion has been tasked with training the new Legionaries."

"And that's why this camp looks temporary," Alerio ventured. "Am I here to train the recruits?"

"We have the room, facilities, and ranges to train a half Legion," Claudius detailed. "Except, the Senate has not released the funds. All this is ready and yet we are training one ten-man contubernium at a time. In reply to your insistent questions, you are not here to train Legionaries."

"I'm going to Sicilia to train the new Centuries?" Alerio inquired.

"No," Claudius responded.

Being out of questions, Alerio took a sip and waited for the Battle Commander.

"With the growth of the Legion comes unverified officers," Colonel Claudius described. "Some are proving to be less than competent."

"We've always had Centurions and Tribunes who gain a position but don't measure up," Alerio stated. "Usually, the Legion sorts them out."

"Things are happening too fast for the normal weeding out process," Claudius described. "Gaius Sulpicius Paterculus and Atilius Calatinus, our new Consuls, want an inspection."

"Inspection for what and where, sir?" Alerio asked.

"Profiteering off Legion supplies, scams, and outright theft," Claudius listed. "As to where? Every place a Legion or a fleet is forming."

"For fleet and Legion supplies, Ostia has the most activity," Alerio proposed. "When do I meet the inspection team, sir?"

"If Tribune Sisera and a wagon full of accountants roll in," the Battle Commander pointed out, "the rats will cover their tracks and go into hiding until you leave."

"Then how am I supposed to inspect the Legions, sir?" Alerio questioned.

"The same way you hid from being a staff officer when you came into my office," Gaius Claudius told him. "Undercover and in disguise."

"Any suggestions on my covert identity, Colonel?" Alerio asked.

"None at all," Claudius responded. "As I said in my letter, I need the opinion of a staff officer I trust."

The Battle Commander handed over a folded piece of paper coated in wax.

"What's this, sir," Alerio asked while balancing the waterproof missive on the palm of his hand.

"That is your authorization from the Consuls," Claudius replied. "It's sealed because the letter pardons you for any crime less than treason. And even then, it is open to interpretation. Do not show the letter unless it is necessary."

"How serious is the theft, Colonel?" Alerio inquired while still holding the letter.

"The Republic is moving thousands in trade goods and massive amounts of coins to feed, pay, and house the Legions and the fleet," Claudius responded. "It doesn't take much for dishonorable men to become dangerously greedy."

"You'll store my armor and gear here, sir?" Alerio requested.

"I certainly have the space," Claudius confirmed. Then he asked. "What else do you need, Tribune Sisera?"

"An old horse, a two wheeled cart," Alerio answered. He peered down at his hobnailed boots and added, "and a pair of broken in sandals."

Act 2

Chapter 4 – The River of Forgetfulness

The horse had years on her as did the old cart. Balanced over the axle of the two wheeled transport and centered between six barrels, the teamster nodded with the bumping of the cart and the gait of the mare.

"You sleep around here, and you will end up looking for your rig," a voice called from another wagon.

Peering out from under his hood, Alerio eyed the other porter.

"And what about you?" he inquired.

The other man held the reins loose between his fingers as he sprawled on his back. His head positioned comfortably on sacks of grain with a view of the sky and not the road.

"It'll be a sad day when brigands can get the better of Hamus Ivo," the other driver declared. He kicked his legs, swung them off the grain sacks, and dangled his feet over the side. "Say, you aren't one of Tristis' lads, are you?"

"I don't know," Alerio admitted, "who is he?"

"If you were, you would know," Hamus decided after a moment. "He is a transport agent in Ostia."

"Having an agent sounds like a good idea," Alerio offered. "My name is Sisera."

Without directions, the horses moved off the road and onto an open field. Hamus did not seem alarmed, so Alerio allowed his mare to follow the other horse. They stopped next to a stream.

"What are you hauling?" Hamus inquired.

He hopped down and walked around to the horse and set planks under the shafts. With the load supported, Hamus unharnessed his horse.

"Barrels of spearheads," Alerio responded as he blocked his cart and freed the mare.

"Ah, a military contract," Hamus Ivo said with a hint of envy. "Sisera, are you sure you aren't one of Tristis' drivers?"

"The load is a favor from my old Optio in the Capital," Alerio half lied. The contract for the barrels was from a Sergeant, but as a favor to Colonel Claudius. "I asked him where a man could earn some honest coins. He pointed me towards Ostia. And supplied me with a load to get me started."

"What is he paying you?" Hamus inquired.

"A half bronze per mile," Alerio told him.

Both men pulled oat bags from trunks mounted on the shafts behind the horses. The location of the boxes kept their personal gear dry and off the valuable space of the cargo bed.

"I hate to tell you, but you got cheated," Hamus informed Alerio while he fed his horse. "You should have gotten at least two bronze per mile. But now I know."

"Know what?" Alerio asked.

"That you aren't one of Tristis' gang," Hamus replied.

"I thought he was a broker?"

"Oh, he is. But there are rumors," Hamus remarked. "I have dried beef. Dinner is on me as I am getting two and twenty-five bronze for the trip."

"Nineteen miles of travel," Alerio did the math. "That's four silver and two and seventy-five bronze. I agree, you should provide dinner."

"You cook, and I'll explain how we independent transporters survive," Hamus exclaimed. He pulled a package out of his trunk and handed it to Alerio. "The first rule, never take less than two bronze per mile."

"What's the second rule?" Alerio inquired. He stacked firewood then struck steel to flint.

"Never take more than a silver per mile," Hamus warned.

"Who would pay ten bronze per mile?" Alerio questioned.

"From what I hear, Tristis does," Hamus told him. "For overnight hauling, once the Legion sentries let down their guard."

"That's a lot of coins," Alerio suggested, "for hauling a load."

"But is it worth your life?" Hamus questioned. "Because if the Legionaries catch you, you'll enjoy sunrise at the top of a cross."

"Along with the sentries who were asleep at their post," Alerio added.

Sisera thought as he prepared the meal. Taking did not become theft until the pilfered items were moved away from their rightful place. He may not have a hint who was organizing the stealing of Legion supplies. Or who was buying the illicit merchandise. But he had a possible lead on the transporter. And that was a good start.

Happy to have made progress before reaching Ostia, Alerio busied himself with fixing the meal. He added water to the vegetables to boil them, and to the biscuits to soften them.

"You were in the Legion," Hamus observed. "I can tell by the comment about the guards being punished and the way you cook. Proficient with no wasted effort. Sicilia?"

"No. I was up north in garrison," Alerio lied. "Mostly we chased outlaws."

**

The next afternoon, Alerio continued towards the military base while Hamus turned off.

"There's an empty lot on the north side of town," Hamus called as his cart headed into Ostia. "If you don't discover better accommodations, come camp with me. You can buy dinner."

"And you will cook?" Alerio asked.

"I am a terrible cook," Hamus Ivo admitted.

Alerio guided the horse further down the road. At the main gate, he turned the rig onto an open area across from a pair of sentries. From his vantage point, he could see the sprawling military complex. Besides the two Legionaries standing guard duty, two off duty infantrymen were loitering at the gate.

"Delivery for the armory," Alerio told the sentries.

"How much do you guys make sitting on your tail?" one of the idle infantrymen asked.

He swaggered across the road, moved behind the cart, and peered between barrels at the teamster.

"I made nine and a half bronze for the trip down from the Capital," Alerio answered.

"Sitting all the way," the Legionary pointed out. "I made six and a sixty-sixth bronze over two days. But I ran twenty miles this morning."

"Buy a healthy horse and a fine cart," Alerio offered. "Then you too can be a wealthy man."

"Are you saying you are better than me?" the infantryman challenged.

Legionaries were trained to fight. The aggression and lack of fear driven into their hearts and minds came out at odd times. It seemed Alerio was facing one of those instances.

As a weapon's instructor, Alerio could teach the young man the error of poking at an unknown enemy. Or as a Legion officer, he could beat sense into the infantryman. But as an independence porter, he needed to remain meek.

"I apologize if I gave you that impression," Alerio begged. "Please accept my word that I meant no harm or insult."

"You aren't such a big deal now, are you?" the Legionary sneered.

While they talked, the second loitering infantryman strolled to the side of the cart. When he reached between barrels and grabbed, Alerio rolled over backward to avoid the hands.

As Alerio's feet arched over, he made a slight adjustment in the position of the balls of his feet and rapped the first infantryman in the forehead. The Legionary hit the ground as Alerio rolled out of the cart.

"Excuse me," Alerio gasped in shock. He bent down and offered a hand. Except the hand became a fist and unseen by the two on duty, he punched the man in the temple. Dazed, the infantryman rolled over and moaned.

The other Legionary came at Alerio.

"Help," Alerio yelped. "There's something wrong with him..."

The Legionary lowered his shoulder, turned the corner of the cart, and rushed at Alerio.

"He needs help," Alerio shrieked loud enough for the two men on sentry duty to hear.

Sidestepping the charging infantryman, Alerio wrapped an arm around the man's neck while punching him in the gut. The Legionary stumbled but with Alerio's help, he stopped and stood over the groaning man on the ground.

"Listen to me," Alerio threatened. He pounded his fist into the infantryman's midsection again. "I am not going to kill you. But if you harass me again, it will be my knife in your side and not my fist."

The infantryman vomited all over his partner. Feeling the wet, warm chunks, the man on the ground began crawling away.

"Help! He's ill," Alerio summoned the guards. "Come here. Help him."

Both jogged across the road just as Alerio eased the infantryman to the dirt.

"Look, I've been on the road for two days," Alerio pleaded. "Can you point me to the armory?"

While one of the sentries tended to the two Legionaries, the other pointed to the supply area.

"Thank you," Alerio said.

He did not bother climbing back into the cart. Taking the reins, Alerio snapped the leather straps from beside the cart. Then, he and the horse walked into the Legion post.

Behind the teamster, an Optio marched from a building. A big man with a nose broken too many times, the NCO appeared relaxed until he caught sight of the sentry post. Seeing two men on the ground and his sentries out of position, the NCO ran to see what was wrong at the gate.

Relief flooded Alerio from having dodged a confrontation with the Sergeant of the Guard. While Alerio could explain himself, he knew the Optio would back men from his Century over a civilian porter. Brawling at the main gate was not a great way to stay undercover or healthy.

Unfortunately for Alerio, the loyalty of the Optio with the crooked nose extended beyond his duty as the Sergeant of the Guard.

***

The military camp had grown. From a naval base guarding the mouth of the Tiber river, it spread to include permanent fortifications against an invasion and structures for housing men and warehouses for supplying ships and Legions.

"What do you have?" a Centurion asked.

Alerio pulled the reins. The horse and cart stopped in front of a long building.

"Barrels of steel spearheads," Alerio replied. Seeing an odd look on the combat officer's face, he added. "from the Capital, sir."

"I figured as much," the Centurion complained. "What do I need with them? They should have gone to Central Legion for recruit training and equipment. I have metalworkers here who forge everything the fleet and the Marines need."

"The supply Sergeant in Rome said to deliver them to Ostia," Alerio assured the Centurion.

"I don't know what's wrong with the procurement department," the officer mumbled. "They send excess gear and then I have to ship it back. Deliver the barrels to the rear of this building. See the clerk at the depot's shipping and receiving department for payment."

"Thank you, sir," Alerio acknowledged.

On the trip around the building, Alerio admired a garden the supply men had planted. The plot was lined in a double row of large river rocks placed in artistic wavy lines. At the rear, several Legionaries helped unload the six barrels. Once they were rolled into the storage building, Alerio went to the office.

"You are new at this," ventured the clerk after looking over the invoice. "At one bronze per mile, I'm tempted to hire you to transport them back."

"I was told the minimum is two per mile," Alerio countered.

"It could be a half bronze a mile and I still couldn't use you," the clerk admitted. "My Tribune wants us using porters secured by Tristis."

"Where can I find the broker?" Alerio asked.

"In town," the clerk replied. He counted out nine and a half bronze coins, then advised. "Almost any teamster can tell you where to find Tristis."

Alerio's experience with supply consisted of a few weeks working as an officer at a depot. But for most of his career, he performed as an infantryman or a combat officer. Both placed him at the terminus of the supply chain as an end user.

The problem with his load of steel spearheads made him realize the complexity of shipping gear to various units. And the drudgery of having to make good on bad shipments by forwarding the gear to where it rightfully belonged.

He stepped out of the backdoor of the supply building and all thoughts of the supply system faded.

***

Lingering next to his cart were four off duty Legionaries and the Sergeant of the Guard

"Good morning, Optio," Alerio greeted the NCO.

"Is that the porter?" the Sergeant asked.

Unlike the Optio in his armor, the four men wore civilian wool tunics. But their physiques and mannerisms identified them as Legionaries.

"You don't want to do this," Alerio warned.

"That's the teamster, Optio Noxalis," one of the infantrymen confirmed.

"You laid hands on two of my men," Noxalis accused Alerio.

"It was self-defense," Alerio protested, "and I went easy on them."

"Then we'll go easy on you," Noxalis promised. But there was no grace in his tone. "Or we can take your cart and horse."

"On the road from the Capital, I expected to meet bandits," Alerio stated. He took several steps away from the building. "But I never expected to meet Legion robbers in Ostia."

"You hurt my men," Noxalis scoffed. "Now we are going to hurt you."

"That may prove to be more costly than you can imagine," Alerio declared. He tossed off his hooded robe.

From a porter in a long robe, Alerio emerged as a scarred and muscular man. His appearance might have caused a normal citizen to hesitate. But Legionaries were trained to be tough and robust. Alerio's level of fitness and the battle scars had no effect.

The Legionaries spread out and moved towards Alerio. No weapons flashed, so no one countered with a blade of their own. It would be fist and feet. Based on the odds, Alerio assumed a painful aftermath. One positive, he would retain his horse and cart.

In a shield wall, a shoving match, or a group attack, weight matters. As does the absence of mass. Shifting to his left, Alerio lined up on the biggest infantryman. Once the man was down, Alerio stood a better chance against the other three. Provided the Sergeant remained a bystander. If not, then armor mattered.

Big men were accustomed to people avoiding them. As a result, he under reacted when Alerio ran at him. Planting a foot on the large infantryman's hip, Alerio vaulted to his head, dropped an elbow on top, and continued over while the heaviest Legionary crumbled to the ground.

The other three spun to face Alerio.

"What in the lower reaches of Hades is going on here?" a voice demanded.

"Tribune Flamma," Noxalis blurted out. "Like you, sir, I just arrived. You men separate. What is the meaning of this?"

"A case of mistaken identity," Alerio submitted to the staff officer and the NCO. "They thought I was a thief. But I am not, I can assure you, sir."

Tribune Flamma strolled away as if he had not stumbled across the fight.

"You were saved by the river Lethe," Noxalis exclaimed.

"The staff officer has sipped from the river of forgetfulness?" Alerio asked.

"No, he is studious," the NCO replied. "Always has his head in a scroll. Too smart for a Legion officer, if you ask me."

"I'm getting my cart and leaving," Alerio stated.

"This is not over," the Optio threatened. "I'll see you in town sometime. And we will settle this."

Alerio didn't reply. He got the horse in motion before jumping onto the cart. Soon, the warehouse and Legionaries were far behind. The horse trotted through the gate and Alerio guided her towards the town of Ostia.

Chapter 5 - Ingot Iron or Fish Heads

Alerio had a revelation as he rode through the streets of Ostia. Porters were specters. If not complete shadows, they were faceless forms barely rating a second glance. People stepped out of his way, but they also did that for swarms of gnats.

Unnoticed by the population, he urged the mare to a northward running street. At the end, he waved to

Hamus Ivo and headed his rig towards the other teamster's camp.

"Sisera. I thought you would land a military contract and a bed," Hamus teased. "You know, live the good life for a day or so."

"No bed for me, and certainly no Legion commission," Alerio reported while unharnessing his horse. "It seems the supply depot only uses teamsters brokered by Tristis."

"Ingot iron or fish heads," Hamus muttered.

"What?" Alerio inquired. His shoulders and head vanished into the storage box. When he stepped back, he held a package of salted pork and a sack of beans. "I didn't catch what you said."

"One is a heavy load that pays well but requires allegiance to a questionable master," Hamus replied. "The other, a smelly low paying job where you keep your self-respect even as your dignity gets tarnished."

"What's wrong with fish heads?" Alerio asked. He squatted and restacked the logs in the campfire. After a few powerful blows on the embers, the fire caught properly. "Not only can't you cook, but you lack fire building skills."

"Do not insult your host," Hamus scolded. "It's uncivilized."

Alerio glanced at the back of the houses and businesses in the town and the open meadow where they were camped.

"Let me apologize for insulting your grand villa," Alerio offered as he shoved a stick through the pork.

"Apology accepted," Hamus stated.

"That's a first for today," Alerio told him. "You were saying?"

"Fish heads and fish guts smell," Hamus exclaimed, "and after you unload, you must scrub your cart. It's a terrible load."

"At my father's farm, he plows fish heads into fields he is resting," Alerio described. "He finds them as useful as manure."

"Also, not a load most porters want to deliver," Hamus added.

They were silent while the meat cooked. When the skin browned, Alerio cut slices and placed them on plates with the beans.

"I noticed something on the way here," Alerio mentioned as he handed a plate to Hamus. "We are not acknowledged on the streets."

"Like a bird on a branch," Hamus started to explain. He took a bite and declared. "I so hate my own cooking. This is delicious."

"A bird on a branch?" Alerio questioned.

"There are hundreds of birds all around us," Hamus answered. "Yet, you don't notice them unless you are hunting. We are like birds, we fly around."

"If people don't pay attention to us, how do we find work?" Alerio inquired.

"Some submit to a broker," Hamus commented. "Or, if you are independent, you use other methods to be recognized. Me, I sing like a bird."

"Singing," announced Alerio. "I am also fond of singing. Sing us a song."

Hamus Ivo, in a clear high voice, began.

"Hear me administrator
I have an empty cart
You have craftsmen's art
From the bench
Products from forge or loom
Even a tanning room
Delivered to a factory floor
A retail store
or the seashore
From hay to manure
Barrels to iron ore
Regulator be smart
I have an empty cart."

"You are suggesting to businesses how to use your services," Alerio exclaimed. "What a great idea. Sing it again."

"There's more verses because some days are slow and I don't want to be a nuisance," Hamus informed Alerio. "Potential customers should be drawn to my availability. Not driven off by the repetition of my song."

Then he started another verse.

"Hear me administrator
I have an empty cart
And a will to depart
A strong back
A sturdy horse ready to go
But alas no cargo
Not seeking to agitate
Just a crate
Some Freight
Anything to accelerate

All at a fair rate
Regulator have a heart
I have an empty cart."

"Tomorrow, I will sing for my loads," Alerio declared.

"Singing works for me," Hamus confirmed. "Now tell me about your delivery to the Legion complex."

***

The next morning, Alerio and Hamus packed up and drove their rigs into town. Once near a group of commercial businesses, Hamus sang.

"Hear me administrator
I have an empty cart
From here to the mart
Are miles apart."

Proprietors came from their buildings and waved at Hamus.

"Nothing this morning," one promised. "But swing by this afternoon. I'll have a load for the docks."

"I'll be back," Hamus pledged.

Other owners called for him to come back later or tomorrow or the day after.

"I can see the advantage of a fine singing voice," Alerio complimented the porter. "Let me try."

"Have at it, Sisera," Hamus encouraged.

"You have contracts to uphold
Time is a threshold
Don't have your freight wait
I will expiate
For a tiny rate."

"Hold up," Hamus begged. "I just remembered. I have a shipment that needs to be hauled. We should split up."

"Afraid I'll take all of your business," Alerio guessed. "I consider you a friend Ivo and not competition. Out of respect, I'll take my rig and my flowing voice to the docks."

"Yes, yes," Hamus urged. "It's only fair."

"I am blessed of Canens," Alerio explained. "Having the help of the Goddess of beautiful singing truly is an advantage."

"Most unfair," Hamus agreed as he snapped the reins.

Alerio started singing and Hamus hunched his shoulders as if he could discretely cover his ears.

"From your door to the gate
And never late
Regulator be smart
I have an empty cart."

After finishing the verse, Alerio fell silent so as not to attract any of Hamus' customers. Two streets from where he parted with the teamster, three rigs parked at a restaurant drew his attention. He eased the mare to the side of the café and pulled her to a stop.

"Let's see if any of the porters know where I can find this Tristis guy," Alerio suggested to the horse.

He tied her to a post and walked into the eatery.

***

Stacks of vino casks filled one wall and across the room salted hams, cured meats, sausages, and rounds of cheese hung from the ceiling. Between the seasoned

35

wood and the aging delicacies, the aromas caused Alerio's stomach to rumble.

"Quiet, my fine friends. Here's what I propose," Alerio said quoting lines from the Odyssey by the Greek poet Homer. Although in the poem it was Antinous speaking to the suitors', here Alerio spoke to his stomach. He finished the passage as he headed for a table. "These goat sausages sizzling here in the fire, we packed them with fat and blood to have for supper."

His mission briefly forgotten, Alerio sat at the table.

"Sausage and bread," he ordered from the proprietor.

"You'll want watered vino to wash it down," the owner added.

Alerio nodded his agreement while he glanced around the cafe. He was not dependent on the rig for his future. The horse and cart were subterfuge to allow him to move around freely. Oddly enough, the three teamsters in the corner of the restaurant seemed relaxed as if they had nowhere to be. Hamus and other porters Alerio had seen needed to keep moving to make a living. But it didn't seem to apply to the trio in the corner.

The sausage and bread arrived. While he ate, Alerio's focus returned as his belly filled. Once the mission overcame his hunger, Alerio dumped bronze coins on the table and went to converse with the teamsters in the corner.

***

"Excuse, me," Alerio said to the three men. "I'm a porter and I'm looking for a broker named Tristis."

"For a porter you eat good," one remarked.

The man had a burn scar on his right wrist. At some point, he had gotten to close to a glowing hot piece of iron.

"Most men earning a living by the load," another commented, "don't linger over a leisurely breakfast."

"Not to be insulting," Alerio observed. He shifted his feet and bent his legs in case they took offense. "You seem to be honoring Aergia."

Rather than anger, the mention of the Goddess of Laziness and Sloth brought laughter from the men.

"We work for Tristis," the third porter told Alerio. "He pays good and requires we be available when he needs us."

"I'd like to work for him," Alerio stated.

"You don't apply to Tristis," the man with the burn scar informed him. "The broker finds you."

"How does that work?" Alerio asked.

"We were struggling until he pulled us from hauling fish heads and manure," the second porter exclaimed. "Now we haul ingot iron and crates. But like he said. You do not find Tristis. Tristis finds you."

Alerio spun and walked to the entrance. In his mind he turned over the information. There was a universal truth in what the teamsters said. Desperate men will do anything to improve their lot. And a despicable agent could entice them with coins to do his bidding.

The sausage in Alerio's stomach soured because this meant Tribune Sisera had to become desperate. Alerio climbed on his cart and turned the horse down a side street. He had one stop to make before heading to the beach to join the ranks of desperate, dirty, and smelly teamsters.

***

Households had casks of it in storage, businesses stocked barrels of it, and ship's cargo holds were filled with amphorae of the liquid. But few porters, or single men or women, purchased a cask full of vinegar.

"It's good for digestion and to wash wounds," the seller instructed.

"Good to know," Alerio replied as he placed the container in the center of the storage box. Then to himself, he mumbled. "And excellent for scrubbing garbage and filth out of carts."

With the vinegar stored, he flicked the reins, and the mare pulled the rig towards the beach.

Chapter 6 – Haul from the Sea

The horse dropped down a ramp and struggled to pull the cart across the soft dirt. As they neared the water, the gravel and packed sand provided better footing. While moving towards the fish racks, Alerio counted Republic warships. There were two squadrons on the beach, but fewer than half the six thousand oarsmen needed for twenty warships. Hopefully, without the extra rowers to feed, the fishermen would have surplus catch to ship to inland towns.

Ahead he could see three stooped men with worn out horses and badly repaired carts. Here were the desperate teamsters he needed to join.

Higher on the beach, men dumped the morning's haul from the sea on tarps. From the location beside the hot embers under the drying racks, men sorted the fish. Big and medium fish were held for direct selling while the small fish were placed on the drying racks.

"Master fisherman," Alerio called to the group of men tending the fish and fires. "Have you a load for the road?"

"I do. Several in fact," one replied. He separated from the others and approached Alerio. "But before I can load carts, I need salt. You ride and get me sacks of salt and I'll hire you to carry a load of dried and fresh fish."

"What does it pay?" Alerio asked.

"It's only a mile and a half to the marshes," the Master of the Catch answered. "I don't pay for hauling preservatives you need to transport fish. You want the job, or not?"

Even as Hamus' advice to always work for a minimum of two bronze per mile went through his mind, Alerio nodded his agreement.

"I don't have the coins to purchase the salt," he admitted.

"Do you have all of your fingers and toes?" the fisherman questioned.

"I do," Alerio replied.

The Master of the Catch handed Alerio a slip of paper.

"Give this to the warehouse foreman. It is a voucher for fifteen sacks. I expect you to return with a count the same as toes on both feet and fingers on one hand."

In reply, Alerio took the piece of paper. Then he wiggled his toes as if he had no grasp of numbers and finished by jiggling the fingers on one hand.

"I understand," Alero told the Master of the Catch.

Turning the mare, Alerio headed the rig along the beach in the direction of the salt marshes.

***

The route took Alerio from the sand to the ground along the piers. On the seaward side, merchant transports unloaded grain and goods for the fleet and Ostia's Legion post. Teamsters, all well fed with good rigs and healthy animals, hauled the cargo away from the docks. They were Tristis' porters, Alerio had no doubt.

Opposite from the docks, the fortified naval buildings with the reinforced roofs and the bolt throwers stood sentinel over the approach to the Tiber river. Beyond the structures of the pier and the buildings, a raised pathway trekked inland and deeper into the marshes.

A series of square ponds stretched out along the sides of the path. Although ponds might have been giving the shallow basins too much credit. The largest in area and closest to the beach contained maybe a hand's width of seawater.

After baking in the sun and wind, the brackish water drained via two trenches into more shallow basins. At these, laborers raked the surface pulling algae and seaweed from the top of the thumb deep water.

Next in the series were even smaller basins. In these, laborers pulled boards mounted at the end of long poles.

The boards parted the thin film of water while scraping up white granules of salt.

Along the edges of the ponds, the salt piled up and was left to dry in the sun. From mounds sufficiently dried, men with buckets collected the salt.

Using the land between ponds for footpaths, they carried the buckets of sea salt to a warehouse. Alerio followed the harvesters to the same building.

***

"I have a voucher from the Master of the Catch," Alerio informed a man standing at the entrance. He looked at the number before passing over the slip of paper.

The warehouse worker took the voucher, glanced at it briefly, and inquired, "How many sacks?"

"Do you want that in fingers and toes?" Alerio replied.

"Fifteen sacks it is," the warehouseman declared. "Wait here…"

"Hold up," Alerio ordered. "Read the number again. I believe you'll find it's for seventeen bags of salt."

The man bristled as if indignant about something. He studied the chit and finally acknowledged the number.

"Seventeen sacks of salt," he confirmed. "Wait here while I get them."

"In honor of Salacia, leave the paper with me," Alerio instructed.

"What does the Goddess of Seawater and Patience have to do with this?" the worker questioned. He waved the voucher in a dismissive manner as if the page held no significance.

"As I explained to the Master of the Catch," Alerio told him. "I don't have the coins to buy any missing salt. If there is any confusion in the count, you'll quickly grow to appreciate the calm of the Goddess Salacia."

Cheating illiterate porters must be a business deal between the Master of the Catch and the manager of the salt warehouse. When Alerio challenged the count, he noticed the salt merchant flinch. Even though caught, there was no way of him backing out of the sale.

"I get your meaning," the warehouse worker responded. He passed the chit to Alerio and vanished into the building.

Alerio followed but stopped inside the doorway. Resembling stalls for horses, the warehouse was divided into kiosks. In some areas, the salt was as light as fine sand. In those booths, men used scoops to fill bags. In other stalls, bulky crystals of salt were beaten by wooden mallets until they were coarse granules. The rest of the booths had salt in consistencies somewhere between the two.

After sniffing the air, Alerio's nose burned from the salt dust. He stepped outside and marveled at the difference. Sea scented air was refreshing while the warehouse air burned the back of his throat and made his tongue dry.

"It's so odd," he pondered. "We use gifts from Tellus and process the raw materials. Then afterwards, the gifts from the Goddess of the Earth become irritating."

He was thinking of the salt dust, the wasting of lead workers, and the sharp unpleasant aroma from the tanning process. A line of men came from the warehouse carrying bags of salt.

"And then there is the fruit of the vine," he considered while strolling to his rig. "Processing grapes certainly creates a more pleasant product than mere fruit."

At the cart, he placed all seventeen sacks of salt evenly on the bed. When loaded, he handed the warehouseman the voucher and guided the mare back to the raised pathway.

"Then there is cheese," he mentioned to the horse as they rode by the seawater drying basins. "A product far superior to milk in taste. Plus, cheese last much longer."

***

"Let me count," the Master of the Catch stated. He ran his eyes over the load of salt. Then with a roar, he announced. "There are two missing. I only see fifteen. The loss of two salt bags is coming out of your commission."

The way Alerio stacked the bags, there was no way of counting the salt containers without unstacking them.

"But you said fifteen," Alerio protested. He held up a foot and pointed at his toes. "Remember, ten toes and five fingers mean fifteen."

"Either, you didn't count at the warehouse, because you weren't listening," the Master accused. "Or you stole the two bags of salt."

"But I need the work," Alerio protested. "Why would I ruin my chances? I swear, I did not take the salt."

The Master of the Catch pulled bags from Alerio's cart and distributed fourteen to the other teamsters.

"I'll leave you one sack," he said while peering up at the sun. "It's barely enough to cover the load. It is only five miles to Infernetto. If you hurry, you might get there before the fish rot. Oh, and the load pays one bronze one way. Payable when you get back. Take it or leave it."

"I'll take the contract," Alerio agreed, as would any desperate teamster.

Fishermen strolled over and flopped the least valuable of the day's catch onto the cart. Alerio reached in, shuffled, and adjusted the load while sprinkling salt over each layer. In the hot sun, with little salt, it would take an intervention from the God Mercury, the swift messenger of the Gods, to arrive in Infernetto with the load of fish unspoiled.

The other three porters had already departed.

"You picked on me because I was new," Alerio ventured.

He stood by the cart looking at the master's face seeking any sign of remorse or humanity.

"I don't know what you are talking about," the Master of the Catch responded. Then with an evil grin, he added. "You better get going. I believe your load is starting to smell, already."

Alerio climbed in among the fish and snapped the reigns. The horse pulled and the cart rolled, leaving ruts in the hard-packed shoreline. Near the docks, he guided the horse onto the road and the mare picked up the pace.

At the crossroads and the turn off to the town of Ostia, Alerio eased the mare to the side of the road.

"You can't cheat an honest man," Alerio told the horse.

From the storage box, he pulled the two missing bags of salt and packed the granules over the fish creating a shell. With the minerals protecting the fresh fish, he climbed onto the cart and snapped the reins.

"I wonder what the citizens of Infernetto did to the Master of the Catch," Alerio said to the mare. "It must have been bad for him to want them to receive a load of rotting fish."

A few paces later, Alerio laughed, clawed a handful of salt up in his hand, and tossed it over his shoulder.

"But this time, the fish will arrive fresh," Alerio exclaimed. "I wonder how the town will respond to that?"

Chapter 7 - Infernetto

Two and a half miles from Ostia, Alerio reined in the mare. After tying a line to a tree branch, he walked to the bank of a water course. Although wide, it didn't seem deep. But those were not the features worrying him. Splashing and stomping across, he checked the bed of the stream to be sure his cart could traverse the creek. Many a Legion had been delayed when their supply wagons bogged down in a soft clay bottom or had wheels broken on submerged rocks.

"The bottom is good," Alerio informed the mare. He pulled the line and urged the horse down the embankment and into the water. Pausing, he allowed the horse to drink before nudging her forward.

"See, not too deep and the bottom is firm."

Alerio and the rig climbed the far bank. On the other side of the creek, they entered a section of the road with trees on both sides. Deeper into the forest, the road, for no apparent reason, began turning back on itself in a series of switchbacks. Usually, a road with that many curves was the result of terrain. There did not seem to be any reason for the curved design on the miles before Infernetto.

***

The hamlet of Infernetto occupied the corners of a crossroad. Alerio studied the intersection trying to decide which of the roads was more twisted. As the horse neared an open area, he discovered that, like the bent roads, the town square lacked straight edges. The green space was oblong shaped.

"Is there nothing square in this place?" Alerio asked the horse.

Guiding the rig off the curved road, he pulled it to a stop on the edge of the town's green.

"Fresh fish," he announced to passing citizens.

A few walked over.

"The last three loads from Ostia were spoiled," a woman complained.

"These are fresh catch and come with a scoop of salt," Alerio pointed out. "Fresh fish!"

46

Even if they did not want the fish, a scoop of salt more than offset the cost of an individual fish. With the bonus of sea salt, Alerio easily sold a third of his load. A coin count showed he had already recouped the cost of the fish and his transportation fee.

The rest of the profit would be a test of character. Or rather, a test of what would separate him from the other desperate teamsters and get him noticed. Keep the extra coins or turn them over to the Master of the Catch?

"You there, stop your selling," a man followed by a man-at-arms shouted.

Their general direction was towards Alerio but the path they walked weaved along the edge of the grassy area.

"Is there a problem?" Alerio questioned.

"Bring your cart over here and I will buy all of your fish," the man promised.

Over here was about ten steps from the rig. Certainly not a great hike for the man and his bodyguard.

"Why don't you come over here?" Alerio inquired.

From behind Alerio a voice boomed, "Because then, they would be on Curiatii land."

"Ignore him and bring your fish over to Horatii property," the first man encouraged.

Sensing he was in the middle of an ancient quarrel, Alerio urged the horse forward until the cart straddled the wandering property line.

***

The noble from Horatii followed and a few steps later, the Curiatii gentleman reach the rig. The nobles, as

47

Alerio could tell by their expensive tunics and their bodyguards, stood glaring at each other over the cart and the salted fish.

"I'll buy this side of the load," the Curiatii man declared.

"And I'll take the fish from my side," the other nobleman exclaimed.

Both men sent for servants to carry away their purchases. While they waited, Alerio inquired, "Why are the boundaries zigzagged? It must require regular sacrifices to Terminus to maintain the lines."

"More than offerings to the God of Boundary Markers," the Horatii Lord stated.

"Sacrifices and steel are both required to keep the peace," the Curiatii noble confirmed.

"How did you come to live with wavy property lines?" Alerio inquired.

"When King Hostilius ruled the Kingdom of Rome, the subjects lived in fear of the Sabines," Master Horatii explained. "But a dispute with neighboring Alba Longa threatened war. Fearing that fighting would weaken both cities and create opportunity for the Sabines, the rulers decided to select champions."

"Three Curiatii brothers stepped between the battle lines to face the Horatii brothers from Rome," Master Curiatii described. "The armies watched as the six men fought. After much slashing and bashing, two of the Horatii trio lay dead. Although the Curiatii siblings were wounded, they stalked towards Publius the last Roman champion."

"Publius Horatii ran. As he sprinted between the battle lines, the Romans feared he suffered from cowardice," the Horatii Lord told Alerio. "But his run spread out the Curiatii siblings. Once a gap opened, Publius turned about and slew the least injured. Then following the meandering trail of blood, he engaged the second wounded brother. After defeating that one, he again followed the staggered trail of blood drops."

"Publius Horatii, curse his name, reached the most injured of the Curiatii brothers and murdered him," Master Curiatii illustrated by indicating the erratic property line. "To honor Terminus, our ancestors used the blood markings as the boundary between our two peoples. Now we are citizens of the Republic, but we keep the old ways."

"And old feuds, it seems," Alerio observed. Then he suggested. "We should discuss prices for the fish and salt."

"Name your price," the Curiatii noble responded. "If it's fair, I'll pay."

"You seem to be an honest man," the Horatii gentleman professed. "Prove it."

Until then, Alerio had been relaxed. But the easy way they agreed to his setting the price unnerved him.

Men and women arrived and as fish and scoops of salt were removed from the cart, Alerio collected coins. First from Horatii servants, then from Curiatii servants. And while he gathered payments, he observed something else. Everyone was armed with a blade, long steel for the men and short knives for the women.

The piles of bronze coins grew taller. They became a focus of attention for the domestics as they stacked fish on woven trays and clutched cups of salt. Their attentiveness to the money made Alerio anxious and he covered the stacks with his hat.

When the fish were gone and the embattled Lords had departed, Alerio used a horsehair broom to brush the remaining salt into a pile. Scooping up the salt, he carried it to the horse and allowed the beast to lick his palm clean.

"Our business here is complete," Alerio said as he snapped the reigns. "Or at least I hope so."

The thirsty mare veered off the road heading for the village's well. But Alerio pulled her back. Once on the winding road, they left the hamlet of Infernetto behind.

***

Four men waited in the trees at the quarter mile marker. Almost as if designed by a military strategist, the quick turn leading to a second blind curve afforded them invisibility from travelers coming from either direction.

"Remember, we only want the coins," the leader advised.

"But Fulvio, what if he resists?" another of the highwayman inquired.

He flicked the tip of his sword with a fingernail.

"Then, we'll bury the body, sell the horse, and burn the cart for firewood," their leader stated.

The comment brought laughter from the three men. Fulvio always had a plan, it was why he was the leader.

They were relaxing at a pub when the teamster arrived. Usually, the fish porters had poor products.

Because this new guy offered fresh fish and salt, he had earned a lot of bronze. A lot more then a teamster was entitled too, according to Fulvio. Even after paying the Lords their share, he and his partners would make a good profit.

"Don't show yourselves until I give the word," Fulvio instructed. "But when I call, be sure you have your swords drawn. And move fast."

With hand signals, he sent two to one side of the road and drew another back into the trees with him. They waited for the sounds of the horse and cart on the hard-packed dirt.

Rattling and the clopping of hooves on the road reverberated from the direction of Infernetto.

"Draw and get ready," Fulvio ordered.

They could stand in the middle of the road but that would give the porter advanced notice of the robbery. By waiting on the sides, they held the element of surprise and could use the frightening of the horse to stop the cart.

The sounds of the rig drew closer and Fulvio judged the man and cart were around the bend.

"Standby," Fulvio directed.

Then from the curve behind the thieves, a grating sound reached them.

"Is there another rider?" one of the men questioned.

"New plan," Fulvio announced. His three henchmen smiled because their leader always had a plan. He called across the road. "We'll take the cart. You two stop the new traveler."

"It sounds like someone singing?" one of the robbers on the far side of the road suggested.

"You have a brass ear," his partner told him. "You can't tell the difference between a drum's rhythm and the hammering of a tin worker's hammer."

"They both beat in time," the man submitted.

"Pay attention, you two," Fulvio scolded them. "This is business."

***

The grating from behind them became words as the new traveler drew closer.

"Hear me administrator
I have an empty cart."

Alerio started his Legion jog before the bend. As unstoppable as a bull Auroch during rutting season, he charged down the road.

"From here to the mart
Are miles apart."

With his pugio in one hand and a gladius in the other, he brought blades in the hope the highwaymen did not have archers with them. When he slipped by the four men earlier, he didn't see any bows and arrows.

"You have contracts to uphold
Time is a threshold."

As he came completely around the bend, he noted two bandits stepping from the roadside. Both faced him. Two other thieves, with their backs to him, watched the mare and empty cart come around the other bend.

"Don't have your freight wait
I will expiate."

The two highwaymen waved their swords as if to stop a horse or a wagon. The movements did little to hinder Alerio. He came to them bent low. Both arms flashed out and his blades cut the flesh under the leather armor.

"For a tiny rate
From your door to the gate."

Jogging passed the wounded, he dashed towards the other two men. The horse moved smartly as if she had a driver. That kept them engaged and caused the robbers to ignore the cries of their partners.

The rough singing coming from behind them finally caught their attention.

"And never late
Regulator be smart."

Alerio drove a knee into one's back and the Legion dagger into the base of his neck. The man collapsed to the road's surface. Spinning around, Alerio swung his gladius at the last man. His blade caught and was parried by the steel of the highwayman.

***

"How did you get behind us?" Fulvio asked. He maintained pressure on the teamster's blade while circling. The cart and horse shot by without a break in the mare's stride. "And keep the horse in motion?"

"Thirst is a powerful motivator," Alerio replied, "and the horse knows there is a creek not far from here. As far as me sneaking by a group of gullible cut throats, it is what I do as a Legion raider."

"That explains why you don't sound or behave like a porter," Fulvio observed. Then he felt the resistance against his own blade increase. It was too steady to be desperation, yet just enough to keep him occupied. Respect for the other man's strength made him afraid to release the blade. "I don't suppose you would let me walk away."

"You know too much about me," Alerio pointed out. Then he asked. "Would you have allowed me to walk away?"

"Not once you started to fight," Fulvio admitted.

Alerio snapped his wrist counter to the pressure. The tip of the highwayman's sword dipped in response to the lack of resistance. Alerio's gladius free of the force, rotated up and over before driving forward into the bandit's neck.

"I have an empty cart," Alerio sang as he withdrew his blade and turned. Further down the road, he walked by the two wounded thieves and advised. "Both of you are blessed of Coalemus, the God of Stupid. Find another line of work."

He broke into the Legion jog. The horse had a good head start and Alerio wanted to catch her. Mostly, he feared she would reach the creek and drink more water than was healthy. Nursing a sick animal all the way back to Ostia would not make for a pleasant trip.

Chapter 8 – Sacrifice and Stupidity

Late in the day as the sun touched the highlands, the horse and cart trotted by the turnoff to Ostia town. The entrance to the Legion Post fell behind and, in another mile, Alerio reined the mare off the road and onto the beach.

Multiple fires highlighted the warships with full crews ready to launch in the morning. At others, single fires showed they were guarded by a half squad of Marines. Passed the squadrons, Alerio pulled reins and stopped the horse at the fish drying racks.

"Late, I see. Every other porter was back long ago," the Master accused. He spit into the sand and shifted around a cookfire. Strolling to the rig, he growled. "It must have been a miserable trip. Did you at least earn your fee?"

"I would like to report a successful expedition," Alerio announced. He wanted to play it coy and hold back some coins to show he had larceny in his heart. But the man's dour attitude brought out the contrary in the Legion officer. "Infernetto was hungry for fish and willing to pay top coin."

Alerio tossed a heavy coin purse to the Master.

"You owe me five bronze," Alerio demanded as if he hadn't just turned over a large sum.

The Master of the Catch gave Alerio an odd look before opening the purse and counting out six bronze coins.

"Here. I've included a bonus, but don't expect it every trip," he said while dumping the coins into Alerio's palm. "Come back in the morning and I'll give you another load."

"Thank you, thank you," Alerio said while touching each coin with a finger. "Thank you, sir. I'll be back."

Alerio brought the rig around and headed for the road.

"What do you think of him?" the Master of the Catch asked a fisherman.

"I say Top Coin is a bit slow," the man responded. "If he had any sense, he would have kept half of what he gave you. I would have."

"This is more than enough to pay for the fish and the extra salt he took," the Master stated. He judged the weight of the coins before deciding. "Tristis can use a not too intelligent thief. But let's give Sisera one more test."

***

In the long shadows of late afternoon, Alerio pulled the cart to the side of the road. He climbed off the rig and opened the storage box.

Once the cart bed smelled of vinegar, instead of fish, he climbed on and headed towards Ostia Town.

"You are getting in late," Hamus Ivo declared when Alerio arrived at the campsite. "I trust you had a productive day."

"I did," Alerio confirmed. "As a matter of fact, I earned a bonus."

"A bonus, you say?" Hamus pondered while scratching the back of his neck. "I didn't get a bonus."

"It could be your singing," Alerio suggested. "Sing me a verse while I fix dinner. Maybe I can give you a few pointers."

"This morning, I might have argued with you," Hamus admitted.

He cleared his throat and began a new stanza.

"Hear me administrator

56

I have an empty purse
For this is my private verse
You fail to disburse
The gold in your hand
Not even a silver band
If a heavy box falls off
It is my payoff
My small quaff
You will never miss the payoff
When I sell the knockoff
Regulator be smart
Find another cart."

"That is a cynical song," Alerio pointed out.

"Well, I didn't get a bonus," Hamus scoffed.

"Hopefully, a portion of camp stew with fish will cheer you up," Alerio told him. Then as the undercover Legionary stirred the contents of the iron pot, he mentioned. "Wealth, intelligence, and courage?"

"Wealth and, I didn't catch the others," Hamus confessed. "What are you talking about?"

"Somethings are building blocks leading to higher goals," Alerio lectured. "Didn't Aristotle give wealth, intelligence, and courage as examples of steps leading to more complicated actions?"

"What does that have to do with me?" Hamus questioned.

"I'm trying to cheer you up. According to the Greek philosopher," Alerio described, "happiness is the only emotion which stands on its own."

"Tell me a joke," Hamus stated, "or relate a tale of courage if you want to cheer me up. But do not talk in riddles or sing to me. Is the stew ready yet?"

"I believe it is," Alerio responded.

"Then I am happy," Hamus vowed. He shoved a shallow tin at Alerio. "Fill this and I will be happy and no longer hungry."

"I guess that answers the question," Alerio stated while he spooned portions onto the plates, "of which is more filling, philosophy or food."

Alerio peered over his plate at the other porter. Having been trained to use questions to trigger thought, the Legion officer had expected Hamus to spring into a discussion based on Aristotle's premise. Instead, Hamus clarified his attitude.

"Sisera, you are one strange teamster," Hamus professed. "You talk funny, but you make good stew."

***

The day dawned with clouds blanketing the sky. Because of the overcast, it appeared earlier than it was, which might have accounted for the late arrival of the rigs.

"Spent your coins on drinks, did you?" the Master of the Catch projected on the four unpunctual porters. "My fishermen have been out since before dawn even with hangovers. Sisera, you are going to be loaded first."

"Thank you, sir, thank you," Alerio blathered.

"Sure, my pleasure," he replied, dismissing the fool's platitudes.

Fish were placed in the bed. Alerio adjusted the fish before he salted the layers. Then, surprisingly, two full sacks of salt were added to the load.

"That's a valuable cargo," the Master warned. "I expect top coins when you get back from Mostacciano."

"That's the Legion waystation," Alerio announced.

"It is and they pay good for salt," the Master of the Catch informed him. "The fish, those are extra."

"You can count on me," Alerio assured him as he guided the horse away from the drying racks. Then while still in earshot, Alerio added. "May Silvanus grant me safe passage."

For a moment, Alerio feared the reference identified him as an educated, thoughtful man. But no one seemed to notice, and he continued along the beach.

"It'll take more than the God of the Countryside to make you safe," the Master mumbled as he strutted to the next porter's rig.

The trap for Sisera was set. Soon the not too bright but eager-to-please teamster would be in debt. And that was the way Agent Tristis liked his porters.

***

A cloudy day provided three benefits. Alerio rode comfortably, the aroma of the fish remained that of a fresh catch, and the horse moved easily over the surface of the road.

Just shy of the four and a half-mile marker, a large Holm oak spread its branches. On a hot day, the high limbs provided shade for travelers. Although not required on an overcast day, the grandfather tree still signaled the halfway point between Ostia and the posthouse at Mostacciano.

Alerio urged the mare off the road and aimed her towards a spot beside the enormous tree. Moving slowly over the rough ground, the rig almost reached the oak when the horse became skittish.

"Just a few more feet and we will give you a rest," he told the mare, "a bite to eat, and my aching backside a break from the boards."

"Maybe your load is too heavy," a masked spearman suggested.

He stepped from behind the tree trunk followed by a disguised archer.

"We can help remove some of that weight," the bowman offered.

They moved forward and flanked Alerio's cart.

"Goddess Nenia, as Death Caller, I ask that if it is my time," Alerio said, "take me quickly. Else, consider these two highwaymen sacrifices."

With a spear tip on the left and an arrowhead on the right targeting him, any unarmed teamsters would give up the rig, the load, and the horse to save his life. It made sense to civilians and untrained robbers. To a Legion officer who carried the blessing of Nenia, it was almost humorous.

"Please, please," Alerio screamed in a high voice. He stood, turning to face the bowman. "Don't...argh!"

Clutching his chest as if shot by an arrow, Alerio toppled off the left side of the cart.

The spearman, assuming his partner for some reason had launched an arrow at the porter, took his eyes off the falling man.

"Why did you…?"

***

Alerio absorbed the fall with his left shoulder and rolled backward. His legs snapped up knocking the spear to the side. At the end of his roll, Alerio rose to his feet.

Momentarily, the spearman and the Legion officer were nose to nose. Then a knee strike to the thief's groin folded his torso forward. Alerio's other knee jerked upward and smashed the man's face. As the spearman toppled over with blood spraying from a broken nose, Alerio snatched the spear from his hand.

Spinning and diving, Alerio hid behind the cart. A quick peek over the load gave him a fix on the archer. After ducking and shifting to throw off the bowman's aim, Alerio stood, drew back the shaft, and launched the spear.

The arrow shot harmlessly into the sky as the archer fell backward, the weight of the spear toppling him to the earth. Protruding from his chest for a moment, the shaft jutted into the air. Then the soft heart muscles allowed the shaft to slowly tilt unto the end rested on the ground.

No assault to counter an ambush was complete while an enemy lived. Pulling the Golden Valley dagger, Alerio dashed to the spearman and slashed his throat.

Too late to recall Nenia Dea and just before the gushing blood covered the man's arms, Alerio noticed the burn scar on the robber's right wrist.

Stooped over with the dagger extended, Alerio scanned the bushes around the old oak. As he searched for more enemies, Sisera wondered how he would explain killing one, or possibly two of Tristis' teamsters.

While placing coins on the eyes of the first dead man, Alerio suffered a crisis of conscience. If Death Caller had not asked for guidance from his Goddess, would the porters still be alive? He shook off the uneasy feeling as he placed coins over the eyes of the second corpse.

***

Later, Alerio splashed water onto his chest and arms to rinse away the sweat and dirt.

"If they hadn't targeted each other through me," Alerio complained to the horse, "we might have talked. But no, they lined up perfectly. Now there are two bodies buried here and I'll need to stop and make a sacrifice to the Goddess Melinoe every time I pass this spot."

The horse shook her head as if impatient to be away from the oak tree and the graves hidden in the brush. Two horses, obviously owned by the robbers, were tied to the rear of the cart.

"I also would like to be on the road and away from this place," Alerio agreed with the mare. "But first a small sacrifice to the Goddess of Ghosts and Spirits."

Alerio walked a wide circle around the graves spilling offerings of vino. The distance was not out of disrespect. It was so the vino trail would not lead travelers to the bodies.

Act 3

Chapter 9 – Needs and Misdeeds

"Master of the Catch," Tristis exclaimed. "If this teamster is as pliable as you claim, he will fit right into my organization."

"He is better than that," the Master promised the shipping agent. "I would bet when he gets back to the drying racks, he will tell me he was robbed of the salt. Yet, Sisera will turn over all of the coins from the sale of the fish and apologize."

"I don't need honesty," Tristis pointed out. "Larceny, yes, morality no."

"Sisera has a twisted sense of embezzlement," the Master countered. "He stole from me, used the salt, then returned all of the profits."

"I will be interested to hear how he handles today," the agent stated. "Keep me posted."

The Master of the Catch left the villa, crossed a backstreet, and dropped down the slope to the beach. When the fisherman left, a man came into the room.

"What do you think, boss?" Silenus inquired.

As Tristis caravan leader and head porter, Silenus acted as the strong arm of the organization.

"I am thinking, I'll keep this Sisera in reserve," Tristis replied. "We have enough rigs for tomorrow night. But let's make sure everyone is sober and no one gets in trouble. Oh, and have everyone keep an eye on

Sisera. I want to know who he associates with in the evenings."

"I'll get the word out to the porters," the head teamster assured him.

"Don't forget to contact the pair who did the job at Mostacciano," Tristis instructed. "We need their carts for the haul. And remind them, the salt they took from Sisera is mine."

***

Alerio's rig and the three horses traveled the straight roadway for another five miles. While the road ran true, the Tiber curved towards the embankment before angling away. At the curve in the river, Alerio spotted the posthouse compound. It rested on the side of the road across from the river, near a small village. The Legion waystation cared for men traveling under Legion orders. The village provided services, other than water and a safe place to rest at night, to civilians traveling to and from Ostia. Without waiting for directions, Alerio's mare turned off the road and trotted down a driveway.

The posthouse at Mostacciano consisted of a main building, a stable, and a large wagon yard next to animal pens. The horse crossed the yard and stopped at a watering trough. Alerio hopped off the cart, untied the two horses, and pulled them to the water.

"You must be headed far and fast," a yardman observed.

"Why do you say that?" Alerio questioned.

"You're outfitted with three horses," the man replied.

"Not me," Alerio protested. "I found these two walking on the roadway. Can you care for them until their owners arrive?"

"Sure. Let's put them in the pen," the yardman agreed.

He and Alerio walked the robbers' mounts to the corral. They would remain unclaimed for a week. After eight days, a stockman would put them into rotation, making the two horses available as exchange mounts for Legion couriers.

"I have fish and salt for the waystation," Alerio told the man. Then, thinking of maybe building a small shrine at the oak tree, he added. "After I see the station agent, I need a load of river rocks. Is there a vendor in the village? Or do I have to go to the Tiber and fetch my own?"

"There are no smooth rocks along this sector of the Tiber. You have to go miles north of the Capital to find smooth rocks," the man described. He picked up a rough-edged stone and tossed it to Alerio. "The best you'll find around here are these. Not good for slingers, let alone a building project."

After catching the stone and examining it, Alerio decided the dead thieves did not rate a shrine. He thanked the man and went into the main building to sell his load of fish and salt.

***

"Hear me administrator
I have an empty cart
And a will to depart."

Hamus Ivo sang as his rig moved slowly through the streets. Being late in the afternoon, he did not expect much in the way of business. A light, short load would end his day nicely. Guiding the horse down a side street, he aimed to cruise the commercial district once more before heading to his campsite.

"A strong back
A sturdy horse ready to go
But a last no cargo."

Three men stepped from an alleyway. One stopped Hamus' horse, one walked to the other side of the cart, and the third spoke directly to the teamster.

"Ivo stay away from Sisera," he warned. "He'll be a Tristis porter soon and you know the agent doesn't like interference."

"You'll not have that young man," Hamus said with confidence. "I'll keep him away from you, bleating sheep, and your bad shepherd."

"Bleating Sheep?" the man on the far side of the cart challenged.

He reached for Hamus. Automatically, Hamus snapped the end of a rein. Acting as a whip, the leather cracked against the man's face. The assaulter's skin split and blood dripped down his cheek.

"I'm sorry. Sorry, I didn't mean," Hamus begged. "Please forgive…"

While the man with the cut reeled away, Hamus leaned towards him pleading that it was a mistake. Seeing Ivo's unprotected back, the talkative one drew his knife and stabbed between the teamster's ribs.

Pain ripped through his lungs and Hamus fell on his side. Curling into a fetal position, he fought for breath.

"Get him out of here," the knifeman ordered.

The thug holding the horse slapped the beast's rump sending Hamus Ivo and his rig racing down the street.

***

Alerio was pleased. It wasn't much but having a load of broken and torn equipment meant his trip back to Ostia earned coins. Although he played teamster to uncover the thefts from the Legion, he still took pride in making the job a success.

At the main gate of the Legion Post, he eased the mare to a stop.

"The waystation at Mostacciano is turning in a request for new gear," Alerio explained while handing over the order. "And I have the discarded equipment."

The Legionary sentry studied the message and handed it back.

"Go ahead," he instructed.

Several streets from the gate, Alerio eased the mare off the road and along the side of the supply building. As he passed the garden, he noticed the smooth river rocks and wondered briefly where they got so many of them.

After parking in the rear, he marched into the building and presented his chit for two bronze coins per mile.

"I see you've learned your value," the clerk said. He handed Alerio two silver coins. "Get out of here before my Tribune realizes you aren't from Tristis' stable of porters."

"Who is your Tribune?" Alerio asked.

"For the past half a year, it's Tribune Gutteris," the clerk replied. "He's also the staff officer for the right flank of the Second Maniple. That is, once the Legion forms."

"You don't sound happy with the Tribune," Alerio mentioned.

"My books are honest," the clerk stated. "I don't appreciate his scrutiny and changing my numbers."

"He changes the count of equipment?" Alerio questioned.

"Not wholesale," the office worker admitted. "Only a line here and there. I ignore it because for the most part the books balance."

Alerio thanked the clerk and left while juggling three thoughts and two silver coins.

Could a few numbers on an inventory list make much of a difference? Legions lose or break equipment daily. And warships have so much extra gear, it would seem impossible to keep track of the supplies.

Each of the one hundred and two Legion warships in the fleet had spare ropes, animal hide sails, and a least one extra hypozomata, the twisted fibers holding tension between the bow and aft of each warship. A line here and there on an inventory sheet would not make a drastic difference.

Shoving aside the petty theft by Tribune Gutteris, Alerio pondered if he should tell the Master of the Catch about the attempted robbery and murders. If word got out about him killing two men, the Legion would get involved, and Alerio would have to disclose his true purpose. In the end, it seemed a better idea not to tell the Master.

Finally, Alerio tossed both coins high into the air. The silver flipped and sparkled in the late afternoon sun. He looked forward to telling Hamus about his demand for two bronze per mile and thanking the teamster for the advice.

Alerio caught the coins, shoved them into a pouch, and climbed onto his rig. Urging the mare forward, he headed towards the main gate and the fish drying racks on the beach.

***

Early cookfires hazed the beach with smoke. Through the smog, Alerio guided the horse to the fish drying rack.

"Master of the Catch," Alerio called to a cookfire beyond the drying embers.

"Sisera. It is late," the Master acknowledged. He eased between the hot spots and swaggered up to the rig. "I didn't think, I would see you until morning."

The grin on his face seemed pleasant. But Alerio knew it was more smirk than smile. Tempted to wipe the expression off his face with the bag of coins, Alerio paused and checked his throw before releasing the coin purse. As a result, the pouch arched gently over the sand and landed in the Master's hands.

"You owe me twenty bronze, sir," Alerio reminded the Master of the Catch.

The smile vanished as the fish boss balanced the purse and judged its weight against the value of a simple load of fish.

"You had no troubles in route?" he questioned.

"No, sir," Alerio assured him. "The delivery went well, and I got top coin for the salt and fish."

"I can tell," the Master stammered as he jiggled the purse. After counting out twenty bronze coins, he promised Alerio. "If you return in the morning, I may have a surprise for you."

Alerio almost contested the invitation. If the next day was like the last two, it might get him killed. But he did not challenge the offer.

"Thank you, sir. Thank you," Alerio cooed. "I'll be here at daybreak."

Turning the cart, Alerio hurried the horse away from the drying racks. If he delayed any longer, Hamus might start cooking the evening meal.

"And if Hamus Ivo fixes dinner," Alerio called to the mare. "He will expect me to eat his awful cooking."

Picking up on the tone of Alerio's voice, the horse surged ahead almost as if the beast understood the reason for the urgency.

**

At a smart clip, the horse trotted through the streets of Ostia town. On a road near the center of the settlement, the rig turned north and headed for the camp Alerio and Hamus shared.

"I don't see a fire," Alerio said with relief. "He must have just arrived."

The last statement took into consideration that Hamus' horse stood harnessed between the cart shafts. But Alerio could not see his friend even as his rig approached the cold firepit.

"Hamus Ivo. You are a sorry excuse for a singer," Alerio tease. "You could have at least built a fire."

In the twilight, Alerio pulled the reins and searched the gloom for activity. Seeing no motion nor receiving an answer, Alerio leaped off his rig and ran to Hamus' cart. He located a shape laying curled on the ground beside the rig.

The smell of copper, and the stink of a body that had emptied its bowels and bladder, assaulted Alerio. As a result of the battle aromas, he wasn't surprised by the dark, wet circle radiating out from his friend's body.

As Alerio began a prayer for the dead, Hamus coughed weakly and attempted to draw in a breath. Dropping to his knees, Alerio shoved his arms under his friend and lifted him from the ground.

***

Darkness ended the day's activities at Doctor Allocco's hospital. The final patient was discharged, the doors were locked, and a guard posted at the entrance. The apprentice physicians had just completed the steps of locking up when a porter's cart raced from the center of the town.

In a wild and reckless gallop, the horse pulled a rocking and often off balanced cart. At the reins stood a man, his legs braced against the tilting cart bed. His arms snapped the leather straps driving the horse, headlong through the streets, towards the hospital.

71

"Surgeon! My friend needs a surgeon," the driver screamed.

The guard jerked from side to side preparing to dodge to either side if the horse jumped the hospital's short defensive wall. But the beast turned and stopped shy of the structure. Still in motion, the cart slid sideways, halting only when the right wheel tapped the stonework.

"A surgeon," the driver bellowed as he lifted a form from the cart's bed. "Please, my friend needs Doctor Allocco."

Chapter 10 – Duty Delays the Blade

Hamus Ivo did not protest when Doctor Allocco probed the wound. Although when she removed her fingers, bubbles of blood foamed at his mouth.

"It's a knife wound, and it is deep," she reported. "Far too deep to sew up. I'm afraid Tribune Sisera, all we can do is wait."

Alerio gripped Hamus' hand, lifted his chin, and began to chant.

"Nenia Dea
You hover just out of sight
But death is called
To claim his life."

In mid verse, Hamus pulled Alerio down until the injured man's lips touched Alerio's ear.

"Tristis wanted you, Sisera," the teamster choked out. "I couldn't let them ruin you."

Then the tension fell from Hamus Ivo's hand, and it lay limp in Alerio's grip.

"With gentle hands so light
Take him with care
As is a worthy man's right
Goddess of Death, Nenia Dea
Hear our plight
As you hover just out of sight."

Alerio closed his eyes but not in grief. Rather, anger surged through his chest. A mad plan formed in his mind. He would kill the Master of the Catch, Tribune Gutteris, Agent Tristis, any porters associated with the agent, and anyone who got in his way. Then a damp rag dapped gently at his ear.

"You have blood on the side of your face," Doctor Allocco offered. She shoved the cloth into his hand. "I don't know why you are dressed like that, Tribune Sisera. But you need a bath and probably a good night's sleep."

"I'm on an assignment," he explained to the Doctor. "Thank you for the offer but I need to get back to my camp."

"What assignment sends you to live like an itinerant dayworker?" Allocco asked.

Alerio's anger slid back into his control. Her question focused him and reminded the staff officer that he had a job to complete. He could murder those he knew or suspected were involved in the crimes, but then the ones making the most coins from the theft would escape. Vengeance he decided would come once he discovered the people on the business ends of the pilfering.

"Please see that Hamus has a priest and a sacrifice to the God Sancus at his interment," Alerio requested while handing the Doctor a handful of coins.

"Why the God Sancus?" Allocco inquired.

"If there was anyone who lived by his oath, was a friend you could trust, and lived an honest life," Alerio replied, "it was Hamus Ivo."

"I'll see to the arrangements," the Doctor told him. "Where can you be reached?"

"I won't be attending the funeral," Alerio informed her.

"Where will you be?" she asked.

"Stalking prey," Alerio said.

Then with his jaw set, the cold calculating Tribune Sisera marched out of the medical facility.

***

The ride back to the campsite contrasted sharply with the race to Doctor Allocco's hospital. Instead of the insane dash, the mare plodded down the street passed the last row of buildings and arrived at an empty campsite.

Alerio noticed the absence of Hamus' rig and horse. With no way to track the animal in the dark, he set about building a fire and preparing a meal. As he bent to blow the sparks into flames, Alerio caught a sniff of his clothing. Doctor Allocco was correct, he did need a bath. He made a mental note to get to the beach early and wash in the sea.

By firelight, he unharnessed the horse and rubbed her down.

"We've had a long day," he said while drawing a brush down the beast's flank. "Hopefully tomorrow will be less stressful for you. Me? I'm hoping for some answers."

Once he and the mare were fed, Alerio stretched out and fell asleep. Overhead the stars twinkled peacefully, but in Alerio's dreams Death Caller littered the landscape with bodies.

***

Long before daylight, Alerio backed the horse between the cart shafts and harnessed the beast to the rig. He was in a sour mood and forced himself to be extra gentle so as not to take it out on the draft animal.

His tenderness extended to allowing the horse to set her own gait. As a result, they clomped and rolled slowly through the quiet town. Even at that pace, it was still dark when they reached the beach.

"We both need a bath," Alerio told the mare. "But first the cart bed."

Alerio pushed the rig to the water's edge, and with handfuls of sand, he scrubbed Hamus' blood and yesterday's fish smell from the boards. Leaving the cart tilted up to dry, he used buckets of water to wash the horse before brushing her down. Finally, Alerio stripped off his clothing and splashed into waist deep water. There, he washed the woolen shirt and pants. While he cleaned, sunlight peeked over the horizon of the Tyrrhenian Sea. Tossing the wet clothing onto the cart, he turned back to the sea and dove under the surface.

He came up to a view of the rising sun. Some of his anger seeped away at the promise of a new day. Adding to the easing, the gentle waves caressed his chest. He dipped under again and felt the pressure of the water lift his body and his spirits. Coming up, Alerio felt...

"You, porter," a voice growled from the beach. "Come out of there and get your cūlus beat."

Spinning, Alerio used his hands to brush the water from his eyes. Once his vision cleared, he smiled.

"Optio Noxalis, right?" Alerio asked. Under the water, he curled his hands into fists. "You have no idea how happy I am to see you."

Confused by the joy in the porter's voice, the NCO and the two Legionaries with him exchanged glances.

"You won't be so happy when we are through with you," Noxalis warned.

"That is exactly what I was thinking," Alerio replied.

The teamster waded through the surf and, as he emerged from the sea, the Legionaries got a look at a collection of battle scars. Dimpled flesh from arrow wounds in his side and thigh, an old knife injury on his hip, a double track scar on his right shoulder, a small scar over his left eye, another under the eyelid of his right, and a crescent shaped scar on top of his head should have alerted them. But men slighted and seeking redress often miss the obvious. Especially when they were confident in their superior numbers. With their vision narrowed by emotion, two moved to the opposite side of the cart to cut off the teamster's escape route.

If the situation had Alerio teaching the infantrymen, he would warn against dividing their unit when facing an unknown enemy. As it was, the weapon's instructor had other plans in mind.

Alerio allowed his anger to resurface. The flood of rage coursing through his veins was tampered only by his lack of a blade. Being unarmed, plus the awareness that scattering dead Legionaries across the beach would expose him as more than a porter, saved the infantrymen's lives. But it did nothing to spare the Sergeant's pride.

***

When the water reached ankle deep, Alerio sprinted straight ahead. Assuming the porter wanted to get to his mount and ride away, one of the Legionaries stepped away from his partner and grabbed the horse's reins. The action further divided the Legion forces.

Rather than aim for the mare, Alerio shifted and ran onto the drying cart. Halfway up the bed, the rig toppled forward. Riding the momentum of the see-sawing cart, Alerio launched his body at the Sergeant. Not headfirst, but in a cross-body attack.

The Optio could have avoided a head on assault by shifting to either side. But the full length of the teamster, coming from above the NCO's head, provided no escape. The body collided with him and the two crashed to the beach. Once they landed on the soft soil, the real fight should have started. But the porter partially rose, lifted one knee, and drove it into the Sergeant's solar plexus. The brawl ended with the Optio gasping and fighting to draw air into his lungs. To his distress, he failed to defend his gladius.

Alerio drove his knee deep into the NCO. With a satisfying crunch, he recognized the breaking of ribs which meant internal bruising. The Optio would be in pain for weeks from the strike. As he rolled off, Alerio wrapped his fingers around the hilt of the Legion sword and drew it from the sheath as he came to his feet.

"Your first mistake was ignoring the battle damage on my body," Alerio cautioned the two Legionaries. Using his right hand, he tossed the gladius high overhead. The blade flipped and spun, reflecting the morning light. When it came down, Alerio caught the hilt in his left hand. "And your second was assuming I would be an easy victim."

The infantrymen drew their gladii, closed in shoulder to shoulder, and stalked forward.

Alerio ran four steps and jumped the cart shaft. As soon as he landed, one hand slammed opened the top of the storage box.

"You can take the Optio," Alerio told the Legionaries while drawing a second gladius from the box, "and go. Or…"

"Or what?" one of the infantrymen questioned.

Alerio bounced the sides of both blades against his thighs.

"Or you can spend the morning with your friendly Legion medic," Alerio replied. "Getting sewn up from four cuts each."

"Four?" the other Legionary asked. "Why four?"

"One for each of your arms and legs," Alerio informed him.

"You can do that?" the other inquired.

"I was a Legion weapon's instructor," Alerio said. "I am that good. Your choice. Painfully slow stitches or a swift retreat?"

When they sheathed their blades, Alerio tossed the NCO's gladius over their heads in the direction of the naval station. For a moment, the Legionaries hesitated.

"I don't need both blades to hurt you," Alerio advised. "Take the Optio and go."

They lifted Noxalis from the sand and as the three moved away, Alerio placed the gladius in the storage box and pulled out clean clothes. But he did not pull them on. Rather, he snatched his wet and now sandy shirt and pants from the beach and waded into the surf to rinse off the sand.

***

Later and further down the beach, Alerio pulled the mare to a stop.

"Sisera. Good morning," the Master of the Catch greeted him. "I promised you a surprise."

"Yes, sir," Alerio replied. Inside, he burned with the urge to gut the fisherman boss. Instead, he nodded and bowed. "I came early."

"And so, you did," the Master exclaimed. "Tristis has his eyes on you. If you are selected as one of his porters, your life will be improved greatly."

'I can't say the same for him,' Alerio thought. Then to the Master, he inquired. "Is there a load for me?"

"Dried and fresh fish to the restaurants in town," the fish boss explained. "It doesn't pay per mile. It is a per stop contract. Are you interested?"

"Whatever you think is best," Alerio said.

"That's my good lad," the Master boasted.

Fisherman placed varieties of fish on sections of the rig. After loading, Alerio guided the cart along the beach. A short way from the fish drying racks, a horse and rider passed Alerio coming from the other direction. While Alerio continued towards the town, the rider pulled up at the drying racks.

"Tristis wants to know if you've seen the two porters that were sent to Mostacciano," Silenus inquired.

"No. Why would I?" the Master responded. "They don't work for me and aren't my responsibility."

"You like the coins Tristis gives you?" Silenus challenged. "Ask around and see if you can locate them."

"Tell the agent, I'll do my best," the fish boss informed him. "But if he is down two men, remind him, I get a finder's fee for Sisera."

"If he is needed," the head porter informed the Master of the Catch, "you'll get what's coming to you."

Chapter 11 – Coins for Blind Eyes

Alerio had eaten at several of the more established restaurants. In those instances, he had come through the front door as a Legion officer and been greeted cordially. As a fish porter, he entered through the rear and was barely noticed. Once told how many fish, he was left alone to fill the order. Then after coins were dropped into his palm, he was ignored. The initial fear of being recognized as an officer at the better eateries soon vanished.

He went about his deliveries unnoticed, just another invisible teamster. By the seventh eatery, his purse had grown heavy, the cart lighter, and his patience thin.

"The life of a porter is unglamorous. And we are no closer to finding the intelligence behind the thefts," he complained to the horse. Alerio shouldered two large fish, headed to the rear door of the restaurant, and declared. "No glory, no challenge, and no progress in the investigation."

Before he reached the door, a rider reined in beside the cart.

"Are you Sisera?" he asked.

"Yes, sir," Alerio replied. "I am he."

"Sir, I like that," the man said while laughing. "After your last delivery, go to the blue villa overlooking the beach."

"Is there a load, sir?" Alerio asked, again using the term of respect.

"I could grow accustomed to being addressed as sir," the rider suggested. "No load, you are going to meet Tristis."

"The agent?" Alerio inquired.

"Yes, the agent," the rider replied. "There is only one Tristis in Ostia. Are you slow?"

Alerio put a puzzled expression on his face and let his mouth fall open.

"I don't think so," he answered after several long moments.

The rider ran his eyes over Alerio's physique and chuckled.

"Tristis likes his porters with strong backs and weak minds. He'll love you," he exclaimed. "Remember the blue villa. And don't stop off for drinks on the way."

"The blue villa," Alerio repeated as if it was a religious mantra. "No drinks. Blue villa."

"You are perfect," the rider stated as he reined his horse around. Then to emphasize the instructions, he said again. "The blue villa overlooking the beach."

The man and mount rode away and Alerio leaned towards the mare and whispered.

"The blue villa overlooking the beach. Sounds lovely, doesn't it."

With a renewed interest in his deliveries, Alerio strutted into the restaurant.

***

Alerio pulled the mare to a stop in front of the blue villa with a view of the beach. During the last few deliveries, Alerio made sure the fish water and blood soaked into his shirt. And so, with the fragrance of a ripe fisherman, he climbed off the cart and strolled to the iron gate of the blue villa.

"Who are you?" a house guard inquired.

"Sisera," Alerio replied from under the brim of his felt petasos.

When the stranger did not supply additional information the guard questioned, "What do you want?"

"Agent Tristis," Alerio said.

The newly arrived teamster did not have the courtesy to even lift the hat and look the guard in the face.

"But does he want you?" the household guard joked.

"Maybe," came the one-word response.

The guard huffed up and bared his teeth. Before he could open the gate, step out, and teach the smelly, upstart teamster a lesson in manners, the rider came from the villa.

"Sisera, get in here," the rider instructed. "My name is Silenus. I'm the head porter for Tristis."

The household guard opened the gate and Alerio strolled through. As he came abreast of the sentry, Alerio moved close to the guard forcing the man to lean back to avoid the brim of the hat.

Adding to the irritation of the short answers and the brush with the brim, Alerio lifted his nose in the air and announced loudly, "Sisera."

Behind Alerio and Silenus, the household guard seethed at the arrogance of the new teamster. At the first opportunity, he would teach the porter to show respect for one of Tristis' household guards.

***

The villa was moderate compared to the better ones in Rome and the summer estates of the wealthy. However, in the great room, a view of the beach and the sea composed a beautiful feature. Other than in murals, urban compounds lacked the sight.

"It is a nice landscape, isn't it?" a middle-aged man offered when he noted Alerio's attention to the scene. "It's why I bought the villa."

The man stood framed by a backdrop of sand and sea as if a pirate captain on a warship. Moving away from the window, the resemblance did not fade. Tristis carried the muscles of a man who worked with his body and could fight. Maybe a little thicker around the middle than when he was younger, but still a man accustomed to physical hardships.

"Master Tristis, this is Sisera," Silenus introduced Alerio.

"The Master of the Catch speaks highly of you," the agent stated. "What do you have to say about that?"

Alerio yanked the petasos from his head and held it by his side.

"I have his coins," Alerio added. He pulled a pouch from under his shirt and raised it to eye level. "The Master of the Catch will be glad. I got top coin for the fish."

There was something about the delivery of the words that intrigued Agent Tristis.

"And how about yesterday's fish sale?" he inquired.

"Fish and salt," Alerio articulated. "I got top coin for the fish and salt."

Tristis looked across the room at Silenus.

"Head porter, if I asked Sisera how the sale went the day before yesterday," the agent mentioned. "What do you think he would say?"

Before Silenus could respond, Alerio blurted out, "The sale of fish at Infernetto. I got top coin for the fish."

84

"Alright, Top Coin," Tristis announced. "Can you be at the main gate of the Legion Post at moonrise, tonight?"

"Yes, sir," Alerio responded with a brace and a hand salute.

"That's all," Tristis ordered. "Show yourself out."

Alerio stuffed away the coin purse and placed the hat on his head before leaving the great room.

"Silenus, do you know what we have in Sisera?" Tristis asked the head porter.

"A slow teamster who follows orders?" Silenus guessed.

"More than that," the agent explained. "He was a Legionary. A combat veteran based on the scar on his head. And he is looking for a new commander. Did you notice the salute?"

"You got all that from one meeting?" Silenus questioned.

"The tip off was Sisera's honesty towards the fish boss," Tristis revealed. "A head wound may have slowed his thinking. But it did not erase the Legionary's loyalty."

"We'll know more tonight as we move the shipment," Silenus offered.

"Yes, we will," the agent replied.

He walked to the window and, as if posing for a portrait, stood gazing out over the beach and the water.

***

Alerio paused on the steps down to the courtyard and the gate. Bending, he tightened the straps on his sandals and secured the waist tie for his pants. Finally, he reached to the small of his back and loosened the sheath of the Golden Valley dagger.

'Hopefully, the blade will not be necessary,' he thought as he resumed the descent.

"Guard open the gate," Alerio instructed in a voice pitched higher than his usual tone.

In addition to the hysterical and demanding voice, the teamster strutted from the stair well as if he owned the villa. The household guard swung the gate open and, even though the villa resided at the seashore, there was but a weak squeak of a hinge.

"My business is concluded," Alerio said projecting snootiness with each word. "The next time, I expect faster service."

The gateway lay open, and the guard occupied an area beside the brick gate post. It should have been a simple beating. And well deserved as Alerio had agitated the guard from the time he arrived until…

The rust on the hinges made the meekest of shrieks. Just enough for Alerio to twist out of the way of the iron gate. And although it did not slam into his shoulder, Alerio stumbled forward and tripped as if the iron had made contact.

He rolled quickly and caught the boot that traveled towards his ribs. Rolling onto the guard's leg and using the side of the knee joint to push to a standing position, Alerio rose over the guard.

He pounded the back of the man's head with an elbow. Then again, the bent arm rocked the guard's cranium.

"How many household guards?" Alerio demanded.

Reeling from the battering to his brain and not thinking clearly, the man replied, "Six household guards."

"You shouldn't kick so hard," Alerio suggested.

Then Alerio rolled down the outstretch leg, hit the ground, and shoved off the gravel. He rose and fell before rolling away from the dazed guard.

"Enough, please, I apologize," Alerio cried.

Coming to his feet, Alerio stumbled away in the direction of his horse and rig.

Behind him, the guard noticed the result of his kick to the teamster's ribs.

"Next time keep a civil tongue when talking to me," the household guard warned. Then he scolded himself. "Hold back on those kicks. The knee hurts and you've given yourself a headache."

The household guard ambled back to the gate satisfied with beating respect into the new teamster. On the street, Alerio rode away armed with the knowledge of how many men guarded Tristis' villa.

***

An almost full moon peeked over the horizon, but its illumination failed to reach the ground. Clouds blocked most of the moonlight. Even in the subdued light, Alerio could see four other rigs waiting on the side of the road. He eased in behind them.

A mounted rider trotted along the defensive wall of the Legion Post. At Alerio's rig, he pulled up.

"Sisera, you are right on time," Silenus told him.

"Yes, sir," Alerio responded. He tilted his head and the felt hat lifted. From under the brim, he remarked. "The others are early."

"Yes, they were," Silenus acknowledged with a chuckle. "But you are right on time, Top Coin."

"Right on time," Alerio mimicked.

The head porter rode to another mounted man. They exchanged words and both laughed. Shortly after the conversation, the riders and the five carts started forward. When they reached the gate to the Legion Post, the second rider stopped at the gatehouse. He spoke to a stooped Legionary NCO.

While the other carts rolled by the Sergeant of the Guard and the mounted man, Alerio kept his head down and his face hidden in the shadow of the hat. When he came through the gate, a quick glance confirmed the identities.

The injured Optio Noxalis leaned against the side of the guardhouse talking to Agent Tristis who sat on his horse. Something illegal was taking place. The lateness of the loading and the pouch of coins the agent passed down to the Legion Optio confirmed it.

However, Alerio had a problem. He had no idea of the nature of the crime or even proof of a misdeed. Blind to the facts, he urged the horse forward to keep up with the other teamsters.

Head Porter Silenus and the parade of rigs circled a structure. In the dark it was hard to see which building. Only when moonlight streamed through a break in the clouds did Alerio see a double row of river rocks and the black soil of a garden. Then the moonlight faded, and the carts circled the structure to stop at the supply depot's shipping and receiving department.

"Six barrels or containers for each cart," Silenus instructed. He slipped off the horse and walked towards a man standing in the dark. Over his shoulder, the head porter cautioned. "Look for the marked barrels and containers. I don't want us taking any of those that came in over the last few days. For every unmarked barrel you take. You will lose the fee for that container."

The orders sent four of the teamsters rushing for the open doorway. But Alerio took a moment to check the mare. While pulling on the harness, he tried to see the man talking to Silenus.

"Top Coin get in there and help with the loading," the head porter instructed.

Silenus turned to the man in the shadows and said something. They laughed. As Alerio shuffled towards the building, the man turned, probably from curiosity about someone named Top Coin, to face Alerio.

His features were blank in the dark although he appeared short and stocky. Then the clouds parted and Alerio saw a patrician nose and aristocratic features. Other than the black orbs of his eyes from the dark night, the man would not look out of place in the Senate of the Republic. Or leading a trade delegation. Where he did look out of place was at the back of a Legion shipping and receiving area in the middle of the night. Alerio lost sight of the man when he entered the building. But he would not forget the nobleman's face.

The carts rolled away from the building when thirty containers and barrels were loaded. Behind them, the nobleman and Silenus closed the doors to the shipping and receiving department. The Head Porter caught up to the rigs as they left the Legion Post.

Agent Tristis joined them for a short stretch. At the crossroads, the agent took the road to the town while Silenus and the caravan continued northeast on the road heading away from Ostia and the coast.

Chapter 12 – Weight of Expectations

They traveled the dark road, moving slowly to protect the horses' hooves and the cartwheels from obstructions. At the six-mile marker, the sides of the roads became dotted with the embers from hundreds of campfires. The ten-man tents at each campsite and the evenly spaced sentries were familiar to Alerio. They also tipped him off as to why Tristis chose this night to move the goods. The newly formed Legions, under the command of Consul Paterculus, were marching to Ostia.

In the morning, shipping, receiving, and rest of the supply depot would be overwhelmed by the arriving Legions. Whatever had been taken, would not be missed for months, if ever.

"First Maniple," Alerio noted when Silenus rode up next to his cart.

"How can you tell in the dark?" the head porter inquired.

"The lines of the tents must be straight," Alerio said sounding reasonable. Silenus was taken aback by the clarity of Top Coin. But then, the teamster added. "Straight lines, straight pegs, or someone will break a leg.

90

See here Optio, the tents must be straight, lest there be a mistake. And our Tribune marches the Second Maniple in with the first wave."

"That's the Top Coin I know," Silenus stated before riding back to the head of the convoy, "spouting nonsense."

Alerio looked again at the uneven rows of tents and nodded at his observation.

"Definitely, the tents of inexperienced First Maniple Centuries."

***

By daylight, the tail end Centuries of the Legions were breaking camp far behind the line of teamsters. Silenus signaled them off the road and ordered a rest period. While the porters were hungry and stiff, before stretching their legs, the men tended their horses. A little discomfort was nothing compared to losing a horse and trying to pull a cart by yourself.

"How far?" Alerio asked another of the porters.

"We'll raft the rigs across the Tiber at Mostacciano," the teamster responded. "From there it's seven miles to the workshops at Malagrotta."

"Forges?" Alerio inquired. "Metalworkers?"

"You like ironworks, do you?" the porter commented. "Sorry to disappoint. But all you'll find there are barrel makers and a few armorers to check and repackage the equipment."

Alerio nodded and went back to feeding the mare. Whatever they were hauling was not broken or used equipment. And if armorers were involved, the cargo must be armor, helmets, gladius, arrowheads, and spearheads. But what foreign government or tribe would be a customer for stolen Legion equipment?

The caravan finished resting the animals and the rigs snaked back onto the road. Ahead was Mostacciano, the waystation, and the ferry. The men would cook and eat while waiting for their turn to board the raft and cross the Tiber. At least that was Alerio's assumption.

***

Ordered to cross first, Alerio backed the mare and cart onto the raft.

"A little further," a pole man directed.

"I am right here, girl," Alerio coached the horse. He tugged at the bridle. "Step back. Good. Good."

"Hold there," a ferry crewman ordered.

Alerio pulled the horse's head down and scratched her ear.

Once the cart and horse were centered, the rivermen untied from the anchor posts and, using their poles, shoved off from the shore. The polemen allowed the current to turn the ferry until the horse faced the other bank. But the mare could not see the land. Alerio stood beside her, holding a cloth over her eyes while gently stroking and talking to her.

The opposite shoreline resembled the launch area they had just left. Access to the river and solid footing over the soft lowland, required a bedding of crushed rocks and gravel. While the land on either side of the roads leading to the raft landings looked rich, the damp, dark soil on the banks were unsuitable for building or planting.

The color of the Tiber gave rise to a nickname, The Blonde. Alerio watched the yellowish water as the raft plowed through the deepest part of the river. Thankfully, the large raft barely rocked in the current. He had been up the Tiber from the sea to the Capital several times. On each trip, he watched the land slide by without a thought to the width of the Tiber. Further up on the bank, a tall post with hash marks noted historical highs. It gave a visual clue to why the farms and structures were built so far from the river's edge.

The normal flow level of the Tiber vanished several times a year when the 'The Blonde' flooded. According to notches on the post, the launching and landing points for the raft, and the surrounding land, would be 6 to 7 feet below the surging river.

"You must be new," a pole man remarked.

"Why do you say that?" Alerio questioned.

"You are first over," the raft man told him.

"Is first a good omen or a bad sign?" Alerio asked.

"Some of those horses are skittish," the pole man informed Alerio. He nodded in the direction of the launch ramp. "They can't be trusted to stay on the raft while hooked up to the rig."

"If a horse goes over the side, the beast drowns," Alerio summarized. "And the cargo and cart go into the river with it. What's the solution?"

"They send over the carts separate from the horses," the riverman explained. "You have the job of unloading the carts."

"Like in the Legion?" Alerio guessed. "I unload the first cart and when the horse comes over, the teamster unloads the next cart."

"That would be fair and reasonable," the raft man admitted. He pulled his pole from the water momentarily, pointed the tip at the rest of the caravan, and sank the bronze cap back into the water. "If teamsters were fair and reasonable."

Alerio gawked back at five cookfires and the two rigs already backed onto the ramp. Silenus noted Alerio. The head porter smiled and waved, then sat at his fire to stir the content of an iron pot.

***

Two roundtrips across the Tiber later, the mare fought the harness. This was the fourth and last cart and her normal patience had stretched thin. Or maybe she was picking up on her handler's attitude. Across the river the teamsters laughed at the antics.

"Last one," Alerio promised. Calming himself for the sake of the mare, he tossed a strap over her back. "We will eat soon, but first a little sabotage."

Alerio finished hooking up the mare and they pulled the rig off the raft. He guided her to a spot high on the bank where the other three rigs waited. With the carts hiding him from view, he rubbed a rope on one of the rigs with the side of his dagger. Just before the rope holding the barrels frayed enough to begin unwinding, he stopped. Then he led his horse away from the carts while the raft returned to the other side of the river.

At an old fire pit, Alerio stacked wood and struck flint. Three horses and a trio of teamsters boarded the raft. As they floated across, Alerio's flames blazed to life, and he hung a pot of vegetables over the fire. While his meal cooked, he pulled a sack of grain from the storage box and fed his horse.

***

By midafternoon, the landscape changed. From flat ground, hills rose and fell, and the road became rockier. The rolling and bouncing tossed the teamsters and the barrels around. On one rig, the rope holding the cargo in place began to unravel. As the fibers twisted loose, the tilt of the barrels increased.

At the base of a steep grade, a bump caused the containers to leap off the bed and slam against the rear of the cart. As the rig started upward, a final rut shifted the entire load. The rope snapped and two barrels toppled off the back.

"Perfututum, me," the teamster shouted.

"I am perfututum," Silenus echoed when he saw the reason for the curse.

The barrels split and the contents of both spilled down the hill.

Alerio pulled the mare to a stop and leaped from his cart. Strolling forward, he took a quick inventory of gear sprawled down the slope. All of it appeared to be in good condition. Helmets, shoulder sections of armor, chest and back pieces, and sword belts. In the other barrel, he saw helmets, daggers, arrows, and spearheads.

'None of it seems to be broken,' Alerio thought while picking up pieces of barrel, 'and not just repaired, but new.'

"The rope broke," complained the teamster who lost part of his load. "I checked the rope before we crossed."

Alerio froze and waited for Silenus to connect him with the damaged line.

"Did you check the rope after the raft ride?" the head porter questioned. "Or when we reached the hills?"

"Well, no," the man admitted.

"Stash what you can on your rig," Silenus ordered. "And distribute the rest among the other carts. We can't waste the rest of the day repacking the equipment."

Alerio dropped the barrel sections and snatched up an arm load of mixed armor. With the illusion of having helped with the disaster, he went to his rig. While stuffing the armor pieces between his barrels and the open spaces in the corners of his cart, he studied the tradesman's marks stamped into the metal and leather. He didn't recognize them or connect the equipment with a specific manufacturer. What he did notice was the absence of a second brand which would signify the gear had been reworked or repaired. The clean brands confirmed his initial impression. The gear was new.

"Let's move," Silenus called to the porters.

Alerio snapped the reins. As the cart rolled forward, he again pondered the subject of a customer with the coins and the need for stolen Legion gear.

Act 4

Chapter 13 – The Customer

Malagrotta offered little in the way of attractiveness. Small patches of cultivated soil along the road testified to the unsuitability of the ground. Further evidence of poor conditions and lack of water were displayed by widely spaced stands of stunted trees. Rocky gullies and dirt mounds seemed to be the dominant features of the area.

Yet, when the caravan topped a hill, a complex of small buildings and work lean-tos came into view. And despite the lack of local resources, the collection of structures resembled a thriving town complete with a walled estate to the east.

"Take the carts to the storage building," Silenus advised. He indicated a structure on the other side of Malagrotta. "Unloaded the cargo and meet me on the west side."

Silenus kneed his mount and rode towards the estate. The five carts, following his directions, weaved through the hamlet. As they moved, Alerio caught site of men standing at work benches. Some inspected gear before scraping and buffing away the existing stamps. Others applied new identification marks to the equipment and did a second inspection. Finally, young apprentices collected the rebranded gear and carried the helmets, sections of armor, and gladii to a packing area.

'There are not enough planted fields to feed a village of this size," Alerio thought as the rigs lined up in front of the storage building. Hopping down, he untied the rope, freeing the barrels. Then he asked a neighboring teamster. "What is this place?"

"This, Top Coin, is the Malagrotta Armory Works," the porter informed him before laughing.

Other than a couple of metalworking stations and workbenches, the village contained little associated with a hot grimy armory.

"Isn't Silenus going to help us unload?" Alerio asked.

"Silenus doesn't sweat since he became Tristis' head porter," the man replied.

"So where does he go while we work?" Alerio pressed.

"Into the villa to drink vino and eat beef with the boss man. And to collect our coins," the teamster responded. "Come on. Help me with my load and I'll help with yours."

They took sides and lifted the first barrel. As the teamsters carried the container to the storage building, Alerio wondered how he could get close enough to lay eyes on the man buying the stolen goods.

***

The sun rested low in the eastern sky and to keep it out of their eyes, the teamsters from Ostia sat facing westward. It was why the arrival of the convoy took them by surprise.

One of them twisted around, peered into the bright sunlight, and inquired, "I wonder what they are hauling?"

Alerio squinted eastward while lifting a hand to the brim of his hat to shade his eyes. It took several moments to make out the cargo on the rigs. Once sure of the loads, Alerio strolled to his storage box and exchanged the wide brimmed petasos for a snug fitting woolen hat. Then he lifted out a wineskin and hung the strap on his shoulder.

"Are those your night caps?" a teamster joked.

"Don't need a brim at night," Alerio stated with authority.

"Top Coin, it is a miracle that you can feed yourself," another of the porters teased.

The four men shifted, once again placing their backs to the sun. Alerio, however, strolled away on a path that would intersect with the convoy.

"Where is Top Coin going?" one asked.

"I don't know," another porter replied. "And I don't care where that fool goes."

One poked the campfire while the rest settled back to wait for Silenus and their pay.

Away from the camp and out of sight, Alerio picked up his pace. He needed to choose the correct cart and make friends with the driver before the convoy reached Malagrotta.

Of the six rigs, two lagged far behind as if hauling something heavier than grain, vegetables, or meat. Alerio gave the slower ones only a glance because he had selected his target.

"Travel far?" he asked while falling in step with the second cart.

"We left the high country two days ago," the teamster replied.

"My group came out of Ostia yesterday," Alerio told him. Then he patted the wineskin. "Think we can trade?"

"I can do an even weight," the man offered. "If you help me unload."

"I have a taste for beef," Alerio said before agreeing. "It's a deal."

He handed the wineskin to the teamster. While the man took a stream of vino, Alerio reached under the goatskin cover and sliced off a section of meat.

He held up a red mass of dried beef that covered his hand.

"Good?" Alerio questioned.

"Yes," the teamster acknowledged. "I have three hindquarters and the guards never offer to help."

"Guards?" Alerio asked. "Who gets the delivery?"

"The beef always goes to the villa," the porter reported.

"Who owns the estate?" Alerio asked.

"Some priest from the Capital," the teamster answered. "I don't know which temple. All I care about is he pays and doesn't cheat me."

"I can understand that feeling," Alerio concurred.

The convoy moved into the village and became visible to the Ostia porters. To avoid questions later, Alerio stooped a little to hide behind the horse as the rig moved away from the other carts.

As his rig approached the estate, the porter called to the guard, "Open the gate."

"What are you hauling?" a household guard demanded.

The guard's mannerisms were odd. Most estate sentries were untrained muscle or men who had served in the Legion. This guard stood erect and only pivoted his head to look in the direction of the cart. His head movement, almost as if he were a statue, puzzled Alerio.

"Beef for the villa," the teamster replied. He pulled back on the reins and the horse stopped a cart's length from the gate.

"Wait there," the guard ordered.

He marched away and Alerio had his answer about the sentry. Legionaries marched to stay together during Century movements. The other reason to march was for parades or exhibitions. In those, Legion stomps were used to keep the ranks in unison.

The measured gait of the guard, leaving no knee lift for the stomp, and his stiff neck revealed the household guard's true profession. He was a Temple Guard. And not from a small Sanctuary to a minor God, but from a major Temple with lots of visitors. Enough worshipers that the guards needed to be visible to keep order, but unobtrusive to the inflow of bodies and coins, and accommodating to the outflow of blessed citizens.

The observation did not tell Alerio who the priest was, but it did eliminate an easily dominated celebrant. The owner of the estate and the buyer of the stolen gear had the backing of a powerful Temple. While thinking about the delicate nature of accusing a priest of buying stolen gear, Alerio peered at the convoy's last two carts.

"For every unmarked barrel you take," Silenus had warned. "You will lose the fee for that container."

Thinking of that remark, Alerio visualized the garden at the shipping and receiving building. River rocks outlined the garden, although the Tiber River at Ostia did not have any large rocks. Then, peering at the loads on the last two rigs, he realized the extent of the theft. And conversely, who the ultimate customer was for the stolen Legion gear.

"Are you coming?" the teamster questioned.

"Yes. I was just admiring the river rock on the carts," Alerio answered.

"They ship them to Ostia as ballast for warships."

"That sounds reasonable," Alerio lied.

In fact, warships did not use ballast of any kind. Alerio accompanied the rig into the compound. As they moved beyond the guard and gate, a realization occurred to him. The smooth rocks were shipped to Ostia, but not to the port and not as stabilizers for vessels.

***

The hindquarter of beef weighed as much as a man. It took Alerio balancing the odd shape on his back and the teamster taking the weight of the leg to transport the meat. They stumbled from the cart to a series of tables placed side by side. While they offloaded the first piece, the butcher stood at the rig inspecting the other two sections.

"The meat appears properly aged," he declared.

The butcher slapped the meat to test the firmness just before Alerio hoisted the second quarter onto his back. As the porter and Alerio walked the meat to the tables, the butcher punched and poked the last hindquarter.

"Three excellent hinds," he stated. Then glancing into the cart, he spied the hand sized piece of steak. "What's this? A loose piece of meat."

"That's his payment," the teamster informed the butcher pointing at Alerio.

"Then let him earn it," the butcher directed. He stepped back to allow the men to reach into the rig.

Alerio and the teamster pulled the quarter to the edge of the cart and struggled to lift the huge dogleg shaped hind. Once up, Alerio slipped under the beef. Then he and the porter carried it to the tables.

"Here is your fee," the butcher said.

He held out a coin purse to the teamster but held the steak close to his side.

"What about my payment?" Alerio inquired.

"It's the master's beef," the butcher informed him. "And not the porters to offer. If you have a problem with the pay, talk to the teamster. Now leave the compound."

"We made a deal," Alerio shouted. He moved forward and crowded the butcher with his chest. "A deal is a deal."

"Guards. Remove these two," the butcher shouted.

His call brought three Temple Guards. And a pair of men from the backdoor of the villa. Silenus was one of the two.

"Top Coin, what are you doing?" the head porter asked.

A man in a silver edged robe stood beside Silenus. Lean of face, he could have been a businessman or a politician. Even his small squinty eyes disclosed a man who studied accounting scrolls more than the landscape.

"They took my payment," Alerio complained. While his demeanor displayed nervousness, Alerio secretly studied the man in the expensive robe. "I worked for the steak."

The teamster's description of the villa's owner being a priest put the man's dress in perspective. But there was no jewelry to identify which temple.

"Do you know this man?" the priest asked Silenus.

"Top Coin is strong and a good teamster," the head porter acknowledged. "But he is slow. Master Tristis believes from fighting with a Legion."

"You there," the priest barked.

Alerio braced and saluted the celebrant, then added, "Yes, Senior Tribune."

The priest smiled at the assumed rank before asking, "Where did you serve?"

"Flaccus Legion at Volsinii, sir," Alerio replied. "Were you there?"

"Very interesting," the priest said ignoring Alerio's question. "Keep the steak."

The priest turned and Alerio panicked. He needed more information. While he formulated a strategy to keep the man engaged, Silenus delivered the intelligence.

"Fetial Mattia, thank you for your generosity," Silenus remarked.

"It's the least I can do," Mattia assured him. "I advised Quintus Gurges to go and put down the revolt at Volsinii. Unfortunately, the Consul got himself killed and most of a Legion murdered. Flaccus had to go in and clean up the mess. In a way, I feel responsible for the young man's injury."

"Still, sir, the steak is a mark of your charitable nature," Silenus advised.

"So it is," Mattia acknowledged.

The priest and the head porter vanished into the villa. In the rear yard, the butcher offered the meat to Alerio.

When he did not reach for it, the butcher advised, "Take the steak or I will keep it."

The porter grabbed the steak and Alerio's arm.

"We are leaving," he advised. After pulling a stunned Alerio onto the cart, the teamster snapped the reins and guided the horse to the gate. "Friend, you have a peculiar way of accepting a gift."

Alerio was not play acting at being Top Coin. In this instance, he really felt brain addled as well as afraid.

The Fetiales were a sect of celebrants dedicated to Jupiter. As the Sky Father and the God of Good Faith, Jupiter offered insight into commerce and treaties. The Fetiales deciphered Jupiter's wishes and spoke for the God to the Senate in matters of trade negotiations and foreign affairs.

Accusing a Fetial Priest of theft would put Alerio uncomfortably close to the top of a cross.

"You keep the steak," Alerio told the porter. "I've lost my appetite."

Chapter 14 – Accused Not Convicted

The four porters from Ostia and Silenus slept late. In the soft light of dawn, Alerio studied the fading stars. They offered no council for his dilemma. When wagons rolled and drivers called to teams of horses, Alerio climbed to his feet to see what was happening.

Three large wagons, each pulled by a pair of horses, left the hamlet. Then from the estate, a cart raced to fall in with the transports. Finally, Fetial Priest Mattia and two Temple Guard trotted from the villa. They caught up with and rode passed the wagons.

"Where are you going, Top Coin?" Silenus asked. He propped himself up on an elbow and watched Alerio harness his horse to the cart.

"My sister is in the Capital," Alerio replied. He stopped and held up a purse of coins. "She will like that I earned top coin."

"I'm sure she will," the head porter offered. "When you are finished visiting family, come to Ostia. With the Legion comes business and we need you and your rig."

"I will be in Ostia," Alerio told him.

With a gentle urging, the horse moved away from the campsite. Alerio allowed her to pick her way around Malagrotta. Even when the cart reached the road heading east, he did not pressure the beast. Mostly because an empty cart could not catch riders on horseback but could easily outpace three heavily loaded wagons.

He knew the destination of the priest and could make a guess about the wagons. But he wanted to be sure where the barrels and crates went. So, while a chase, it was not a race. He sat on the bed of the cart and let the mare pick her own pace.

***

At the five-mile marker, the land changed drastically. Green grass and crops grew in sweeping fields. Yet, while the land was cultivated, there were no permanent villas or farmhouses. Only utilitarian and replaceable buildings dotted the landscape and all the structures used rough lumber for their construction. Upon closer inspection, Alerio noted debris from river flooding wrapped around the trunks of hardy trees. Just two miles further on, the Tiber River flowed, for now, within her banks.

Alerio guided the mare off the road and pulled back on the reins. Ahead, the three wagons and the cart stopped as well. Once sure no traffic approached from the far bank, the teamster on the first wagon climbed down and positioned himself at the front of his team. Then he tugged and led the horses onto the bridge name Pons Sublicius. It was called that because it was a bridge resting on piles.

Below the bridge and under the fast-flowing water, sharpened logs had been hammered into the bottom of the river. On the pilings were affixed crossbeams that linked the neighboring piles and the road boards that spanned the Tiber. Over its lifetime, the bridge suffered damages many times from natural catastrophes. Only once had it been purposely ravaged. Two hundred and fifty years ago, shortly after the Senate removed their King, the Romans demolished the Pons Sublicius to stop the invasion of an Etruscan army. Shortly afterwards, it was rebuilt to allow the bridge to carry commerce back and forth over the Tiber River.

The bridge wobbled slightly as the heavy wagon rolled over the boards. Speaking softly and reassuringly, the teamster kept a firm grip on the horses. Kickboards, only an ankle high, ran along either edge of the bridge. Without railings, a panicked horse could easily take its harness mate and the wagon over the side.

Alerio waited for the three wagons and the cart to cross before he urged the mare back onto the road. The horse moved briskly until they neared the bridge. Then she stopped in the middle of the road.

"Just a little further," Alerio suggested.

But the mare wanted no part of the steep embankment, the water below, and the narrow bridge. After stepping down, Alerio moved to her head and patted the animal's neck.

"We'll walk it," he told her. "You keep your eyes on the boards. I will tell you what you are missing."

A tug and half a step persuaded the horse that Alerio intended for the cart to follow him onto the narrow path.

"It's solid underfoot," he bragged. But Alerio resisted the tendency to stomp his foot to demonstrate the sturdiness of the decking. "The big wagons and teams made it across. You should have no problem."

The mare's ears flicked back and forth rapidly, and she hesitated. Seeing the signs of anxiety, Alerio patted her and cooed.

"When we get to the other side," he promised. "I will fill your bag with oats. That sounds good, doesn't it?"

His voice and the firm pressure on her buckle strap kept the horse moving.

"To our left is Tiber Island," Alerio informed her. "The building, don't you look I'll describe it for you. The building is the Temple of Aesculapius. It was built during a plague in hopes the Greek God of Healing would stop the disease."

At the center of the bridge, the mare's muzzle tightened, and her mouth pursed. The tension warned Alerio of her stress and worry. He needed to get her focused on him and not on the possibility of falling off either side.

"What's that you ask?" he teased in a relaxed tone. "Did the pestilence stop with the building of the Temple?"

They passed the halfway point.

"I don't know about that one, but there have been other plagues since," he said. "But Aesculapius is a foreign God, and you can never tell about those Greeks."

They reached the far side and Alerio looked at the crowded streets searching for the wagons. When he could not locate them, he selected a road and walked the mare in that direction.

***

Taking advantage of the narrow cart, Alerio dodged through alleyways. When they reached a wide plaza, he pulled the mare to the side of the road and got out her feed.

"You made it across, and I am proud of you," he said as he poured her a generous portion of grain. "Now let's see if I am correct."

He peered across the plaza at the Legion warehouse. Wagons arrived and others departed. For years, the garrison Legions requisitioned from craftsmen or constructed their equipment from the regions where they were assigned. But the heavy use of marching Legions to stem the aggression of the Qart Hadasht Empire required infantry equipment. While the number of Legionaries needed for the fleet, and the addition of a permanent half Legion in Sicilia brought about the need for a central distribution point. As Colonel Gaius Claudius pointed out, the Legion was changing.

From a street several blocks away, the three wagons from Malagrotta came into view. The teamsters drove the horses around the plaza before turning off and heading for the Legion warehouse.

Here was confirmation of Alerio's assumption. Although hurtful, he knew the customer for the stolen Legion equipment. The criminal enterprise sold not to a foreign military but peddled the Legion's own gear back to the Republic's procurement department. With a sick feeling in his stomach, Alerio climbed on the cart and ordered the mare forward.

He needed a bath and advice. In Rome there were several quality baths. But only one where he could get trusted advice from a politically powerful man.

***

Several blocks from the forum and the Senate building, Alerio pulled the mare off the main road and onto a driveway. At a statue to Bia, he eased the horse to a stop.

"Goddess Bia, thank you for the strength of my body and my drive," Alerio prayed to the statue before hopping to the pavers.

When the door to Villa Maximus opened, a scowling Belen charged out. Behind him, two men-at-arms moved through the doorway and flanked the secretary.

"Deliveries are made at the rear gate," he instructed the teamster in the dirty clothing.

"If I had anything to deliver except me," Alerio replied while facing Belen. "I would gladly use another entrance."

"Master Sisera, I did not recognize you," Belen gasped. "Please come in."

"The mare is a good draft animal," Alerio described. "But I'll need a mount to get back to the Central Legion at Ariccia."

"You aren't staying?" Spurius Maximus' secretary inquired.

"No. But I need a bath, a change of clothing, a conversation with my father, and a good meal," Alerio told him. "Then I have to go."

"The bath, food, change, and horse we have available," Belen advised. "The Senator, however, is at a luncheon feast."

They moved to the villa and Belen deferred to the master of the villa's adopted son. Alerio walked through the doorway and waited for the secretary to catch up. Leaning over, Alerio whispered.

"How hard is it to convict a Fetial Priest of criminal activity?" he inquired.

"Accused, unfortunately for a beloved of the Senate, is not legally punishable," Belen responded. "And your testimony against a Fetial Priest, who speaks with the authority of Jupiter, is far from a conviction."

"You are saying it's hard," Alerio guessed.

"Most likely impossible, Master Sisera," Belen added. "Before we speak any more, may I request that you bathe?"

After scrubbing, scraping, and oiling his body, Alerio ate while writing a letter to Senator Maximus. He laid out the criminal organization and the ways and means of the crimes. At the end, he added a warning about Fetial Mattia and a request that the Senator and the Senate handle that part of the investigation.

Once finished, he went to the stables and selected a horse. Shortly after noon, Alerio kicked the mount into motion. He rode across the city to the southern gate. Once outside the wall, he relaxed and let the horse carry him towards Central Legion's training camp.

Chapter 15 – Vengeance of the Wronged

The buildings of Albano Laziale rose in tiers with the hills. The sun dipped low to the east casting bright light on the faces of the structures while creating shadows on their sides. Before reaching the town, Alerio guided his mount off the Via Latina and onto an unpaved road.

Five miles later, he stopped at the gate of the Legion camp at Ariccia.

"Tribune Alerio Sisera," he told the sentry. "I can break out my orders but that would take time I don't have."

"Sergeant of the Guard," the Legionary on gate duty hollered. Then to Alerio, he ordered. "Stay right there, sir."

He added the sir because to ignore the possibility of the rider being a staff officer was to invite trouble.

"Name, sir?" an Optio asked while crossing from a post building.

"Tribune Alerio Carvilius Sisera," Alerio replied.

"Go ahead, sir," the NCO instructed.

Alerio kneed the horse and as the mount moved into the camp, the Legionary turned to his Sergeant.

"Do you know him, Optio?" he inquired.

"No, I don't," admitted the Sergeant of the Guard. "But I recognize battle wounds. And that Tribune has seen more combat than almost anyone in this camp. Scars like his tell of an impatient man and not one to be held up by the likes of us. Understand?"

"Yes, Sergeant," the sentry acknowledged.

***

Alerio reined in at the headquarters building, leaped to the ground, and marched into the office.

"I need to see Colonel Claudius," he announced to the staff.

"The Colonel is hosting a dinner," a Centurion replied. "Come back tomorrow and I'll put you on the schedule."

Alerio about faced and marched from the office. On the street, he broke into a jog. Two blocks away, he marched onto the porch of the Battle Commander's private quarters.

"Name, sir," the Legionary on duty asked.

"Alerio Sisera," Alerio responded. "I need to see the Battle Commander."

"Tribune Sisera! You are unexpected," Gaius Claudius called through the open window. "Come in."

Alerio crossed the threshold, walked to the main room, braced, saluted, and began to sweat. Along the walls were the Colonel's bodyguards, a scattering of Junior Tribunes, and several young priests. Their presence being normal, they barely registered.

The Battle Commander lounged at the head of a table. On either side of the room, staff officers holding cups of vino occupied couches. They also were of no consequence to Alerio. However, the Priest of Jupiter on the divan next to Gaius Claudius caused perspiration to break out on his forehead.

"Sir, can we talk in private?" Alerio requested.

"This is my command staff," Claudius announced, "and my honored guest, Cleric Rastellus. So, speak up."

"Sir, I think it's best if we…" Alerio started to say.

"Tribune Sisera. I am not accustomed to repeating myself," Gaius Claudius exclaimed. "I sent you on a mission. Report!"

Not sure if the Battle Commander was showing off and feeling the need to display his authority. Or, if the vino had overwhelmed his senses. In either case, a request from the Colonel amounted to an unquestionable

114

order. Before Alerio could formulate a response that concealed information from the priest, Claudius added.

"I sent Tribune Sisera, the adopted son of Senator Spurius Maximus, to investigate the theft of Legion equipment at Ostia," Gaius Claudius informed everyone in the room. "After that build up, Tribune Sisera, don't disappoint me."

Chapter 16 – Race for Results

"As you said sir, I went to Ostia to investigate the missing gear," Alerio began.

"Nonsense Tribune, you did more than investigate," Claudius beamed. "You went undercover."

"Undercover?" Rastellus, the Priest of Jupiter, inquired. "I traveled from the Capital to visit Jupiter's Temple at Alban Hills. There was an odd donation, and I wanted more details from the priest. When the Colonel asked me to dinner, I almost declined. But now, I am enthralled. Please continue."

Alerio guessed a Fetial Priest would not be traveling to smaller temples inquiring about donations. But Cleric Rastellus did represent the main Temple in Rome and that meant he was acquainted with members of the Fetial Sect.

"I worked my way into the gang of teamsters. When they transported the stolen equipment, I was one of them…," he described the evolution of events. Then Alerio paused and debated how much to include at the end. Finally, after seeing the Battle Commander give him an out-with-it motion, he said. "We transported the goods to a villa in Malagrotta."

Barely visible, the tremor of the priest's hand revealed Rastellus' knowledge of who owned the country house. To Alerio, it became a race to see who would be first to arrive at the villa in Malagrotta and at the Legion warehouse in Rome. If Claudius' Centuries got there fast, they would find the stolen gear, the work benches, and the barrels of repackaged equipment. If the Legionaries were delayed, people from the Temple would remove any sign of the crime.

"I traced the wagons and the equipment to the Legion distribution center," Alerio concluded. "After watching them enter the Legion warehouse, I rode here, sir."

No one questioned his cleanliness or the clothes he wore. For now, the stop at Villa Maximus would remain undisclosed. Alerio was not sure why, but keeping his adopted mother, Aquila, out of the affair seemed prudent. While Senator Spurius Maximus could decide for himself if he wanted to be involved.

"What is our next step?" Gaius Claudius asked. He seemed more somber and business like than before.

While Alerio replied, a young priest answered a hand signal from Rastellus.

"Colonel. We need two detachments," Alerio blurted out. "One for the villa and one for the warehouse."

Alerio wanted to add a warning about the Fetial Priest Mattia. But a Battle Commander, despite his military expertise, had no business going to war with a

Temple. Especially against clerics who commanded the ears of the Senate and carried Jupiter's thoughts on their lips.

"I want two Senior Tribunes in charge. Take at least one Junior Tribune with you, and a Century of infantry," Claudius directed. "Put cavalry out front and move fast. Secure the two locations until I arrive."

The young celebrant fast walked to the door. Once out of the main room, he broke into a sprint. Alerio took his departure as an indication that Mattia was as good as warned.

"Rastellus, please excuse me," Claudius solicited. "I may be a while, if you care to wait."

"No, thank you Colonel. It was a most enjoyable feast," the priest acknowledged, "but I have business at the Temple."

"As you wish," Claudius responded. "Sisera, walk with me."

Alerio followed the Battle Commander out of the main room. Down a hallway, they entered the Colonel's private quarters.

***

"I am not a garden, and I don't appreciate having merda spread all over me," Gaius Claudius said while moving to a wardrobe. "Transport and storage of stolen goods is only half the story. You are too smart to have stopped your investigation there."

"That is correct, sir. A Tribune named Gutteris in Ostia orchestrates the thefts," Alerio informed the Colonel. "On the buying and repackaging end is a Fetial Priest."

"A Priest of Jupiter?" Claudius stated. He stopped pulling on his Battle Commander's armor and glanced at the door. As if envisioning his guest in the great room, he observed. "Rastellus is from that Temple."

"Yes, sir," Alerio confirmed.

"And I told him your parentage," Claudius admitted. "For that I am sorry."

"Colonel, I left word about the Fetial with my adopted father," Alerio explained. "It's best to let Senator Maximus decide on how to deal with the priest."

Colonel Claudius gnashed his teeth together before allowing a smile to ease his features. Then he buckled on a sword belt and squared his shoulders.

"We may not be able to challenge him. But the Legion can hurt the thieving holy man," Claudius offered. He walked towards a stand where his helmet was mounted. "If we get to Malagrotta and find evidence, I'll personally order the dismantling of the estate. That at least will cost him. Come with me."

"Sir, I need to get to Ostia before the news reaches there," Alerio cautioned.

"That's right, the disloyal Tribune," Claudius expressed his anger by spitting out the words. "Do you need an escort?"

"No sir," Alerio replied as they walked out of the private quarters. "Phobos and I will make better time alone."

"Get him arrested, trussed up in knots, and sent to me in a slop cart," the Battle Commander ordered. "Stealing gear leaves the Legions short. Unequipped

Legionaries die because of other men's greed. If I could, I would crucify Gutteris without a trial."

"He is a Tribune, sir," Alerio reminded the aggravated Colonel. "You cannot simply execute a Patrician."

"I am glad to see you are starting to sound like a nobleman, Sisera," Claudius observed. "And less like, what's that the Legionaries in Sicilia called you? Death Caller."

"Yes, sir. But my warning is not as a nobleman," Alerio corrected. "I am an infantry officer watching out for his Battle Commander."

"When you are done, get back here and make a proper report," Claudius advised. "Until then, take care of things in Ostia."

"I intend to, sir," Alerio promised as they walked out of the front door.

Colonel Claudius' staff and a mounted contingent of First Century infantrymen sat waiting for him. Alerio saluted the Battle Commander and ran for the stables.

***

The chestnut horse held his head aloft and walked the rut that ran along the back rail of the corral. It seemed the beast was purposely ignoring his master.

"Phobos. You can remain here," Alerio advised the stallion. "For all the good you are doing me, I can ride a pack mule to Ostia."

"He is a mean one, sir," a stockyard man cautioned. "Bites he does, and kicks anyone who get close."

"There is a horse from Villa Maximus tied up at the headquarters building," Alerio instructed. "Be sure it gets back to the Capital."

"Want me to fetch you another ride before I go, sir?" the man questioned.

"No, I'll be taking this one," Alerio assured him. Leaping the fence, Alerio walked to the middle of the corral, stopped, and turned his back to the horse. Then he spoke to the night sky, his voice easily reaching the stallion. "Phobos, let's go. Unless you think I would be better off with a new horsehair blanket, and an icehouse full of horse meat?"

A nudge in the back shoved Alerio half a step forward. He spun around to face the horse.

"I lied to the Colonel," Alerio told Phobos as the man and the horse strolled to the stables. The stallion pushed Alerio with the side of his head as if scolding him. "Well, it was more like a sin of omission. Somehow in my report, I left out Agent Tristis and any mention of my friend Hamus Ivo."

Alerio located his saddle and picked it up by one of the two front horns. Then, he tossed it over Phobos' back and attached the rear strap, the belly tie, and the chest strap.

"We need to get to the Legion Fort. But first we have a stop to make," Alerio informed the horse. He led the animal out of the stable. "The Legion will execute Tristis for his part in the theft, anyway. At least with me, he has a chance."

Phobos shook, most likely to settle the saddle and holding straps. But Alerio took it as a question.

"I know, it's not much of a chance," he replied. "But you have to admit, fighting me will be faster than him hanging on the boards, watching his last sunset."

Alerio tied Phobos to a post and walked to the entrance of a supply tent.

"Who is in charge here?" he demanded while throwing aside the flaps of the tent. "I need a few things from my bundle."

***

Despite the darkness, the big horse cantered effortlessly along the dirt wagon trail. Equipment bags hung from the two rear horns of the saddle. One held a matched set of swords and a dual harness rig. On the other side, the sack contained a change of clothing. Both were for the mission at Tristis' villa. One for cutting his way in, and the other clean clothing so he was presentable at the Legion Fort when he left the compound.

"Up ahead, we should intersect the road to Ostia," Alerio told Phobos. "The going will be easier."

The stallion rocked his head back as if to brush aside the offer of a smoother surface. He seemed content to be out of the corral and on the march.

"Nenia Dea," Alerio prayed. "Is it right that I plan to deliver Tristis into your arms? If so give me a sign. If he delivers me, I beg you to take me quickly."

The moon raced from behind the clouds and dyed the landscape in a silvery sheen. In the moonlight, the turnoff for the paved road to Ostia appeared. As the chestnut stallion left the dirt trail, Phobos increased his pace. Almost as if the horse named after the God of Fear was rushing Alerio to his fate.

Agent Tristis and his household guards slept. They dreamed unaware that Fear carried Death Caller, bringing revenge for the murder of Hamus Ivo to their villa.

Chapter 17 – Field Justice

At the rear of the supply warehouse in the Capital, the Legionaries assigned to the procurement detachment had set up a barracks area. Other than off duty Legionaries, teamsters due to leave early from the Legion distribution center could use a corner of the space. Between the telling of stories and the throwing of dice, the evenings could get rowdy. By late into the night though, the warehouse complex and sleeping areas quieted down. The only sounds were men snoring, the occasional whinny or bray from draft animals, and the clicks of hobnailed boots as sentries patrolled the warehouse.

A loud pounding overrode the subdued noises. The sentries jogged towards the sound while sleeping men rolled over, trying to ignore the rapping on the main door.

"Who is it?" a Legionary demanded.

The two other guards arrived as a voice responded, "Your Optio, you fatuus. Unbar the door."

Being call a simpleton did not bother the sentries. They were happy all three were there and not caught napping on duty by their Sergeant. The bar lifted and the doors swung open on the dark plaza of the city and an impatient NCO.

"What's up, Optio?" one Legionary inquired.

"The loads for Ostia," the NCO replied. He carried a lantern and used the light to identify the three sentries as he entered the warehouse. "We need the wagons loaded and on the way to the shore."

"Right now, Sergeant?" another questioned.

"Have you been touched by Echo?" the Sergeant demanded.

He held the lantern up as if looking into the Legionary's ear.

"No, Optio. I'm from right here in Rome," the guard protested. "I've never seen a mountain nymph."

"Well, she seems to have found you and affected your hearing," the Sergeant uttered. "Yes, now. Get everyone up and load those barrels and crates."

From the silence of midnight, the warehouse filled with the grunts of men rolling barrels up ramps. In the wagons, other men spun and positioned the crates and barrels. The teamsters backed pairs of horses into place and strapped on their harnesses. When the three wagons were loaded and the cargo tied down, the teamsters climbed onto their benches, snapped the reigns, and shouted for the animals to step off.

As the calls for the teams to move reverberated off the roof, Legion cavalrymen raced across the plaza. The horses galloped to the entrance and formed a semicircle.

"You might as well climb down," a Centurion of Horse instructed the drivers. "You aren't going anywhere."

"By whose orders, sir?" the Optio asked.

He expected the hold up was a mistake or the mounted combat officer was exceeding his orders.

"By the authority of Colonel Gaius Claudius, the Battle Commander of the Central Legion," the cavalry officer replied. "This location is locked down. No one in or out until the Colonel releases you."

"And how long will that be, Centurion?" the NCO asked. "We have supplies to deliver."

"That, Optio, is not up to me," the Centurion responded.

***

Being up and awake, the teamsters and the Legionaries not on duty pulled out rations and ate breakfast. The others talked to the mounted Legionaries. It was this festive looking siege Gaius Claudius found when he rode across the plaza.

"Centurion, report," he ordered.

"Sir, these three wagons were about to leave when we arrived," the mounted officer replied.

"Get a couple of barrels opened and let's see what they are carrying," Gaius instructed.

Three cavalrymen jumped onto the wagon, untied the load, and rocked one of the barrels to make room to work. In their haste, another barrel rolled to the edge then toppled off the wagon. It crashed to the floor, cracking open.

Battle Commander Claudius bent over the neck of his horse and stared at the spilled content.

A layer of armor pieces rested on top of a layer of river stone. Alternating strata of equipment and rock continued to the bottom of the barrel. Without opening the container, the rocks would make the barrel weigh as if it were full of heavy gear.

"Open every crate on the three wagons," Claudius ordered. "And arrest everyone in the warehouse."

"But sir, we don't have…" the mounted officer began to say he lacked the manpower to seal every approach to the warehouse. But he stopped.

The sight and sounds of a Century of heavy infantry jogging across the plaza ended his protest.

"I want those barrels inventoried and the gear sorted," Claudius directed. "I'll question the personnel later. But first, I have a villa to inspect."

The Colonel and his entourage spun their horses around. Kneeing the mounts, they galloped across the plaza.

Secretly, Gaius Claudius let out a long breath. While he trusted Tribune Sisera, a man with the nickname of Death Caller and with so much blood on his hands was suspect. Obviously, the barrels at the warehouse were part of a swindle and that proved part of Alerio's allegations. Feeling empowered by the evidence, the Battle Commander looked forward to what he would find in Malagrotta.

***

The horse moved faster than was safe in the dark. But the messenger faced punishment or even exile from Jupiter's Temple if he failed in the mission. With fear for his future driving him, he kicked the mount and charged into the darkness.

A dip in the road, perhaps from a washout during a rainstorm, or simply a depression caused by traffic would not be difficult to navigate during the day. At night however, the rut caught one leg and the mount fell. The future priest tumbled over the beast's shoulder and landed on his back. The horse recovered, walked carefully on the leg, and realized it held weight. Before the youth had an opportunity to stand and test his own limbs, the horse walked away and vanished into the night. Horseless, the messenger pushed to his feet and began jogging towards Malagrotta.

***

Without Fetial Priest Mattia in residence, the two guards kept slack routines. Their patrols of the grounds shrank to almost nil as they figured one sleeping in the villa prevented burglary and one at the gate covered the road. Satisfied their choices were enough to protect the estate, they both dozed overnight.

"Attention, villa," a breathless voice called from a distance.

"Go away beggar," the guard on the gate scolded the voice. "Let an honest man get his sleep."

Closer now, the voice insisted, "Attention, villa."

The guard identified the caller as a young man.

"Begone, child," he growled, "or I will thrash you."

A sweating youth, dirty from the road, stooped in the lantern light. He inhaled trying to catch his breath. With one arm he waved at the guard and pointed to the villa.

"I told you to go away," the gate guard insisted.

"The villa…the Priest…," the young man squeaked out.

"Priest Mattia isn't here," the guard told him. "Even if he was, I would not wake him for the likes of you."

Straightening, the youth exhaled several times.

"I am a messenger from the Temple of Jupiter," he got out before starting to cough.

"If you are a messenger, where is your horse?" the guard demanded.

"The beast stumbled and threw me," the youth responded. "You are directed to remove the Priest's iron bound chest from the villa and take it to the temple."

"Why?" the guard questioned.

"The Legion is coming here, looking for stolen equipment," the messenger said. "Also, warn the craftsmen before you leave."

Having completed his mission, the youth dropped to the road.

"Attention at the gate," the guard yelled.

Moments later, the second Temple Guard arrived.

"We are supposed to take the iron bound chest to the temple," the first reported.

"Says who?" his partner asked.

"The messenger," the one at the gate responded.

"What messenger?"

"The lad sitting in the dirt," the guard pointed out.

"Since when do we take orders from street urchins?"

Before the gate guard could respond, the rumble of hooves came from the dark. In a few heartbeats, a unit of Legion cavalrymen crowded the gate.

"Open it," a Centurion ordered.

"We are Temple…"

A javelin appeared in the guard's chest.

"The Centurion said open the gate," the cavalry's NCO exclaimed. He focused on the second guard. "You. Open the gate or do I have to bury you as well?"

The second guard opened the gate and stepped back.

"Optio, secure the town," the officer instructed.

"Yes, sir," the Sergeant acknowledged. "Give me two squads to the east and two to the west. Two squads stay with the Centurion. The last two, follow me."

No one mentioned the murder of the guard. Then again, no one would. Orders from a Legion combat officer were to be carried out, immediately. The mounted Legionaries split up by squads and rode to surround the town of Malagrotta.

"Disarm him," the officer instructed as his mount passed the gate.

A foot shot out and kicked the Temple Guard in the head. He fell and a Legionary slid off his horse to remove the guard's sword.

Again, no one questioned the Legionary's tactics because the Centurion had ordered it. If the officer wanted mercy or the guard treated gently, he would have added it to the order.

Seeing the fate of the Temple Guards, the youthful messenger faded into the dark. In a stand of trees, he hid among the trunks. After seeing what transpired, he would begin the long walk back to the Capital and the Temple. As he squatted, his mind turned over thoughts of how to explain to Fetial Priest Mattia the loss of his iron bound chest.

***

Colonel Claudius, his bodyguards, and staff rode around a jogging Century. Ahead, the Battle Commander could see the outlines of lean-tos and sheds in the early morning light. A walled estate was the largest structure in the village.

"Where do you want the infantry, sir?" a Tribune asked.

"In the village," Claudius responded. "I want to know if they have stolen Legion gear."

"Yes, sir," the staff officer acknowledged.

He pulled up and trotted back to inform the infantry.

Gaius Claudius led his staff through the gate and reined in at the entrance to the villa. A man in quality armor sat off to the side with two cavalrymen guarding him.

"Look through the house for any contraband," Gaius instructed his staff officers. Then, as he dismounted, the Colonel studied the man being guarded. "Who is that?"

"A man-at-arms from the villa," the Centurion replied. "He keeps asking if I know who owns the house and compound."

"Remove him," the Battle Commander ordered. "If we find Legion gear around here, it won't matter who owns the embers."

At a signal from their officer, the two cavalrymen jerked the Temple Guard to his feet.

"Don't you know…," the Temple Guard shouted.

The combat officer made a fist and swung it across his chest. In reply, one of the mounted Legionaries slammed the hilt of his sword into the guard's face. His jaw shattered and his knees buckled. They hoisted him by his shoulder armor and walked him away from the officers.

"I have a feeling this villa is trouble, sir," the Centurion offered.

"Not for us," Claudius assured him.

One of the Tribunes reappeared on the porch.

"Sir. You need to see this," the staff officer insisted.

"Show me," Claudius said. He followed the Tribune into the house.

***

A chest, the lid once held in place by iron bands, sprawled on the tile floor. Its content spilled out in a wave of expensive fabric.

"Who broke it open?" Claudius asked.

"I did, sir," a nervous Junior Tribune admitted. "They appear to be priest robes."

"I wouldn't know," Gaius lied.

He walked to the chest and nudged it with his hobnailed boot. It felt heavier than it looked. To test the idea, the Battle Commander tapped the wood with his toe. The chest rocked and a bulging sack tumbled out.

"What do we have here?" Claudius pondered.

Reaching down, the Colonel lifted the bag and shook it. Inside the cloth, small pieces of metal clinked together.

"It's a massive coin purse, sir," a Tribune guessed.

Colonel Claudius faced a dilemma. If they did not find stolen gear, he would have to visit the Fetial Priest, return the coins, and apologize for invading his country home. Then, the Centurion called from the front of the villa.

"Colonel, if you please," the combat officer requested. "I need you to see this."

Claudius walked through the house having to strain one arm to hold the coins in one hand. When he walked out of the front door, he no longer worried about visiting the Priest.

"Explain that," Claudius directed.

There were five separate stacks of helmets, another five of chest and back armor, and several more with shoulder rigs.

"The separate piles are from different craftsmen," the Centurion described. "All the gear is new. Sir, in my opinion, this equipment is stolen."

"Burn the villa and put men to the task of dismantling the walls," Claudius ordered. "And after you finish with this place, I want the village burned and every tool broken. Malagrotta has been stealing from the Legion. Therefore, the Legion will turn this place into a dump."

Act 5

Chapter 18 – Better than a Cross

Alerio allowed Phobos to walk slowly through the town of Ostia. Early risers moved between shops and villas, but they were too busy to pay attention to a lone rider. A couple of streets off the main throughfare, Alerio caught a view of the sea. A short distance down the block, he approached the blue villa.

"Why, my friend?" he asked, reining in the horse near the wall. While the rider and saddle were out of sight, Phobos' nose was visible through the iron bars.

"Why what?" the guard at the gate asked. "Come forward if you want to talk to me. I'll not converse with a nag."

"Why, my friend?" Alerio asked again.

"I will not hold a conversation with a man through iron bars," the sentry complained. "Especially one I can't see."

"Why, my friend?" Alerio repeated.

Frustrated and maybe bored from standing sentry early in the morning, the guard unlatched the iron barrier and opened it. Then he stepped outside the wall.

As the gate began moving, Alerio jumped up on the saddle and leaped to the top of the defensive wall. Dangling momentarily, he peered over the wall and into the courtyard.

A single cart rested beside the stable. His bravado of seeking vengeance during the night ride had faded with the sunrise. But seeing Hamus Ivo's rig in Tristis' possession rekindled Alerio's anger. With a kick, he swung his legs to the top of the wall and rolled off the opposite side.

"What?" the guard shouted when he saw a riderless horse and a pair of legs vanish over the wall.

Stepping back, the sentry gripped the gate, preparing to close it before going after...

Phobos reared up and smashed the iron bars with his front hooves.

The gate slammed shut then rebounded, throwing the guard savagely to the ground. With the entrance unobstructed, the stallion pranced into the compound, looking for his master.

Pushing off the ground, the sentry dashed into the courtyard, sprinted around the horse, and ran right into one of Alerio's blades.

"Why, my friend?
Amicitia sends few friends my way
The Goddess blessed me with one
But he seems to be misplaced."

The sentry slid to a stop, drew his sword, and dashed Alerio's aside. While he parried, the Legion officer rapped the man in the head with his second blade.

"They never see that one coming," Alerio observed.

He continued singing as he ran for the stairs on the far side of the courtyard.

"I see signs of his passing this way
I best find him in your bath

Or your black heart
Will feel my wrath."

Another of the household guards jogged from around the stable. Seeing the gate guard on the ground and an intruder heading for the villa's entrance, he drew a dagger, brought it up to his ear, and sighted in on the man's back. At this distance, he rarely missed.

Focused on Alerio, the knife throwing guard failed to pay attention to the chestnut stallion. Before he could pitch the dagger, Phobos rose high into the air and came down. A hoof crushed the man's shoulder.

Hearing the disturbance, Alerio stopped and looked back at the horse. His mount stood menacingly over an injured guard. Unfortunately, the guard moved which angered Phobos. The heavy stallion pawed on the man's back until the guard stopped moving.

"The stockyard man was right. You are crazy," Alerio submitted to the horse. "But you just saved my life, and I will not forget it."

Phobos cocked back his head as if acknowledging the promise. Alerio finished the verse while heading for the stairs.

"Why, my friend?
Answer me if you can."

***

Alerio dashed up the first three risers then stopped. Blocking the stairwell were two more household guards coming from the other direction.

"Why, my friend?"

134

The men-at-arms exchanged puzzled looks, then together, they drew their swords. Their opponent chanted.

"He was not extraordinary nor a Prince
But told good lies around the campfire
His tales they made me wince."

Most people assumed a fighter with two swords preferred offensive moves. What they failed to understand, while one blade attacked, the other acted as a shield. Further confusing the guards facing Alerio, most swordsmen favored their right hand especially if they were former Legionaries. The Legion trained exclusively right-handed to benefit their shield formations.

The men-at-arms on the stairs with Alerio believed these things. They had no way of knowing the intruder was a sword prodigy and ambidextrous.

Alerio poked weakly with his left hand and slashed in an uncontrolled manner with his right.

Two blades, two offensive moves, and the guards relaxed. Taking out this amateur should be easy, they thought.

"A wise man yet too young to expire," Alerio sang.

The blade on the right went from thrashing to countering the opposing sword. While that one blocked, the left blade stiffened and slammed the guard's sword up and out of position.

Alerio's sword swirled in a half circle before snaking under the guard's wrist. The tip and a length of steel pierced the man's forearm. As the blade withdrew, the guard dropped his sword and grabbed the wounded arm.

The move to stem the blood flowing from the arm left the guard on the right alone in the fight. And the swordsman sang.

"Explain why he was killed
Or your rotten heart
Will be skewed and grilled."

Alerio put his arms close together and stabbed with both blades. The remaining guard defended against one sword. It was the other that stabbed him in the neck.

Alerio hopped over the wounded guards and crooned as he moved up the steps.

Why, my friend?
Answer me if you can."

***

A spear made a devastating weapon system. Given room to use the reach and an enemy forced to come from one direction, a spearman had the advantage. The intruder emerging from the stairwell satisfied the directional requirement and the wide hallway provided space.

To the surprise of the household guard with the spear, the intruder sang as he reached the top of the stairs. Even when he saw the steel spearhead, the man, although off key and sounding as if his throat was being tortured, warbled on.

"Why, my friend?
A man's journey is a lonely staircase
With a few rest stations for the heart
Some for tender embraces."

Alerio came level with the second floor and began to spin. His blades held away from his sides as his body rotated. Combined with erratic steps, the revolutions made his torso a blurred target.

Chancing a stab, the spearman jabbed. A snag of fabric caught, then ripped away.

Alerio felt the cloth tear and judged the location of the spear shaft. Reaching across, he hacked into the wood and left the blade in place. Still spinning, he followed the pole.

The spearman was attempting to shake the weight of the impaled blade off his shaft. If he could, the intruder would eat either the spear head or the blunt end of the shaft. Confusing the situation, the interloper sang as he spun.

"Rarer are cases of companionship
Cursed reveal his fate
Or your evil heart
Will be shredded on a grate."

Alerio brought the sword around with his spin and stopped. Buried deep into the spearman's throat, the blade was halted by the bones at the back of the guard's neck.

"Why, my friend?
Answer me if you can."

Alerio retrieved both swords. Then he proceeded along the corridor.

***

From the hallway, Alerio could see into the great room. Agent Tristis stood at the big windows gazing out at the sea.

"Why, my friend?
When you cleaved him from my life
You gouged out a piece of my soul."

Alerio moved rapidly towards the room and the criminal transporter. Just before he reached the doorway, Tristis turned.

With a smile on his lips, the agent greeted Alerio, "Welcome back, Top Coin. Come in. Let's talk."

Something gnawed at the back of Alerio's mind.

"In the emptiness that is left
I am filled with hurt and distress."

Alerio reached the end of the hall, bent his knees, and dove into the room. An arrow shot across the threshold. If he had walked in, the sixth household guard would have sunk an arrow into his chest.

"Tell me before it goes badly
Or your cold heart
I will cut out gladly."

Rolling forward, Alerio came up on a knee, cocked his arm back, and threw one of the swords. The blade tumbled through the air before stabbing the guard. From attempting to notch another arrow on his bow, the archer grabbed the blade stuck in his gut.

"Are you coming with me to face crucifixion?" Alerio asked Tristis. "Or will you fight."

"Why would I fight a Legionary?" the agent asked.

"Because it's better than dying on a cross," Alerio replied.

Tristis pulled a knife and drew a sword.

Alerio answered by singing as he stalked forward.

"Why, my friend?

Answer me if you can."

***

Alerio stripped off his tunic while descending the staircase. Thinking about saving the soiled garment, he inspected the bloody cloth before tossing it to the steps. He made it to the bottom step and stopped.

The guard he knocked unconscious and the one with the arm wound were pressed against the villa wall. Phobos towered over them. The stallion watched the humans as if daring them to try and escape.

"Where is the well?" Alerio asked as he crossed to the horse and pulled a bag from the rear saddle horn.

One of the cowering men-at-arms indicated the other side of the villa.

"I'm taking Phobos to the well for a drink," Alerio offered. "While I clean up, I suggest you head for Doctor Allocco's clinic."

Taking the reins, he led the mount towards the well. Supporting each other, the guards stepped away from the wall, and rushed for the gate.

After cleaning the gore from his flesh, Alerio dressed, and mounted. Then he guided the horse from the villa and headed for the Legion Fort. The job of bringing an end to the criminal organization was not finished yet.

Chapter 19 – Messages for Three

The morning sun beat down on the young messenger. High enough to disperse the shadows in alleyways, it scorched the pavement, and drained the last of the lad's energy. Stumbling into a wall, he collided with the bricks then decided to rest for a moment. Everything hurt. Some parts from falling with the horse and other body parts from dodging Legionaries as he ran back from Malagrotta.

'The priest must have the news about the Legion raiding his estate,' the youth scolded himself.

With his destination still several blocks away, the dedicated messenger pushed off the wall and staggered towards Capitoline Hill and The Temple of Jupiter.

***

Fetial Priest Mattia never developed an appetite for grain or vegetables. Almost wolf like, he craved beef. His two other passions were power and gold. As a young Fetial Priest, he discovered that power did not necessarily bring riches. Advising the Senate on foreign trade and declarations of war brought him influence and the ability to twist people and situations to his will. But it did not bring wealth. For the gold, he needed to formulate other schemes.

Sadly, the recycling of stolen Legion equipment had been discovered. But his thoughts were not on the fate of his accomplices. His concerns were on the loss of income.

A knock on the door drew his thoughts away from his problems.

"Come in," he instructed.

The door to his apartment opened and a sentry poked his head inside the room.

"Sir, there is a messenger for you," the Temple Guard informed him.

Mattia's eyes glared at the guard over the piece of meat the priest held in his hands. Almost as if defiling the guard's flesh, he ripped off a piece of beef with his teeth.

"Send him in," Mattia instructed while chewing the meat.

The exhausted, dirty, and aching messenger appeared in the doorway. Although he attempted to stand erect, he failed when a stitch in his side caused the youth to bend sideways.

"Well, what is it?" Mattia demanded.

"Sir, my horse threw me, and I was late getting to Malagrotta," the lad, who wanted to be a priest, admitted.

Mattia's stomach revolted, and he was barely able to swallow the mouthful of meat. In frustration, his fingers sank into the piece of beef causing juices to run down his fingers.

The messengers' eyes bulged at the succulent meat and rich liquid.

Mattia enjoyed the want in the lad's face for a moment before stating, "And then what happened?"

"The guards at the villa argued with me," the lad described. "Before they were convinced of my authority, Legion cavalry arrived."

"And my chest with my personal belongings?" Mattia demanded.

"I have to assume the Legion has it, sir," the messenger informed him. "I am so, so sorry."

"I know," Mattia agreed. "You look exhausted. Go to the kitchen and have something to eat."

"Thank you, sir," the lad stated while backing out of the room.

Moments after the messenger left, Mattia did some quick calculations. He needed to get out of the Capital to avoid having to answer questions about the stolen goods.

"Guard." At Mattia's call, the sentry walked in. "Get me a pair of escorts and have three horses saddled. I'm going to visit the temple at Alban Hills."

"Right away, sir," the Guard replied. "Anything else?"

"Send someone to the kitchen," Mattia added, "and have that urchin thrown out of the Temple. He is unfit to be a Priest of Jupiter."

***

Alerio rode to the gate of the Legion Fort and reined in Phobos.

"I am here to see Fleet Praetor Sudoris," Alerio stated before the Legionary could question him. "It is official business."

The man on the horse wore a clean tunic adorned with a Tribune's ribbon. For that reason, the man on sentry duty did not call Optio Noxalis or ask to see the officer's orders.

After lifting the barrier, the guard saluted and said, "Have a good day, sir."

Answering Alerio's nudge, the horse stepped off. Then as Phobos moved through the gate, the stallion nipped at the Legionary.

"Typical staff officer's horse," the Legionary complained. "Maybe I should have delayed the Tribune and that mean horse by calling the Sergeant of the Guard."

As a result of Alerio passing through the gate unchallenged, Optio Noxalis had no idea that one of Tristis' porters had returned as a Legion staff officer - One with knowledge of the Legion NCO's habit of taking payments to allow access to the fort.

Alerio rode to the command building, dismounted, and marched into the office.

"Tribune Alerio Carvilius Sisera to see Fleet Praetor Sudoris," Alerio said using his full name but only Zelare Sudoris' last name and title.

The form of address hinted at an imbalance between social standings. It made Alerio seem to be from a more important family than the Praetor.

"Yes, sir," the clerk responded.

He went to an inner office and quickly returned.

"The Praetor will see you now, Tribune," the Centurion instructed. "Go right in."

Alerio marched to the office, stepped over the threshold, and saluted.

"Sisera? What are you doing at Ostia?" Zelare Sudoris remarked. "I thought you were managing your father's farm."

"I was sir. But Colonel Gaius Claudius drafted me for a mission," Alerio replied.

He pulled the waxed piece of paper from a pouch, broke the seal, and peeled back the wax.

"Here in Ostia?" Sudoris questioned while taking and reading Alerio's letter of authorization.

"You have a theft problem in supply," Alerio described. "I was sent to investigate."

"I saw a report, but it only showed a few items missing. This hints at a much more extensive crime," the Praetor offered. "Are you here to check the books? If so, you better hurry. The fleet is getting ready to launch."

"The investigation is complete, sir," Alerio told the Fleet Commander. "We need to question Tribune Gutteris, Optio Noxalis, and the Tesserarius who keeps the books."

"Those are your witnesses to the theft?" Sudoris inquired.

"Only one is a witness, Praetor," Alerio informed him. "The other two are guilty of cheating the Legion out of thousands of coins by stealing supplies."

"I'll have Tribune Gutteris collect the other two and we'll meet later today," Sudoris offered.

"That is a problem, sir," Alerio corrected. "Tribune Gutteris is one of the conspirators, as is the Optio."

A sour look flashed over Praetor Sudoris' face.

"Senior Centurion, come in here," the Fleet Commander called to the outer office. The fleet's senior combat officer appeared in the doorway. Before he could report, Sudoris spoke. "Take three squads from First Century. I am ordering the arrests of Tribune Gutteris and Optio Noxalis. And have the supply Corporal brought here as a witness."

"Right away, sir," the Centurion responded.

"Now I have a problem, Sisera," Sudoris announced by waving the letter in the air.

"What's that, sir?" Alerio asked.

144

"Tribune Marcus Flamma left to join the Legion in Sicilia yesterday," Sudoris replied. "With Gutteris removed, the Legion assigned to the fleet is short two Tribunes for our Second Maniple."

"That is a problem," Alerio agreed. "What will you do, sir?"

"I have an experienced Centurion I can move to the right side," Praetor Sudoris informed Alerio. "For the left side? Let me welcome you to Paterculus Legion East."

"I am being drafted into the Legion assigned to the fleet?" Alerio questioned.

"That is correct, Tribune Sisera."

***

Fetial Priest Mattia, his two bodyguards, and a cart with his luggage passed the five-mile marker. Moving at a slow but steady pace, they were far enough southeast of the Capital that the Servian Walls had vanished into the distance.

"Rider coming, sir," one of the Temple Guards warned.

In response, the priest eased his horse to the side of the road to allow the faster traffic to get by. Soon the noise of galloping hooves on the road came from behind him. Easily overtaking the small procession, a messenger came abreast of the Priest then jerked back on the reins.

The horse squatted, the rider angled back to keep from being thrown over the mount's neck, and the animal halted beside the priest.

"Sir, a letter from the guard at Malagrotta," the courier stated.

He handed Mattia a folded piece of paper. The Fetial Priest ripped off the seal and scanned the words.

"Any reply, sir?" the courier inquired.

"No," Mattia barked.

He kicked his mount and raced away. The action took the guards by surprise. They looked from the cart to the shrinking back of their charge.

"Go," one ordered. "I'll stay with the cart."

***

The Fetial Priest and his guard reached Jupiter's Temple at Alban Hills long before sunset. Left ten miles behind, the cart and the other guard made their way up the steep winding path to the temple long after dark. While the wheels squeaked in the night, the refectory of the usually sleepy regional temple buzzed with activity.

Beyond the visit of Supervising Priest Rastellus, the Temple at Alban Hills also hosted a Fetial Priest. Celebrant Evandrus was busting with pride and personally oversaw the preparations for the feast. He succeeded as succulent aromas wafted through the air when the guests sat around the table.

"Fetial Mattia, what brings you to our humble temple?" Evandrus asked.

"Recently, I lost something dear to me," Mattia replied while spearing a piece of lamb. "I thought a change of scenery would help me heal."

"Between the fresh air, the evergreens, and the view," Evandrus extolled the benefits of the location. "Jupiter's Temple at Alban Hills is an excellent place to regain your balance."

"Not likely, but I do appreciate the sentiment," Mattia acknowledged.

Priest Rastellus loaded his plate, pulled it close to his stomach, and took a mouthful of food. As he chewed, he held up a finger. The other priests waited for him to speak, even though he had not been asked a question or solicited for a comment.

"I had the oddest experience yesterday," Rastellus finally said after swallowing. "At a feast with the Legion, a young staff officer burst in to speak with Colonel Gaius Claudius. He had been undercover investigating theft at Ostia. It was all extremely exciting, until the name of Malagrotta came up. I sent a runner to the Capital because I know you have a country estate there, Mattia."

"I am afraid I didn't receive the missive," Mattia lied. The message was the reason the messengers went to warn the Legion supply warehouse and to the town of Malagrotta. "You didn't happen to get the name of the officer?"

"Carvilius Sisera, or something like that. His father is Senior Spurius Maximus," Rastellus responded.

"Alerio Carvilius Sisera?" Evandrus asked.

"Yes, quite right," Rastellus confirmed.

"His adopted mother lives in the City of Tusculum," Evandrus reported. "The family has a large farm several miles away on the flatland."

"The Carvilius Maximus family is why I am here," Rastellus informed the others. "I am curious about the gift of gold they donated to the Temple."

"Gold?" Fetial Priest Mattia remarked. "What's the name of Tribune Sisera's adopted mother?"

"Aquila Carvilius Maximus," Evandrus told him. "I can escort you to their villa if you would like to visit."

"That won't be necessary," Mattia brushed aside the offer. "I'd rather she met a Fetial Priest for the first time, alone."

"Right. We wouldn't want to overwhelm a rich temple donor," Rastellus commented. "We'll let Fetial Mattia pass on our thanks and blessings when he visits Aquila Carvilius."

"If you think that is best," Evandrus said in defeat.

He feared his underhanded control of the Maximus farm would come up. If it did, the Temple of Jupiter at Rome might want a larger share of his earnings from the scam. But a regional priest did not challenge a Fetial Priest. Evandrus would have to depend on fate to keep his secret from the other Temple representatives.

Chapter 20 – Sharp Edge of Reason

Three days after Tribune Sisera took command of six Centuries of the Second Maniple, a mounted messenger, leading a chestnut stallion rode into the city of Tusculum. After asking for directions, he guided the horses to the gates of the Maximus country estate. A brief discussion with the gate guard saw him riding to a side door of the villa.

"I have a letter for Lady Carvilius," he told to the household guard, "and a horse with the temper of Furor."

"Not the God of Mad Rage," the man-at-arms corrected the courier. "That's Phobos, the God of Fear, and he is Tribune Sisera's horse."

"I don't care who owns the monster," the messenger described. "I just want the beast out of my charge."

"You have a dispatch for the Lady of the house?" the guard insisted.

Along with the letter, the messenger attempted to hand over the reins.

"I'm not taking that stallion," the man-at-arms advised. "I'll have a stable man come around."

Inside the villa, the household guard handed the letter to the estate manager. As the man-at-arms went to find the animal handler, the servant took the missive to a sitting room.

"Lady Carvilius, you have a letter from Master Sisera," he announced.

"From Alerio?" Aquila asked with a smile. "Give it here."

The Lady Carvilius broke the seal and read the words from her adopted son.

***

The Lady Aquila Carvilius Maximus
Mother Carvilius,
I pray this letter finds you in good health with the necessary stamina to keep the estate in order. Senator Maximus is also receiving a letter, but I wanted to tell you personally about my situation and my whereabouts.

The Second Maniple was short on staff officers, and I was pressed into service. We sail for Sardinia tomorrow to push the Qart Hadasht forces into the sea. After the campaign, the

149

Empire will no longer threaten the Capital from the island. Rest assured that I plan to be careful and will return to you safely in late Spring.

Hopefully, Centurion Accantus is meeting your approval and the farm is planted. I look forward to seeing the ground broken for your grape vineyard when I return.

Alerio Carvilius Sisera, Citizen of the Republic, Tribune of the Legion, and your proud son.

***

Aquila clutched the letter in her hand and felt pressure building behind her eyes. Just as when her husband marched off to war years ago, Aquila Carvilius worried about her son. Her apprehension faded when Spurius Maximus discovered a passion for politics. Although it kept Spurius in the Capital most of the year, at least she knew he was safe. The Lady Carvilius reread the letter, knowing she would have many sleepless nights until Alerio returned from the Legion.

***

The next day just as the sun reached the top of the sky, three horses turned onto the drive leading to the Maximus estate. A household guard, seeing one of the riders wearing a fancy robe, hobbled into the villa on his bad legs. Almost all older Legion infantrymen suffered pains in the knees. If he had been fit, Aquila Carvilius would have had more time to prepare. As it was, she issued lunch orders then scurried to the front door. Stepping onto the porch, she calmed herself as the riders approached.

"Lady Carvilius. I am Fetial Priest Mattia from Jupiter's Temple in Rome," the robed man announced.

"Where is Celebrant Evandrus?" Aquila inquired. "We only met socially a few times, but he represents the local temple at Alban Hills."

"Yes, I've heard of your family's generosity," Mattia offered as he walked up the steps. Without waiting for Lady Carvilius' invitation, the priest strolled into the villa. Then from inside, he asked. "Are you coming Aquila?"

***

Shocked at the Priest's impudence, Aquila rushed in preparing to scold the rude man.

"Recently, I have lost something dear to me," Mattia confessed.

Feeling remorseful towards the Priest, Aquila allowed him to lead her to a sitting room. He selected a couch, and she sat on one as well.

"I am sorry to hear that," Lady Carvilius offered. "Was there nothing you could do about it?"

Mattia waved at his escorts. To Aquila's horror, the young bodyguards pushed her older household guards from the room.

"I need privacy," Mattia directed, "and beef. Alert the kitchen."

Aquila fought to keep from yelling at the man's boorish behavior. Instead, she calmed herself, controlled her breathing, and studied the priest's expensive robes.

She had never met a Fetial Priest but knew they consulted the Senate on foreign matters. It appeared to her, they also reaped financial benefits from the association.

"There was nothing I could do to prevent the loss," Mattia explained. "Because I wasn't there when your son took it from me."

"My son? Alerio?" Aquila asked in confusion.

One of the bodyguards came through the doorway with a platter of meat. He placed it on the table beside the priest then left the room.

"Not him in person," Mattia stated. After cutting a piece of beef, he shoved it into his mouth. While chewing, and with juices running from the corners of his lips, Mattia slurred. "Tasty. Not personally but, as a direct result of your son's actions."

"That, my dear priest, seems to be a matter you should discuss with my son," Aquila ventured. "Unfortunately, he is not here."

"Alerio is a Legion officer, and your husband is a Senator," Mattia exclaimed. "Do you know what I am?"

Lady Carvilius stopped herself from voicing an unladylike response.

"A Priest of Jupiter," she replied.

"Ah, my dear Aquila," Mattia corrected. He paused to pull a piece of gristle from between his teeth. He examined the twisted gray mass before dropping it on the floor. "I am Fetial and speak with the authority of Jupiter. On my word, your son's Legion could be instructed to attack a Qart Hadasht stronghold. With a wave of my hand, I can cause your husband's trade agreements to evaporate. And with a whisper, you become an outcast from your social circles and the produce from your farm becomes cursed and unmarketable."

Aquila's entire frame shuddered. Thinking of her fear for Alerio while he fought in Sardinia and the commerce that supported her husband in the Senate, the Lady Carvilius' head felt as if it would explode. And while the threats to her loved ones were paramount to her, being ostracized from her friends and being poor, added to her heartbreak.

"What did my son take from you?" Aquila questioned.

"Three hundred gold coins," Mattia declared.

With her eyes bulging and her mouth hanging open, the Lady of the house staired at the Priest of Jupiter. Moments passed as she processed the information and uttered an opinion.

"You barge into my villa and menace my family," Aquila cried, "because you lost a few gold coins?"

"To you, they represent purchasing power. To me, gold is dear," Mattia admitted. "And due to the actions of your son, a sum of gold has been taken from me."

Crushed by the brutal honesty of the unstable man, Lady Carvilius lowered her head.

"What do you want?" she asked.

"That is simple, Lady Carvilius," Mattia informed her. "The return of my three hundred gold coins."

"And for that, you will leave my family alone?" she inquired.

"I may. Or I may not," the Fetial warned. "But if you don't pay for the sins of your son, I will vent the power of Jupiter on your life and the lives of your husband and son."

"But I don't have that much gold," Aquila told him.

"So, you admit to having some on hand," Mattia said picking up on her use of the word much. "Plus, you have land that you can sell."

"I can't get it all at once," Aquila advised.

"That is fine," Mattia acknowledged. "As long as I have the total amount by the time I return to Alban Hills for the Festival of Jupiter."

"That's only seven months away," Aquila pleaded.

"I am heading back to Rome in three days," Fetial Priest Mattia imparted. "I expect a down payment before I leave."

He stood and strutted from the room. Behind him, Lady Aquila Carvilius Maximus trembled and wept.

Act 6

Chapter 21 – Southern Coast of Sardinia

Rain poured down and wind lashed the wet and miserable oarsmen, sailors, and Legionaries. Along the beach at Solanas, no tents or covers protected the men. As a matter of fact, no men were on the sand. Four miles away at Baccu Mandara beach, the rest of the Roman fleet suffered in the same wretched conditions.

"I have a new goatskin cover," an oarsman boasted.

Shaking his head, he attempted to avoid the rain that fell through the overhead decking.

"A lot of good it's doing you today," another rower remarked.

He ran a palm over his head to clear the water. Then he shoved the hand back under his armpit to rewarm it.

"Stop your complaining," the deck officer instructed. "You'll soon be warm enough."

"I'd be plenty warm if we were on the beach, Second Principale," the oarsman protested, "with a fire, a pot of boiling oats, and my new goatskin cover."

"Get over it," the deck officer instructed then pointed out. "We are all exposed."

To keep peace with the rowers, the Second Principale did not have on his waterproof wrap. He strolled the rowers walk getting splashed with cold rain from above, the same as his oarsmen. From the Stroke section at the stern, by the big rowers of the Engine at midship, and the light oarsmen of the Bow, he moved back and forth encouraging his charges.

"The rain can't last all day," the deck officer advised.

"You might want to consult with Tempestas about that," suggested a big oarsman from the Engine section.

"General Paterculus made an offering of a sacred chicken to the Goddess of Storms," the Second Principale advised. "His Augur read the signs and the Gods are happy with the plan."

"Maybe," offered a rower from the Bow section. He cupped a hand and caught a stream of water then poured it out. "And maybe not. At least, we're not infantry or sailors."

Below them, sailors scooped pails of water from the bilge and passed the buckets to the upper deck. In a smooth loop, empty containers got handed down where they were refilled. Since before dawn, the ship's sailors had been bailing water. Although tired, they were warm.

On the deck overhead, Legionaries huddled. They could use bulky rain gear but were restricted from moving around the deck. All areas had to remain passable at a moment's notice.

Five men stood on the steering platform watching the rain fall.

Ship's Centurion Naulum squinted up into the gray sky.

"We need a break in the weather or an order to stand down," he offered.

"I can't argue that sir," First Principale Dormivi replied. "Should I signal the fleet commander?"

156

He looked towards the flagship where General Gaius Paterculus and his staff stood in the rain. On the decks of the quinqueremes separating the warships, the muted shapes of crewmen were barely visible in the blowing rain.

"From what the General told us during last night's briefing," Naulum reported. "His priest read the signs in the chicken entrails and assured us the fleet could row out."

"Tribune Sisera, you haven't said anything," the first deck officer pointed out. "What's your opinion?"

"I was trained as a heavy infantryman," Alerio answered. "We are taught to ignore heat, cold, and discomfort."

"Does it help?" one of the two navigators on the rear oars inquired.

From under an oiled hide near the steering platform a Legionary responded, "No."

One upmanship was a time-honored tradition in the infantry. If someone tossed out a response, someone else was duty bound to top it. Without thinking and probably because he was tired, wet, and bored, Alerio participated in the ritual.

"I don't know about chicken gazing," he announced. "My personal Goddess is Nenia. We're better at eviscerating chickens than reading their guts."

"Rah!" was shouted from under several of the covers.

While Alerio had endeared himself to the infantrymen, his crude admission drew hard stares from the Ship's Centurion and the First Principale.

Before they could scold him about blasphemy on a seagoing vessel, the rain stopped, and the clouds parted. Flags on General Paterculus' warship flashed messages and the crews on the nearby ships went into action.

"First Principale, beach the launch team," Naulum ordered, "stand by the oarsmen, and ready the musician."

"Yes, Centurion," the deck officer acknowledged. "Third Principale, send out the launch team."

On the rowers walk below deck, the Principale reminded the oarsmen, "I told you. You wouldn't be cold for long. Launch crews, get to the beach, and stand by."

The third deck officer followed a third of the ship's oarsmen to the upper deck and over the side. Once on the sand, the deck officer shouted up to the steering platform.

"First Principale, ready," he bellowed.

From up on the platform, the first deck officer instructed, "Launch the warship."

The Third Principale called down the Port side, "Get Sors' Talisman wet."

Then at the Starboard side, he repeated, "Get Sors' Talisman wet."

Responding to the muscles of the rowers, the warship, named after the God of Luck, slid off the beach and into the sea. Running and splashing, the launch team climbed on board. Last up, the Third Principale ran for his bow lookout position.

Along the beach, only eight of the quinqueremes and two of the triremes slid into the surf. Four of the large warships carried the five hundred men and officers of Alerio's half maniple line. The other four heavy warships hauled a compliment of seventy-five Marines, the heavy corvus boarding ramps, and sported two bolt throwers. They would, along with the triremes, attack and prevent the Qart Hadasht ships-of-war from launching. While they targeted the enemy fleet from the sea, Tribune Sisera's combat line would land and attack, occupying the mercenaries to delay them from reaching their vessels.

It was a good plan, endorsed by the Gods according to the Augur Priest. However, it only took one God to declare his displeasure to throw the entire operation into disarray.

***

"Hadad is displeased," ventured a Qart Hadasht Lieutenant.

He stepped away from the doorway and faced the room.

"It does seem our God of Rain has his temper up," Senior Captain Barekbaal concurred. "Don't you think so, Admiral?"

Hannibal Gisco shifted in his seat. Ever since the naval tribunal in Carthage, where he barely escaped execution, the Admiral had been careful with his words. Because of envious Gods, ambitious politicians, and vengeful royals, he guarded against saying anything that could be used against him.

"The will of the Gods is the will of the Gods," Gisco replied.

"There is one benefit to the storm," the Senior Captain offered.

"And that is?" Gisco questioned.

"The Republic fleet cannot row out either," Barekbaal replied. "They are as beached as our fleet."

"Are the crews and our mercenaries comfortable?" Hannibal Gisco inquired.

"They are here to do our bidding," Barekbaal declared. "Their exposure to the elements is of no importance."

Major Vinzenz of the Noricum mercenaries bristled but remained silent. His Celtic height and muscularity easily dominated the room. Compared to the lean shape of their Qart Hadasht masters, Vinzenz and the warriors in his Companies were almost all above average height. It was the reason Hannibal Gisco chose a unit from the Noricum as his bodyguards on Sardinia.

"Men cannot fight if unrested and hungry," Gisco offered. "Lieutenant, we have thirty ships-of-war on Porto Botte beach. Go check on every one of the sailors and mercenaries. Then report back to me if any are lacking supplies."

Major Vinzenz did not say anything, but internally, his heart filled with respect. Hannibal Gisco was a commander who understood fighting men. It was the reason the Noricum officer proudly provided bodyguards for the Empire Admiral.

***

The attack warships had sailed for a good part of the morning when trouble struck. Sors' Talisman and the other nine warships of the squadron ran into an isolated squall. To save their masts and sails, the materials were rolled.

"This could be bad," First Principale Dormivi warned.

"I see blue sky ahead," a navigator on one of the rear oars described. "This may be a last kiss from Tempestas before she departs."

"Let's hope so," Ship's Centurion Naulum stated. "If the rest of the fleet thinks the rain is returning, they might not launch."

"Where will that leave us, Tribune Sisera?" Dormivi asked.

"Without orders to the contrary," Alerio responded, "we continue the mission."

"We are still on the southwest heading," Naulum described. "Once we reach Chia, we have to decide. Turn back, or cross the bay, round the point, and row into Empire territory."

"I believe, sirs, the General will see the clear sky," Dormivi suggested. "And the fleet will arrive as planned."

"So, First Principale, you agree with the Tribune," Naulum explained. "But if our fleet isn't at Sulci Bay and enough Qart Hadasht ships-of-war get off the beach, our squadron will be destroyed. Not to mention the Second Maniple being stranded on the beach. Are you sure Tribune Sisera?"

"Centurion, the infantry goes where we are ordered," Alerio answered. "I have confidence my Legionaries can do damage with few losses until the fleet arrives."

The shower stopped and Naulum stiffened and watched the coast of Sardinia slide by. Then he shifted

161

his eyes southward and studied the land where it ended at the edge of a broad bay.

"First Principale, unroll the sails," he ordered. "Keep the rowers at their oars so we don't lose momentum."

"Yes, sir," Dormivi acknowledged before stepping off the platform.

He marched to where he could talk to the Second Principale down on the rowers walk.

On the steering platform, the ships' commander addressed the Legion staff officer.

"Tribune Sisera, I don't have enough ships to land Marines if I'm busy defending the squadron," Naulum pointed out. "This is your last chance to change your mind."

"Centurion, we are the infantry of Second Maniple," Alerio assured him. "My Legionaries are experienced and tough. We can hold until the fleet arrives and delivers the rest of the Legion."

Ship's Centurion Naulum did not respond. He watched ahead for sight of the other side of the bay. And Alerio went to check on the one hundred and twenty-five infantrymen crowding the deck of the quinquereme.

"Are you the officer known as Death Caller?" a grizzled Optio asked Alerio. "I heard you say Nenia Dea was your personal Goddess."

"It's a name I picked up in Sicilia when the Legion first landed," Alerio offered. "Because so many were suffering, I prayed for them."

"And because your personal Goddess is Nenia, they tagged you as Death Caller?" the NCO questioned.

"Yes," Alerio told him. "But it's not…"

"Nineteenth Century will offer a sacrifice to Nenia after the battle, sir," the NCO from his most experienced unit promised. "And we will carry prayers to her on our lips as we fight."

"Thank you," Alerio said accepting the NCO's declaration.

Many units honored their leader's personal Gods or Goddesses. The reverence they hoped would strengthen their commander's attachment to the deity which would curry favor and, hopefully, bring victory. Alerio didn't know if the tradition helped, but he figured it was better than the Legionaries of his detachment being afraid of him.

"Tribune Sisera," a Decanus solicited him. "Second squad of the Fourteenth will also honor your Goddess."

After a brief talk, Alerio moved to another squad's area. Once the Tribune had moved down the deck, a sailor tightening a line leaned down and asked a Legionary.

"Your commander walks with Nenia?" he whispered.

"We all do," the infantryman informed him.

"But you are courting death," the sailor cautioned.

"Our gladii and the muscles of our right arms send her offerings," the Legionary bragged. "It's only fitting, wouldn't you agree, that we honor the Goddess and that our Tribune is known as Death Caller."

"You are all mad," the sailor decided.

"We are heavy infantry," the Legionary countered.

"It appears to me, to be the same thing," the Sailor offered as he finished tying off the line.

Sors' Talisman and the warships of the attack squadron zoomed around the rocky southern tip of Sardinia and sailed towards Sulci Bay.

Then a disgruntled God decided to interfere with General Paterculus' plan. Notus began blowing from the south. While the strong wind hastened the journey of the advance squadron, the stiff breeze swept along the Sardinian coast. The strong headwind almost stopped the progress of the Republic fleet.

Ship's Centurion Naulum realized the wind meant the majority of the fleet would be delayed. Before he could order the ten warships of the squadron to turn about, Porto Botte appeared on the horizon.

***

At the Qart Hadasht headquarters, an Empire officer slammed through the doorway.

"Admiral, the Republic fleet is here," he cried.

"Define here," Gisco requested.

"There are warships on the horizon," the Lieutenant replied. "Orders, sir?"

"If the Captains of my ships-of-war are waiting for orders," Hannibal Gisco complained while reaching for his armor, "then the battle is already lost. Go to the beach. Instruct any Captains, not preparing to launch, to get off the beach."

"Yes, sir," the officer acknowledged before running from the room.

"Admiral, I am assigning more men to your protection detail," Major Vinzenz offered.

"Fine, fine," Gisco said accepting the increased security. "Just make sure they don't get in my way."

The Noricum squads brought up to help guard the commander only knew the Admiral by sight. They had no idea of his affection for his mercenaries. Even so, the Celtic warriors met Gisco and jogged alongside his horse as he rode to Porto Botte beach.

Chapter 22 – A Deadly Efficient Plan

The blessing and the curse of Notus' gift sent the attack squadron racing quickly into Sulci Bay. Arriving shortly after being sighted allowed the Republic warships to attack the first of the Empire ships-of-war to launch. Additionally, the four quinqueremes hauling the half maniple, reached the start of the beach, and began offloading Tribune Sisera's Legionaries.

Conversely, while the wind pushed from the stern, speeding Centurion Naulum squadron, the stiff breeze from the God of the South Wind hit the Roman fleet in the bow and slow them. Isolated and against a larger force, the warships and Legionaries spearheading the plan were cursed with following the scheme, without knowing when or if reinforcements would arrive.

"Centurion Pashalis get them off the ship and formed up," Alerio ordered. He indicated a marching force of mercenaries further up the beach. "Give me a triple line and set a center position."

"Yes, sir," the combat officer replied. He ran down the ramp, jogged by the staff officer, and grabbed the senior NCO of the nineteenth. "Optio, position them in the middle of the beach."

The eighty men of the nineteenth Century and forty Legionaries of the fourteenth trotted away from the warship. Halfway between the surf and the shrubs and trees on the bank the senior Century assembled in three lines while the four squads from the other waited for their officer.

"Strap them on," an NCO directed.

The infantrymen, the two Optios, and the Tesserarius of the nineteenth untied the waterproof covers from their scutums. Once the shields were free, they strapped them to their left arms.

Behind the triple line, Pashalis directed four Centuries into positions on either side of his. The sixth Century he split. Each half of the fourteenth moved to flank the main body of the formation. As the last of the infantrymen took their places, Alerio jogged out front of the formation.

"Second Maniple, left side, stand by," Alerio shouted to the men of the six Centuries.

The Legionaries lifted their right legs, slammed their feet to the sandy soil, and roared, "Standing by, Tribune."

"We did not come here to watch the mercenaries board ships and row away," Alerio hollered. "We came to Porto Botte to fight. Agreed?"

"Rah," came back at him in a wave of voices.

"Senior Centurion Pashalis get us into this fight," Alerio ordered while drawing his gladius.

He held the blade up in a salute as the Legionaries walked towards him, parted to either side, and continued marching forward to engage the Empire mercenaries. Once they passed him, Alerio sheathed his blade and fell in at the formation's center.

***

Ship's Centurion Naulum watched the Legionaries collect their gear. To his surprise, Tribune Sisera was one of the first men off the warship. In the Centurion's experience, staff officers usually hung back unless rushing to meet a senior officer or a politician.

"Get us off this beach," Naulum ordered when the last infantryman shuffled down the narrow ramp.

The oarsmen of Sors' Talisman backstroked until the warship pulled away from the shoreline. Once clear, the ship turned and aimed the ram at the row of beached ships-of-war.

"First Principale Dormivi, set a fast tempo," Naulum instructed. He waved his hand to get the attention of the navigators/rear oarsmen. Pointing to a Qart Hadasht ship-of-war just sliding into the water, he announced. "I want that ship dead."

"Yes, Centurion," the navigators replied.

They adjusted the two rear oars putting Sors' Talisman at the proper angle of attack. Pounding out a rapid tattoo, the musician set a tempo and the rowers dipped oars in time with the beat.

On the Qart Hadasht ship-of-war, men dove overboard as the Sors' ram tossed a rooster tail into the air. When the bronze cap hit, side boards splintered, and the ram ripped a trench along the water line. The Empire vessel rolled away from the ram. When Sors' Talisman veered off, the ship-of-war rolled back. But this time, it continued to roll until the deck was vertical with the water. Then the Empire ship rested momentarily on its side before sinking into Sulci Bay.

"None get off the beach," Naulum called to his first deck officer.

"What about those already afloat?" Dormivi asked.

"Leave them for the warships with corvus boarding ramps and the Marines," Naulum instructed. "Our job is to hold down the odds. Find us another target."

***

The flaw as always with the mercenaries of the Empire were the different customs, languages, and traditions. Ships' Captains and their deck officers ran searched and shouted for their crews and the soldiers assigned to their vessel. In most cases, the oarsmen and the soldiers spoke different tongues. And both had different languages than the ships-of-war officers.

For the few ships-of-war that made it safely off the beach, they ran a gauntlet of Republic warships. Those with soldiers and rowers who reached open water attempted to fight their ships. But the Marines flowing over the corvus boarding ramps turned the sea battles into shield-to-shield skirmishes. The Legion trained Marines relished the opportunity to turn the decks red with the blood of Qart Hadasht mercenaries.

Some vessels collected rowers and soldiers late. They launched only to be skewed by Republic rams. In the ships' deaths, the hulls turned in the tide and the wind, blocking parts of the beach.

Whether lacking crews or courage or being blocked by wreckage, a lot of the Empire ships-of-war remained on the beach during the initial attack. A few rowers collected their belongings and ran inland. But the fleet far outnumbered the ten Republic warships, and as more launched, they rowed clear and began to engage in ram-to-ram combat.

***

About a thousand shipless soldiers gathered on the beach waiting for orders. When Hannibal Gisco and his staff rode among them, they cheered. The Admiral looked out at the Republic warships. His fleet could deal with them if he could clear the beach of enemy forces. Then, shifting his focus to the formation of Republic Centuries, Gisco drew his sword and pointed down the beach.

"Kill them," he instructed.

"Yes, sir," his combat officers responded.

The Captains and Lieutenants separated their Companies into loose formations. Then they stepped off heading for the Republic forces.

***

"Tribune Sisera," Pashalis called over his shoulder. As the most senior Centurion, he would control the Centuries while in combat. Alerio's task was to manage the formation and monitor the enemy forces. "I believe the Qart Hadasht mercenaries have taken notice of us."

"It's about time," Alerio replied. "I was beginning to fear we would have to feed them lunch to get their attention."

"Because you are such a good cook?" an anonymous infantryman teased.

The NCOs tensed waiting for the staff officer to demand the identity of the speaker. Most Tribunes dished out punishment for disrespect as readily as ladling out portions of Legion stew.

"The Goddess Vesta blessed me with the art of cooking," Alerio bragged. Then, far off topic, he announced. "I once stood close enough to smell a Vestal Virgin."

"Not that I'm complaining, sir," another infantry asked. "But what does that have to do with cooking, sir?"

"Honey, lavender, and orange," Alerio listed.

The mercenary formation drew closer. As the distance narrowed between them and the Legionaries, the pace seemed to quicken.

Alerio noticed archers behind the Empire soldiers.

"Stand by shields," he warned.

"Standing by, Tribune," the Legionaries replied.

The archers raised their bows aiming for a high release. There were two modes of targeting for an archer. Straight at the prey as in hunting, or high so the arrow arched over friendly forces before impacting on the enemy.

"Sir, honey, lavender, and orange?" an infantryman inquired.

"Arrows in the air, shields up," Alerio ordered. Then in the quiet while the arrows arched over and began dropping for the Legionaries, he explained. "It's how the Vestal Virgin smelled. And the ingredients to a fine sauce for lamb."

Seventy-five steel tips sounded like rain on the shields. As the arrows drove into the scutums, Legionaries cursed and laughed. Not because anyone was injured by the flight. The anger came because they would need to dig out the arrowheads and sand the faces of their shields before putting on the waterproof covers. And they laughed at a Tribune who managed to combine a story about a good smelling woman and food while facing a superior force.

"Pashalis, return the favor," Alerio instruction.

"Two javelins," the senior Centurion instructed.

"Second line stand by two javelins," the other combat officers shouted.

"Standing by, Centurion," the Legionaries answered their officers.

"Throw."

Two hundred javelins on flat trajectories left the Legion line. There was no delay of weapons sailing gracefully into the sky and arching over. Almost immediately, iron heads poked through shields and into the flesh of unfortunate mercenaries.

Warriors dropped out of the moving line to attempt to pull the javelins from their shields. Soldiers moving to take their place at the front stepped around them and over the wounded and dead. Then, the second flight of two hundred javelins hit and decimated the refreshed front rank of the mercenaries.

"Draw," Centurions Pashalis ordered.

"Rah," screamed the front rank of Legionaries.

Hidden under the response was the rasp of two hundred and forty gladii sliding from sheaths.

"Formation halt," the senior Centurion ordered. "Brace."

The Legionaries stopped, stood rigid, and held their shields firmly against the neighboring scutums. Behind them, the second rank placed their shields against the first rank's backs, adding their weight to stabilize the combat line. In the third rank, the infantrymen waited to see if the first two ranks held.

Alerio stepped back several paces. The Centurions would direct the fighting and rotations along their sections of the combat line. As the staff officer, Tribune Sisera's job included watching for breaches in the Legion formation and warning the combat officers about any sudden shifts by the enemy. For a former infantryman who would rather be locked in on the shield wall, Alerio Sisera found the assignment less than gratifying.

***

Hannibal Gisco rode from vessel to vessel directing crews and soldiers. Soon, he had five fully staffed ships-of-war ready to launch. But he held them on the beach. Watching, he waited for the nearest Republic warship to be out of position.

"Go, go, go," he shouted.

The rowers on the beach could not hear the Admiral and neither could the officers in charge of the launch crews. But they saw the arm movements and ordered the men to push the ships into the surf. Five rams dipped then flattened as oars dug into the sea. Then five dangerous ships-of-war joined the battle of Sulci Bay.

"We should have the Republic warships smashed and drowned soon," the Admiral announced. Looking at

Barekbaal, he asked. "What about the beach. Is it clear of enemy forces?"

"Sir, I didn't know I was in command of our land forces," the Captain blabbered.

"Senior Captain, an Empire commander has to direct the mercenaries," Gisco scolded. "They aren't able to do it themselves."

"Yes, Admiral," Barekbaal confirmed while putting his heels to his mount's flanks.

As the Senior Captain rode towards the fighting on the beach, the Noricum bodyguards pondered the words of the Admiral. The two squads of warriors decided that Hannibal Gisco held the low opinion of mercenaries typical of Qart Hadasht commanders. When Gisco urged his horse up the beach, the bodyguards jogged alongside him. But not out of pride, they were simply following orders.

At the assault line, Major Vinzenz, who felt affection for the Admiral, backed away from the fighting. He needed a better view of the shield wall to see why the Qart Hadasht forces were failing to kill the raiders from the Republic.

Chapter 23 – A Narrow View

In a shield wall, a Legionary's sight was confined to a narrow view over the top of his shield. It encompassed the barbarian to his front, the weapons of the two barbarians behind that one, plus the shoulder and weapon of the man to his left front. Because the three and one-half men were trying to kill him, the Legionary dared not look away.

Behind the Legionaries, the Optio and Tesserarius watched segments of the Century's combat lines. For the NCOs, the battle consisted of judging the state of their men and the positions of the opposing mercenaries to maybe three deep and twenty shields wide. As if a latticework, the Legion formation held together because each element dominated a small sector. If a Legionary fell, he was quickly replaced to maintain the pillars of the framework.

Behind, and scanning his entire compliment of Legionaries, the combat officer studied his NCOs, the action along the full combat line, as well as his Century's place in the maniple formation. Most Centurions stalked behind their shield walls as if caged wolves.

The aggressive posture accomplished four things. To Legionaries rotating off the front line, the sight of an angry officer gave them heart. To the enemy across the shield wall, the prowling officer put them on notice that a furious force of will backed up the Legion line. The movement also allowed the Centurion to position himself near a breach. From there, he could kill any barbarians who broke through the shield wall. And finally, the back and forth stalking allowed the Centurion to watch his staff officer for directions without turning away from the battle line.

Tribune Sisera perused the formation and beyond. Whenever he caught the eye of a combat officer, he acknowledged the Centurion with a reassuring nod.

"Optio of the fourteenth," Alerio shouted to the flanking squads on the seaward side. "You have mercenaries trolling in the deep. Gig them for me."

In response, twenty Legionaries threw javelins. Wading through waist deep water, several Qart Hadasht soldiers attempted to get behind the Legion formation. They vanished below the surface. Their floating graves marked by the sinking shafts of the javelins.

"Thank you," Alerio shouted.

"Our pleasure, sir," the NCO replied. As he turned back to his squads, he whispered. "Death Caller. It fits the staff officer."

On the right side of the combat line, the Empire soldiers were big men. Obviously, Celts but Alerio could not place the tribe. But several shattered and torn shields stacked behind his line attested to the size of the warriors and the sharpness of their swords. More worrisome than the broken equipment, five Legionaries from that section were being treated for broken collarbones.

"Centurion of the eighteenth," Alerio yelled. "Come see me."

The combat officer from the right side sprinted to Alerio.

"Is something wrong, Tribune?" he asked.

"Good question. You tell me why my right side is suffering so much damage," Alerio responded.

The officers did not look at each other. They faced forward keeping their eyes on the distressed Century.

"Celtic muscle and, I swear, enchanted swords," the Centurion admitted. "I've had the second line stabbing to keep them back. But one of those swords will break a shaft and another of the big bastardis will step up and cripple one of my Legionaries."

"Then we need to put fear into them," Alerio advised, "and back them off."

"I am open to suggestions, sir," the combat officer admitted.

"Follow along with me. See the bay and squads of our fourteenth flanking that side?" Alerio directed the Centurion's attention to seaward. "Notice the bunched warriors to the right and front of our line? And the Celts at your Century's position? Now observe the rest of the fourteenth on our right flank. Do you see all of that?"

"Yes, sir," the combat officer admitted. He was noticeably confused. "I can see it all."

"Good," Alerio told him. "You are acting Tribune. What's the name of your Optio?"

"Modus, sir. But I'm not a staff officer."

"You are now," Alerio told him. "Do not lose my maniple."

"Sir, you can't just…"

"I am," Alerio stated. "I need to know what we are facing."

"You want a closer look?" the Centurion questioned.

"Look? No, not a look," Alerio informed him. "I want to taste the Celts blood and feel the enchantment of their steel. I am taking a spot on the shield wall."

"That's almost certain death for an officer, Tribune," the combat officer pointed out. "Especially for a staff officer. Ah, you'll draw them to your position."

"If we don't do something, they will break through and we'll have a melee on our hands," Alerio reasoned. "It's my call. Be sure the formation is here when I get back."

Alerio jogged away.

"Your call, my hairy cūlus. It's more of a death call," the Centurion mumbled. A disturbance in front of the left of center alerted him to trouble. The crowd of soldiers parted as a group carried something through the ranks. "Centurion of the sixteenth. You have a battering ram headed your way."

The combat officer saluted his acknowledgement and turned back to his line.

***

"Optio, if we allow a ram through," the officer of the sixteenth asked. "Can we reseal the break?"

"No sir," the NCO replied. The Optio peered over the shield wall until he located the movement. "They have too many bodies and will flood any breach."

"Give me javelins. I want a circle of death around the battering ram," the Centurion ordered.

The NCO pulled men off the third row of his section. Gathering twenty Legionaries, he described the situation and made sure each man had three javelins.

"Ready, sir," the Optio alerted the officer.

"Rain down death," the Centurion ordered.

Throwing one right after the other, the Legionaries chucked the javelins high. Before the first flight landed, the second grouping was in the air. As if clawed from the heavens, the soldiers carrying the battering ram were nailed to the ground by iron tips. Once the men toting

177

the log fell, javelin tips impelled those standing near the battering ram.

A hole opened in the ranks of the Qart Hadasht mercenaries as men moved away while searching the sky for more deadly javelins. The combat officer from the sixteenth Century waved a salutation at the acting staff officer as a thank you for the warning.

After returning the salute, the temporary Tribune shifted momentarily and focused on Tribune Sisera and his suffering eighteenth Century. Then duty overcame his curiosity. Shaking off the narrow view, he expanded his field of vision and continued his overwatch of the entire formation.

***

"Optio Modus, I need a shield," Alerio told the NCO of the eighteenth Century. "And four of your hardest strikers."

"I've got four men who can stand at Vulcan's forge and match the God stroke for stroke," the Optio boasted before admitting. "But not enough healthy Legionaries for all of the shields. What are you thinking, sir?"

Alerio sorted through a stack of shields and selected one.

"We are going to teach the Celts respect," Alerio promised as he strapped the shield to his left arm. Once it fit properly, he added. "And back us up with five strong shoulders."

Modus shuffled his Century until ten selected Legionaries stood in front of the staff officer. Five were impressively muscular while the other five displayed forearms thick from gladius work.

"You five are on javelin duty," Alerio instructed the broad-shouldered Legionaries. Then to the other five, he explained. "We are going to demonstrate the fundamentals of Legion training for the Qart Hadasht soldiers."

"You mean us, don't you, sir?" a squad leader challenged, "because that helmet will draw a crowd."

Men who make their living an arm's distance from hostile blades tended to be blunt. Alerio wanted aggressive. The question told him that was exactly who the Optio picked for the mission.

"No, Decanus, I do mean us," Alerio assured him. "In my horsehair combed helmet and my Tribune insignia, just like I am dressed. Let's go teach the Celts a lesson in combat."

***

Major Vinzenz grasped the reality of a battle along a shield wall. Warriors gained experience not by dying on enemy shields but by living to fight another day. That wisdom translated to caution when facing the barrier of oversized Legion shields. While his Noricum warriors were chipping away at the wall's defenders, none of the other mercenary Companies seemed to be making progress. And that was the reality, few soldiers wanted to sacrifice themselves on Republic blades to break the shield wall. They were waiting for the Noricums to break through.

"Why haven't we breached those shields?" the senior Noricum officer asked.

"We have reduced their numbers," a Captain replied. "We expect a breakthrough and a rout, soon, sir."

And there was the ugly truth. No one wanted to die for an isolated beach on the island of Sardinia. Before Vinzenz could light a fire under the butts of his soldiers, a commotion at the Noricum section of the shield wall drew his attention.

***

Alerio's view of the battle shrunk to the back of a man on the third row, and the Legionaries in his peripheral vision.

"Keep your blades high for three rotations," Alerio described to the pairs of Legionaries flanking him. Then, he drew his gladius and called to Optio Modus. "Rotate us in."

"Eighteenth Century stand by to rotate," the NCO bellowed.

Repeating the alert, the Decani passed the order onto their squads. A response returned, "Standing by, Optio."

Alerio and his four-man team of strikers turned sideways and squeezed between the third and then the second rank. They waited momentarily in spaces between legs and raised shields.

"First rank, advance, step back, rotate out," Modus ordered.

Echoes of 'advance, step back, rotate out' ran through the eighteenth Century. On the front row, shields shot forward, gladii sliced and, as the rank stepped back, they continued backward, flowing between the second and through the third row. Rested Legionaries replaced them along with Tribune Sisera and his four blade-specialists.

Alerio popped to the front, and the brim of his helmet and the top of his shield reduced his vision to a narrow bar. While his field of vision minimized, the horsehair comb on the helmet flew as if a flag, helping to identify him as a Legion officer. And although Tribune Sisera could not see beyond the soldiers to his front, a flock of Celtic warriors noticed him.

"Do you have a death wish, Tribune?" the Legionary on his left inquired.

"If it's my time," Alerio replied, "I hope Nenia takes me quick."

"I heard she was your…"

***

The words were crushed under the war cries and growls of Celtic warriors. They fought each other, crowding in, and attempting to kill the Legion officer.

"Gladius drills, three rotations, high," Alerio shouted.

The five blades cut left twice, then backhanded to the right once for a single rotation. On the second series of the drill, the Noricum Celts at the front countered the blades with their shields and hacked with their swords trying to cut the Legionaries and their officer.

Without a doubt, the elevated heartrates, blood lust, and fear clouded men's thoughts. In a shield wall fight, the mind searched for comfortable patterns, such as the one defined by the Legion gladius drill. By the third repetition of the drill, the Celts anticipated the two hacks from the left and easily blocked the return slash.

"One drill low," Alerio shouted.

And the shields of the Celtics dropped to stay even with the downhill dip of the gladii. At knee height, the blades swung inward.

In a moment of confusion, the Noricum warriors defended low with their shields while reaching forward to cut over the Legion scutums. With their swords descending from overhead and their shields positioned at their knees, the pose left their faces and necks exposed.

"Javelins," Optio Modus ordered.

Usually, the weapons were thrown. Typically, a delay accompanied the use of the pilum as it flew to the target. Not so when five thick shouldered Legionaries shoved the iron tips into the eyes and breasts of the Noricum Celts.

"Hold them up," Alerio instructed.

As they came up, Alerio and his four Legionaries balanced the weight of three dead and two injured Celts on their shields.

Noricum soldiers attempted to pull their dead and wounded comrades off the javelin tips. A tug-of-war developed when the Legionaries holding the shafts of the javelins pulled back. Trapped on the barbed heads, the dead flopped back and forth, and the two still alive screamed in agony.

"Kick their swords behind us," Alerio directed.

Five heels hooked the five dropped Noricum swords, dragging the blades back to the second rank.

"Are we done here, Death Caller?" one of his gladius experts asked.

His eyes were on a Celt who screamed when he was pulled back to the extent of the thorny iron tip. And cried out for mercy when the javelin slid in deeper as he was tugged in the other direction.

"No, they haven't learned to respect us. Yet," Alerio informed his team. "Break them loose."

The five stood and used their shields to push the dead and dying away. Then by lifting their shoulders, they pried the javelin shafts from the hands of the Legionaries in the second rank.

With the release of resistance, the Noricum Celts tugging on their fellow warriors fell back with the bodies. They tumbled into their third rank. Warriors tripped and the bodies flopped to the ground.

"Same drill," Alerio told the four men of his team. "Stand by."

"Standing by, Tribune," the team replied.

Chapter 24 – Noric Steel

Major Vinzenz bellowed when his Noricum warriors funneled to the center of their attack formation. He could make out the horsehair comb on the helmet behind a Republic shield and recognized the prize. But he also saw the trap of everyone wanting to kill a Legion officer. Bunching up reduced the pressure on the shield wall by his front rank and made each of his Celts less efficient. Then, five of his best rose above the shoulders of their fellow Noricums and began flopping back and forth.

"Captain, get in there and unclutter that rubble," Vinzenz barked to a senior officer. "Pull us back until we can coordinate our attack."

The Noricum Captain used his arms to push and pull men aside as he waded into the formation. By the time he reached the center, the third rank lurched when the second rank stumbled.

"Pull back, pull back," the Company commander ordered. "Check with your Lieutenants and regroup."

Almost as if daring the Noricum warriors to come and get him, the Legion officer lowered his shield. Exposed, the Republic commander resembled a lamb offering his neck to a pack of jackals.

"Sir, the Legion officer is right there," a Noricum Lieutenant pointed out.

"I see him," the Captain admitted. "Fall back and form up your men. We will get him when we break the Legion's formation. But first, we need to restore discipline."

The warriors of the two Noricum Companies adjusted their lines as the bodies of the five dead warriors were carried through the formation. Although the tips of the javelins were bent so the shafts rested on the torsos to prevent further mutilation, the effect angered the Celts. Every warrior bristled and fought the urge to run at the Legion shield wall and kill Legionaries.

Then, with the disgruntled attitude in the ranks at its peak, Captain Barekbaal charged up. The Qart Hadasht commander glared at the Noricum Major.

"Vinzenz why are your people pulling back?" he screamed. "Are your warriors that weak of heart? Short on courage? I am ordering you to get back into this fight."

The outburst drew the ire of the Celtic warriors. Most restrained themselves but several felt the insult to their Noricum pride. The offended gripped their swords more tightly.

"Barekbaal, keep your voice down," Major Vinzenz instructed. He checked the expressions on the faces of the warriors closest to them. "and keep a civil tongue in your head."

"You and your mountain herders should remember who I am," Barekbaal advised. "My Empire rules the world. Qart Hadasht pays you to do my bidding. Now, order your oversized cows to fight, before I have all of you punished."

Between the tone and the verbal abuse, a hot-blooded warrior boiled over and lashed out. The tip of his sword slashed a gash in Barekbaal's thigh.

The Qart Hadasht officer assumed the wound was a precursor to an assassination attempt and panicked. While Noricum warriors wrestled the attacker to the ground, Barekbaal kneed his mount and raced away from the Companies.

"Aren't you going after him, sir?" a Lieutenant asked. He held up a treatment bag containing ointments, needles, thread, and bandages.

"It wouldn't do any good with that one," Major Vinzenz offered. "His head is so far inserted into his own cūlus, he has to open his mouth to see daylight."

One of the selected gladius experts leaned over and spoke to Alerio.

"I don't think they want to play with you, sir," he announced. "For the life of me, I have never seen an orchestrated public execution spontaneously held between shield walls."

"I don't blame the Celts for backing off," another of Alerio's flankers reflected. "You are a caller of death, sir, that's a demonstrated fact."

Alerio glanced to his right and left. Along the combat line, the other mercenaries, having seen the Noricums back away, followed the Celts' example.

"I think we have installed the proper amount of fear in our foes," Alerio stated. "Rotate back."

"Are we done, sir?" another of his team inquired.

"The left side of Second Maniple came to Porto Botte to prevent mercenaries from boarding their ships-of-war," Alerio lectured. "We are not here to hold a parade formation on the beach. No, we are not done."

Rolling back, his four blade experts slipped through to the third rank. Alerio paused at the second row.

"Good work with the javelins," he offered to the wide shouldered Legionaries. "Your timing saved my life and I appreciate it."

"Just doing our job, Tribune Sisera," one beamed.

"If you need muscle, we are your guys, sir," another of the powerful Legionaries added.

"I'll remember that," Alerio promised.

Then he shifted through the third rank.

"Orders, sir?" Optio Modus requested.

"I'll leave that up to your Centurion," Alerio responded. He was three steps beyond the NCO when he scooped up one of the Celtic swords and stopped. Turning, Alerio raised the sword over his head and shouted. "Eighteenth Century of Paterculus Legion West. It was my honor to fight with you."

"Rah!" the Legionnaires responded.

Alerio saluted with the foreign blade. Then he marched to their Centurion.

"I'm glad you are back, sir," the combat officer exclaimed.

He did not look at Alerio but continued to scan the Legion formation and the mercenaries beyond the shields.

"I believe we solved the mystery of the enchanted blades," Alerio offered.

"Magic, sir?" the Centurion questioned.

"No, just great steel," Alerio explained. Pulling his dagger, he tapped the Celtic blade. It rang like a bell while bouncing the dagger off the hard surface. "This metal is excellent. I'd give my right hand for a gladius made of this steel."

"But then you couldn't use the gladius," the Centurion cautioned. "Remember Tantalean's punishments."

Alerio was studying the mouth of the bay and missed the officer's point.

"Excuse me," Alerio begged.

"Tantalean, sir. He was punished by standing in a pool of water with the branches of a fruit tree overhead. When he reached for the fruit, the branches moved and

187

when he tried to drink the water receded," the combat officer explained. "It is a cautionary tale about those who have good things but are not permitted to enjoy them. If you lost your right hand, you could not use the new gladius."

"That's true," Alerio acknowledged. "Return to your Century. We need to get back into this battle before some other maniple comes along and claims our victory."

"Another maniple, sir?" the Legion officer questioned.

Alerio indicated the mouth of Sulci Bay and the line of Legion warships rowing to engage the Qart Hadasht fleet.

"Did we do good, sir?" the Centurion asked.

Alerio peered up the beach. For as many Empire ships-of-wars that adjusted to meet the Republic fleet, just as many were sunk or still on shore.

"We did make a difference. But we are not done," Alerio declared. Raising his voice, he asked. "Centurion Pashalis. Are Legionaries paid to stand around looking pretty?"

"Tribune Sisera, we have our fair share of Narcissus worshipers," the experienced Centurion respond. "But not one of them is pretty enough to pose for a travertine statue."

"Then get us moving," Alerio instructed, "because I know we get paid to fight."

***

The attack had gone on long enough for fearful oarsmen to have run away. Those dedicated began searching and finding vessels in need of their services.

Admiral Hannibal Gisco and a few Captains were directing stray rowers and groups of mercenaries onto ships-of-war.

"Admiral, we need to get you on a ship and out of Sulci Bay," a ship's officer advised.

"Not until Major Vinzenz and his Companies arrive," Gisco said into the Captain's ear. He whispered so other mercenary units didn't know he favored the Noricum officer and his warriors. "Did you send the runner?"

"Yes, sir, the Major and his soldiers should be here shortly," the Captain reported. "Will you board now?"

"Put them on those two ships," Gisco directed, indicating a pair with oarsmen but no soldiers. "I need to return to my quarters for a few personal items."

"Sir, you should leave now," the Captain begged. "I will go and collect your things."

"No. I am in command here," Gisco stated. "Keep launching the ships. But save one for me. I will be back shortly."

Gisco nudged his horse around and walked the beast through groups of detached oarsmen and mercenaries. When he reached the top of the beach, he kicked the mount and galloped away from the chaos, leaving his bodyguards behind.

***

The path to his headquarters had small groups of fleeing oarsmen going towards the mountains.

"Admiral, Admiral," a voice shouted from behind.

A peek over his shoulder showed Captain Barekbaal racing towards him.

Gisco passed a group heading in the opposite direction. An old man, lean and frail looking, reprimanded five healthy, young men as they walked back.

"Run away will you," he scolded. "I am old. I do not want to die on Sardinia. We need to be on a ship if we are to get…"

A cry of pain followed by shouts of outrage, so strong, they caused Gisco to rein in his horse. Behind him, the old man lay twisted and still on the path. Barekbaal's horse galloped away from the dead man, obviously having trampled the ancient oarsmen.

Without thinking, the Qart Hadasht commander walked his horse back to the five men.

"Who was he?" Gisco inquired. "I'll make a sacrifice…"

"Admiral, the Noricum are revolting," Barekbaal complained as he brought his horse back to the scene of the accident. "Look, I've been wounded."

A long scratch, with only a few drops of blood, stretched down the Qart Hadasht Captain's leg.

"I was asking about…" Gisco advised while pointing at the ground.

"Him? He is no one," Barekbaal sneered. He almost spit on the crushed body. "I am talking about mutiny. I…"

The rock came from one of the old man's escorts. It clobbered the Captain in the temple. He toppled off his horse. Lucky for him, he fell away from the thrower. Unfortunately, Gisco sat erect on his horse making an easy target for the young men's anger.

A second and third rock knocked Gisco off his mount. Both horses, frightened by the ungainly dismounts of their masters, trotted away.

"He was our grandfather," another of the five youths yelled before throwing the next stone.

Gisco and Barekbaal curled into balls, tucked their heads, and attempted to protect themselves. But the rocks kept coming. Bigger, faster, and harder until the two Qart Hadasht officers lay as still and broken as the old man.

One of the youths walked to Admiral Hannibal Gisco, bent down and freed Gisco's sword belt.

"What's that," his brother questioned.

"A good belt and sheath," he replied while drawing the blade and examining the weapon. "And a sword made from Noric steel."

Act 7

Chapter 25 – Spoils of Sulci

The six Centuries of the Second Maniple fought and pushed the mercenaries back. Without the Noricum warriors to brace up the defense, the Legionaries were able to fight their way forward. Their success was partially due to the lack of a Qart Hadasht officer. Without a commander to unify them, the Empire units battled in separate and isolated groups.

"The big Celts are escaping," the Centurion of the fourteenth notified Alerio.

With his Century being divided to cover the flanks, the officer travelled from one side of the formation to the other. On this trip, he paused to point at two ships-of-war that had just left the beach.

"Do you hunt lynx barehanded?" Alerio asked the combat officer.

"I don't understand, Tribune," the Centurion remarked.

"I would put my coins on Legionaries against the Noricum warriors in a one-on-one fight," Alerio explained. "But when we landed, we faced odds of more than two-to-one. Even now, the mercenaries outnumber us."

"You are saying catching a lynx without gloves and weapons would not go well," The Centurion ventured.

"Just as fighting the Celts while holding off the other mercenaries wasn't favoring us."

"We got mauled badly," Alerio pointed out. He jerked a thumb over his shoulder. "Back there are the casualties of the mismatch."

"The next time we'll have the Legion to handle the other mercenaries," the Centurion commented, "while we introduce the Noricums to Deimos."

"If it is the will of the God of Dread and Terror," Alerio submitted. "Good job protecting our flanks."

"Thank you, Tribune," the least experienced of Alerio's Centurion responded.

***

Tribune Sisera watched the two Empire ships-of-war. The pair cut across the water to the opposite shoreline before swinging seaward and rowing for the mouth of Sulci Bay. One Republic warship turned to give chase. But the distance proved too great, and the Legion quinquereme veered off to find easier prey.

Alerio pulled his gladius and compared it to the Noricum sword. Nicks and folds along the edges marred the blade plus a little piece of tip was missing from the Legion sword. A professional grinding and sharpening were required to keep it serviceable. In comparison, the sword made of Noric steel only needed honing to bring the edges back.

Noricum warriors, a wounded mercenary named them, were muscular, organized, and carried almost magical blades. Staff officers and Centurions needed to believe in the infallibility of their Legionaries and in the tactics of the Legion. Most of the time, Alerio did. But today, deep in his heart Alerio was glad to see the Noricums row away. Losing Legionaries for a miserable section of beach in a forgettable battle held little appeal. For the Tribune, there was no post battle prize worth the cost.

At the far end of the beach, a Legion warship backed to the shoreline and began depositing Legionaries onto the sand.

"Centurion Pashalis, hold here and go on the defensive," Alerio ordered. "We've done enough for today."

"Yes, sir," the Centurion acknowledged. Then he shouted. "Formation halt, step back, and brace."

The Empire mercenaries, no longer pursued by Legion shields and blades, continued to move away.

"Left side, Second Maniple, Paterculus Legion West, rest," Centurion Pashalis instructed. "Officers set a watch for your section and give me work details. Let's bring our wounded and dead up to the formation."

***

Along the shoreline, Legion warships landed. In the shallows, other vessels hooked and towed sunken ships-of-war away. When the approaches opened, more Republic vessels, along with captured Empire ships-of-war, beached. Guards marched prisoners off those vessels.

At collection areas, squads stood guard over the prisoners while other squads patrolled along the water's edge. Qart Hadasht soldiers and rowers, lucky enough to swim to shore, were collected and marched to the holding areas.

Tribunes strutted around checking on their Centuries making sure none of their men had fallen overboard during the sea battle. And at the center of the beach but high up on the bank, Legion engineers cleared and marked off a giant circle.

A large tent went up in the middle, then the engineers tamped and leveled the ground around it. Once prepared, three smaller tents were lashed to the large center tent. Before the Legion headquarters was completed, squads of the First Century jogged to positions around the structures. Tribunes and Centurions from the command staff wandered over to wait for the General.

While the construction progressed, General Gaius Paterculus walked the beach inspecting the trophies of the battle. In front of each captured ship-of-war stood the Centurion from the warship that captured it. And each of the ships-of-war abandoned on the beach had an infantry officer claiming it.

"We should have claimed all of them instead of just two," Tribune Sisera complained. "We bled for them."

"Sir, we were a little occupied to worry about bragging rights," Centurion Pashalis suggested.

"Centurion, what do we do about that?" a Corporal asked.

Out on the bay and heading towards the beach was a large fishing boat. Alerio dug into his coin purse and extracted a gold coin.

"Go to the water's edge and hold this up for the fishermen to see," Alerio instructed.

"Why am I doing that, Tribune?" the Tesserarius inquired.

"You are telling him that you want to buy his fish," Pashalis explained. "Now hurry before he lands on a different part of the beach."

The NCO sprinted to the water's edge and waved the coin. Late afternoon sunlight reflected off the metal. Seeing the glint of gold, the fishermen rowed their boat to the end of the beach.

"How was the fishing today?" Alerio asked as he and Pashalis joined the Corporal.

"We have fish, both big and small," the fisherman exclaimed. "How many will you take?"

"Where are you out of?" Alerio questioned while peering into the boat.

"If I knew this was going to be an inquisition, I would have put in further up the beach," the man complained as he hopped out of the fishing boat. In the sand he traced a map of the coastline to his village. "If you must know, Portoscuso, about thirty-fives miles sailing northwest of here."

"You have a fine boat," Alerio commented. "And your haul looks fresh."

"It is. We caught them in deep water."

A messenger came running to the group.

"Tribune Sisera. Senior Tribune Vergilius requests your presence at Legion headquarters," the runner told Alerio.

"Buy all the fish and make sure our Centuries get as much as they want," Alerio directed while handing his coin purse to Pashalis. "Sell the extra. And keep in mind, I would like to have some coins left when I get back."

"Yes, sir," Pashalis responded. Then to the fisherman he offered. "I'll pay a half bronze for the small and a full one for the biggest fish."

"For that, I might as well dump them back into the sea," threatened the fisherman. "A full bronze for the small…"

Alerio walked to his equipment. As he slipped on his scarred combat armor, he heard Centurion Pashalis protest, "For that amount, I could put Legionaries in the water and catch my own fish. Let us talk about reasonable prices."

Alerio tucked the Tribune helmet under his arm and hiked away. Based on the Centurion's negotiation skills, he felt confident there would be coins left after the sale.

***

First Century Legionaries parted to allow Alerio access to the command tents. His easy passage reflected his rank and status. It was a far cry from when he was an infantryman and had to explain himself whenever he walked close to a General's tent. It was good…

Alerio's sense of entitlement ended when he pushed through the tent flap.

"Tribune Sisera, you could have cleaned up and put on more appropriate dress," his direct superior scolded.

Most, no, all the staff officers and quartermaster officers wore clean tunics or ceremonial armor. Even the maniple Tribunes and combat officers were unsoiled. None had blood stains, fresh scratches, or dirt on their armor.

The conflict between Alerio and Second Maniple's Senior Tribune started when Alerio joined the Legion. Few Patrician/Tribunes trained with their Legionaries. And an even smaller number participated in shield and gladius drills with their Centuries. Only one, according to Senior Tribune Vergilius brought the shame of brawling with Plebeians to the staff officer's mess.

"At least change out of the infantry armor," Vergilius declared after their fourth or fifth conversation about the matter. "Remember Tribune Sisera, an officer must dress the part to get the respect."

As a result, Alerio had purchased a set of ceremonial armor. The armor was stored with his possessions on Sors' Talisman.

"I apologize," Alerio said with no enthusiasm. The pretty Tribune armor could not stop a spear thrust or a dedicated sword strike. Had he donned it for the beach assault, he would be in the arms of the Goddess Nenia on the way to Hades. "There wasn't time to get to Sors' Talisman and change."

"I guess we will excuse you this time," Vergilius blustered, although no one else in the tent seemed to care. "But remember, you represent the Second Maniple and I expect you to be professional in the future."

A reply welled up in the pit of Alerio's stomach and he almost vomited it all over the Senior Tribune. But the General and his Battle Commander pushed through a flap from a side tent and prevented any more exchanges.

"Where is Sisera?" Colonel Leporis Damocles asked.

"Here, sir," Alerio responded.

The Colonel studied Alerio's armor then shifted to the General.

"You held the beach?" General Paterculus inquired.

"General, Second Maniple, left side held the beach," Alerio replied. "I was honored to be assigned to lead them."

"All well and good, Tribune," Colonel Leporis Damocles said. "Are your Centuries fit to fight?"

"Yes, Colonel. We have four dead and six critical..."

"Fine, fine," the Battle Commander interrupted. "Give your report to the Senior Centurion."

"What Colonel Damocles is getting at. And we do not have a lot of time," Gaius Paterculus exclaimed using the shorted sentences with little meaning that Senators practiced keeping from committing to anything. "Well. I'll let the Battle Commander fill you in."

"Legion Paterculus won a great victory here today," the Colonel declared. "To keep pressure on the Empire, we row for Tharros in the morning. That means the Legion will go back into combat the day after tomorrow."

Alerio, angry at his Senior Tribune for singling him out, chewed on the bile, and allowed the blood to pound in his ears. Thus, he ignored the Battle Commander's speech. Then a few things broke through his ego induced deafness and he flinched.

"After this last push, we will have driven Qart Hadasht from Sardinia," Damocles announced. "No longer will the Empire threaten our Republic from this island."

Applause and cheers, the most enthusiastic from the noncombatants, filled the command tent.

"Allow your Centuries to rest," Gaius Paterculus urged the officers, "for tomorrow we row for glory."

More clapping with the flat of the palm and verbal endorsements followed the General's words. When it died down and before anyone else could speak, Alerio did.

"Tharros is home to the Qart Hadasht infantry on Sardinia," Alerio cautioned. "Do we have any intelligence on their strength, Colonel?"

"We know the Empire is there and that's all we need to know," Damocles chastised Alerio. "Are you having a crisis of courage, Tribune Sisera?"

Alerio bristled and he began to lift his hand, point at the Battle Commander, and give him the facts of the matter. A cautionary hand gripped his wrist and tugged hard. Centurion Siglum, the acting Tribune for the right side of Second Maniple, added a twist to impress on Alerio the dangerous path he walked.

Tribunes argued with Colonels at their own peril. Then, Alerio's counterpart released his arms and the Centurion stepped away. Because the only person in more danger than an unruly staff officer, was a Centurion seemingly supporting the Tribune in a stand against a Battle Commander.

"Sir, I was in Tharros a few years ago. It was fortified then," Alerio described. "There is a chance they improved the walls and ditches. Let me go in tonight. You'll have a report on the facilities and strength tomorrow."

"Tomorrow, we plan to be halfway to Tharros," Leporis Damocles advised.

"That is perfect Colonel," Alerio brightened. "I can go in, snoop around, and meet you with the details."

"Perhaps I wasn't clear Tribune Sisera," Battle Commander Damocles said with a set of his jaw. "The Legion rows out in the morning. The next day, we attack Tharros. Think for a moment. Would you want a man who knows your plans to walk into an enemy camp?"

"No, sir," Alerio confessed. "I understand, sir."

"Now that the junior staff officer is satisfied, let's go take care of our Legionaries," Damocles advised. "And because of the work by the Second Maniple, left side, you Tribune Sisera will be in reserve, guarding the warships."

Later, in the waning light, Alerio thought about his attitude as he and the other officers left the briefing.

The Battle Commander had a point about security. But Alerio still believed the Colonel was making a mistake going blindly into Tharros. His attitude didn't perk up until he reached his Centuries.

Smoke laced with the aroma of roasting fish drifted to his nose.

"I have two questions, Centurion Pashalis," Alerio remarked.

"Tribune Sisera, I have coins for you and three cooking fish," Pashalis responded. "What do you need?"

"That about covers it," Alerio replied. He slipped the purse into a pouch and began unstrapping his armor. "We row out at daybreak. Pass the word. And pass me a fish."

Chapter 26 – Staging for the Assault

The close quarter maneuvers used by the Legion transferred readily to sea battles. Moving in coordinated lines, both Legionaries on land and warships at sea proved efficient at breaking their opponent's formations. The other tactic favored by the Republic's land warfare machine dealt with the location for staging before an assault.

Most armies gathered near the point of attack and camped nearby the battlefield to save their warriors from an exhausting march. But the Legion favored a distant staging area.

From the prospective of the defenders, they woke in the morning, saw no threat, and sat down for breakfast. Then, after jogging for miles, the Legion appeared. And soon, Legionaries were bashing the defenders, storming the walls, and cracking open gates. All orchestrated from miles away. The scheme suited a naval assault as the oarsmen did the hard traveling at sea and allowed for the delivery of fresh Legionaries to a fight.

"Two days ago, we were first off the beach," Ship's Centurion Naulum grumbled. "Now, our squadron and your Centuries are last."

"This time, we are the reserves," Alerio pointed out. "It won't get interesting unless the fighting reaches the beach."

"And what would it take for that to happen?" Naulum inquired.

"The Empire forces would need to defeat twenty-four hundred heavy infantrymen," Alerio listed, "eight hundred Velites, and dodge fifteen staff officers."

"Why staff officers?" the Ship's Centurion questioned.

"On the shield wall, heavy infantrymen always discuss what to throw when they run out of javelins," Alerio told him. "The consensus always comes down to throwing Tribunes as a last resort."

"First Principale, where are we in the launch order?" Naulum inquired, as he turned away from the crude staff officer.

"As near as I can tell, sir, our squadron should get off before the sun is fully risen," the first deck officer informed him.

"There is one bright spot," Alerio mentioned to Naulum. "If a Qart Hadasht fleet comes from the south, you'll be their first contact."

"I believe we destroyed their fleet," Naulum remarked. "The chance of that happening is slim. About as slim as your Centuries getting into this battle."

"And there, Ship's Centurion, is the knotty problem with war," Alerio advised. "You can never tell when a slim chance of contact will become a blood bath."

***

The day dawned clear and bright. Warships hauling the First Maniple rowed along the beach. A short distance north of the village of Tharros, the Republic ships spun and backstroked onto the beach. There were no signs of Qart Hadasht ships-of-war or soldiers to challenge the landings.

Tharros sat on an arm of land that formed the seaward limb of a bay. Isolated, the fort had no approach except by water on both sides and to the south where the land ended. Second and third Centuries jogged confidently along the only land route to the wooden palisades of the fort. Coming rapidly behind, the other ten Centuries of the First Maniple followed.

Although inexperienced, the nine hundred and sixty heavy infantrymen had the confidence of Legion training and its esprit de corps hammered into their hearts. Boldly, the leading squads approached a series of defensive ditches.

As planned, they formed two combat lines and locked shields. Light infantry Centuries filtered through the forest along the flanks, checking against mercenary units hiding in the brush and behind trees.

"Tribune, there is no sight of an enemy," a Centurion from the third Century informed his staff officer.

"Acknowledged. I'll pass the word to the beach," the Tribune replied. To a runner, he instructed. "Alert the Senior Tribune that the trenches at Tharros are empty of combatants."

The messenger raced back to the beach and located the maniple's Senior Tribune. But the commander of First Maniple was in a conversation with two other staff officers. Holding up a hand, he waved the courier forward and made an 'I am listening' sign while still talking.

"Sir, First Maniple has encountered no resistance," the courier spoke in a raised voice. "The ditches of

Tharros are deserted with no sight of enemy combatants."

"Very well, return to the combat line," the Senior Tribune told him.

Excusing himself, the staff officer backed out of the conversation. He sauntered to the Colonel and erroneously relayed the message.

"The fort is deserted, sir," the Senior Tribune announced.

The Legion had planned for the First and the Third Maniples to assault the fort. Centuries of both would act as a blocking force for any Empire units coming from the north to help their trapped comrades. A deserted fort changed the assault to an expedition of discovery.

"Hold the Third Maniple afloat. And signal the Second Maniple's right side to land," the battle commander ordered. "We'll sweep through the fort and see if Qart Hadasht command left us any clues as to where they went."

The ships with the hardened veteran Legionaries rowed away from shore while half of the Second Maniple hit the beach. Leisurely, the Centuries moved to set up blocking positions facing north.

***

While most of the fleet remained on the seaward side, Sors' Talisman and four other warships rowed into the bay. From the steering platform, Naulum and Alerio watched the trees slide by.

"The sharpened posts are the top of the fort's walls," Alerio described.

"What do you suppose is happening in there?" Naulum asked.

"I imagine the First Maniple is advancing into the Empire's combat line," Alerio answered. "When they stall, and they will because of their lack of familiarity with combat, the veterans of the Third Maniple will move up."

From the Third Principale at the bow, an alert was passed back, "Movement on shore."

Squads of infantrymen stepped from the tree, marched onto the beach, and waved at the passing warships.

"It's just Legion infantry," Naulum observed.

Alerio moved to the rail and bent forward watching the Legionaries.

"Those are Second Maniple," he offered. "They should be on ships as reserves."

"Why would the Battle Commander order them ashore?" Naulum questioned.

"If the battle at the fort is going badly," Alerio responded, "he would need the Second. Have you seen anything for my left side?"

"No signals or flags for your half maniple, Tribune," Naulum assured Alerio.

***

Qart Hadasht General Hanno observed the five Republic warships rowing around the bay at Tharros. If most of his fleet had not been sunk or captured, he would order the warships attacked. As it was, the General had only a few ships-of-war at his disposal. What he did have were five thousand mercenaries.

"Major Vinzenz you were correct," Hanno complimented the Noricum commander. "The Republic assumed the fleet was my major force."

"Can we begin, sir?" Vinzenz inquired. "My Celts want revenge."

"As do I, Major, as do I," Hanno reassured him.

They ducked back into the tree lines and walked away from the northern edge of the bay.

"General," a man called from a treetop. "We have sighted an arrow from the fort."

"Major Vinzenz, you and your Noricums may take the field of battle," Hanno instructed.

The Celtic commander jogged to a broad trail. In triple lines, his two Companies of infantry waited. Behind them, other mercenary units filled the road.

"Noricums, move fast and strike hard," Vinzenz urged.

Without warning, the Major jogged away. The sudden action by their commander caught the Celts off guard. They raced after Vinzenz without thinking about the danger on the other side of the bay.

Behind them, equally surprised, but not as enthusiastic, three thousand Empire soldiers collected themselves before jogging after the Noricums.

The disparity in attitudes was reflected in a noticeable gap that opened between the trailing units and the Celtic Companies.

***

Sors' Talisman rowed beyond the Legion pickets.

"Was that an arrow?" Dormivi asked.

"An arrow? From where, First Principale?" Naulum inquired.

"From behind the fort," Dormivi replied. "But it happened so fast I wasn't sure if it was a bird or an arrow with long black feathers."

"Tribune Sisera, did you see an arrow?"

"No, Centurion," Alerio responded. "I was looking away from the stockade poles."

As if he could figure out the Battle Commander's reasoning, Alerio continued to study the shoreline and the Legionaries sitting on the beach. To the squad leaders' credit, each squad had two men standing guard while the rest lounged. Alerio pulled his eyes away from the men when the warship turned from the shore. He could not see the far side of the bay, only the horizon and blurry landscape beyond it. But to the north, the white sandy beach, and green trees were clearly in view.

Dormivi's description drifted through Alerio's mind, 'A bird or an arrow with long black feathers.'

In the trees to the north, birds lifted into the sky and flew away. Then another flock, further from the first zoomed into the air. When a third group of birds took flight, Alerio thought of Gabriella DeMarco. Only because thinking of her beauty was pleasant. But also, it led him to connect with her logically minded brother.

'Two points is a line,' Alerio remembered Nicholas saying. 'Three points on a straight line is a direction.'

"Ship's Centurion Naulum. Signal the fleet," Alerio requested. "The left side, Second Maniple is landing."

"Why?" Naulum inquired. "And weren't you ordered to wait in reserve?"

"There is a large force moving through the trees to our north," Alerio told him.

"First Principale Dormivi, flag the rest of the squadron and the fleet, we are landing," Naulum ordered. It was after giving the instructions that he asked. "How do you know a force is there, Tribune Sisera?"

"It was Dormivi's remark and a flock of birds," Alerio informed him. Then to the Century and a half being transported on Sors' Talisman, he instructed. "Get up, armor up, and prepare yourself for glory."

A few men prayed, others joked, most talked, and some remained quiet keeping their own counsel. Each Legionary bringing himself up to a mental and an emotional peak. Glory meant someone would die. In infantry training, the Legionaries were taught that you needed a winning attitude to be sure it was the enemy who died. They donned sections of armor as the quinquereme came about and headed towards the men on the beach.

***

The First Maniple separated the edges of their shields and spread the formation.

"First rank, move forward," the Centurions ordered. "Move slow so the men climbing the ditches can keep up."

Four hundred and eighty Legionaries stepped off the line. In front of several sections, flat trails offered good footing. But many of the Centuries traversed down the slopes and into ditches.

"Arrow," a Tribune announced.

"Sir, do you mean arrows?" a combat officer questioned.

"No, Centurion," the staff officer corrected. "Just one arrow loosed from behind the fort. I don't know what it means."

At the bottom of the ditches a linen and branch framework, hidden under a light coating of dirt, gave way. Legionaries tripped as the ground dropped from under their feet. Sharpened spikes ripped skin or skewed deeply into calf muscles or through the leather of their hobnailed boots. During the cries of pain, shouts of shock, and begging for help, the gates of the stockade fort opened.

Iberian infantry ran out in columns of six. Dividing into pairs, the files raced along the flat trails. If the veterans of the Third or the experienced Legionaries of the Second Maniple faced the threat, they would have collapsed their line and met the enemy on the pathways. But the inexperienced First Maniple hesitated.

The Iberians struck the unprepared combat lines and butchered young, untested Legionaries.

Chapter 27 – Good Steel, Better Tactics

Alerio strapped on his armor and tugged the helmet over his head. When the keel of the warship touched the beach, Tribune Sisera jumped. Splashing through the shallows, he ran to Pashalis and consulted with his senior Centurion. After giving instructions, Alerio sprinted by the squads guarding the beach.

"Trouble is coming from the north," he shouted to them as he ran into the woods.

Centurion Pashalis made a circle in the air with his hand. The five other Centurions from Second Maniple's left side moved quickly to the experienced combat officer.

"We have a large Qart Hadasht force moving from the north," he told them. "Tribune Sisera is going to warn the right side."

"The land is too wide and the trees too thick for a single combat line?" another officer remarked. "What's the plan?"

"We are going with Century fighting squares," Pashalis replied. "Let's start with the fourteenth on this beach. You will also guard the ships. The fifteenth will be on your left and the rest in order up till we link up with elements of the right side."

"The fourteenth is ready, Centurion," the combat officer assured him.

"I hope you are," Pashalis said even though he worried about his weakest Century.

***

Alerio reached the center of the road and found his counterpart standing by himself.

"Centurion Siglum, you have company coming," Alerio informed him. "From the looks of it, a large force stretching back a quarter of a mile."

"I thought we were reserves," the acting Tribune remarked. "Now the First Maniple has been attacked and I had to send in four Centuries to restore order."

"What? You did what?" Alerio asked. "Where is Third Maniple?"

"Still afloat," Siglum replied. "What am I supposed to do with only two Centuries?"

"You are going to go to the beach and tell the Senior Tribune that we are about to be overrun," Alerio replied. "I'm going to reposition our Legionaries."

"Yes, sir," the Centurion acknowledged.

Then the staff officers for the Second Maniple ran for the beaches. One to the eastern shoreline and the other to the western side.

***

The command staff resembled a debating circle. No one was doing anything, but everyone of the command staff was talking at the same time.

"Senior Tribune Vergilius, we are about to get overrun," Siglum announced when he reached the gaggle of officers.

"You mean the First Maniple is being overrun," Vergilius corrected.

"No, sir. Tribune Sisera said there are Empire forces coming from the north," Siglum insisted.

"What is Sisera doing on shore?" the Senior Tribune questioned.

"Sir, obviously, he is warning us about an attack," Siglum replied.

"Vergilius, what is going on?" Battle Commander Damocles asked.

He walked away from a conference with his planning section. As he moved, members of the First Century shifted to keep him in a protective pocket.

"Colonel, Sisera claims we have Qart Hadasht reinforcements coming from the north," Vergilius replied.

"Planning tells me it is easier to load everyone up and row away. I've already suggested the General depart," Damocles stated. His reference to suggesting something to the Consul/General was a polite way of saying he had already put Paterculus on a warship. It would be an unusual politician who ignored his chosen military commander's advice. "Leaving is a lot faster than bringing in Third Maniple and fighting it out. Ideas, gentlemen?"

"But we don't know if the Empire has enough forces at Tharros to defeat us," a supply officer offered. "We could win the battle."

"Runners tell me the First Maniples in a melee slug fest," the Battle Command responded, "and elements of the Second are attempting to extract them. Do we fight or do we leave?"

"A quarter of a mile," Siglum commented.

"What's that Centurion?" Colonel Damocles asked.

"Tribune Sisera said the enemy column stretched out for a quarter of a mile," Siglum explained. "In my experience that is either one thousand warriors. Or two, or even three thousand, depending on the number of files in their formation."

"I think that settles it," Damocles exclaimed. "Disengage the First and Second, get them boarded, and launched."

***

Alerio reached the beach and marched up to Pashalis.

"Centurion, we have an issue," Alerio stated.

"It's combat, Tribune," the senior Centurion of the maniple informed Alerio. "If we don't have problems, it isn't a fight."

"Good point," Alerio confirmed. "How about this? Third Maniple is out on the ships. And apparently the First is in trouble as they sent in four Centuries of the Second to help."

"Sir, we are in deep trouble," Pashalis projected. "I believe…"

A runner broke from the tree line. He glanced up and down the beach before locating Alerio and Pashalis. Once identified, he headed directly for the Centurion and the Tribune.

"Two Companies of Empire soldiers just broke through our lines," he reported. "The Colonel wants the Second to go in and pull the First out."

"Tell the Battle Commander we are moving," Alerio confirmed.

Pashalis took a step in the direction of the nearest Century.

Alerio grabbed his arm, "Hold on a moment, Centurion."

"I was going to have the Centuries break their formations," Pashalis told Alerio.

"The signs I saw were bigger than two units could make if they tried," Alerio proposed. "I think there are more Qart Hadasht forces on the way."

"And if the Second is withdrawing with wounded and guarding the First Maniple," Pashalis summed up the problem, "we will be attacked from behind. But we have been ordered to go in. Is there an alternative, Tribune?"

"We have extra shields and javelins on the ships, don't we?" Alerio asked.

"We do," Pashalis said.

"Take our Centuries and go save the First," Alerio instructed. "But I'm keeping two squads from the fourteenth for a secondary mission."

"Yes, sir," Pashalis acknowledged. "You'll be along, afterward?"

"In a manner of speaking," Alerio replied. "Now go and may Clementia go with you."

"I don't need the Goddess of Mercy and Clemency," Pashalis corrected the sentiment. "Your Goddess Nenia is the one we need for this kind of work."

"I'll ask her to look over your shoulder and guide your gladius," Alerio promised.

***

Centurion Pashalis formed his four hundred and seventy infantrymen into a loose double attack line. He was down ten Legionaries with five wounded and resting on the warships and five others buried at Sulci Bay. They jogged up the road and tensed when the sounds of metal slamming together and men shouting war cries carried to them.

"Straighten your lines and tighten those shields," he barked as the six Centuries reached the fighting.

215

His notification was unnecessary for the experienced Legionaries of Second Maniple. But the reassuring voice of command helped to steady their nerves. And firming up resolve was needed as they encountered a scene of madness out of a battle mural.

Men hung on the lips of ditches, some with obvious wounds and others with agony etched on their faces. On the flat, others crawled away from the fighting. Some to nurse their wounds and others to find a peaceful place to die.

The fighting coagulated around small clusters of Legionaries. Quite a few limped with odd injuries to their lower legs. Iberian and Noricum soldiers surrounded each Legion fighting circle.

"Let's give the stragglers a home," Pashalis remarked. Aware that more Empire units were coming from behind him, he directed. "Face left and double time to the flank."

Both lines faced left and ran in a curved arc until they jogged down the side of the battle site. Before any of the Qart Hadasht soldiers could hit their flank, Pashalis called for a stop to the maneuvering.

"Second Maniple, halt," he shouted. His command voice loud enough that the combat officers and NCOs repeating his order were redundant. "Face right and draw."

Four hundred and seventy gladii slipped from their sheaths. Tucked in behind the big shields, the enraged men of the Centuries waited to be unleashed on the soldiers. Their anger rose from seeing the mutilation of the Legions First Maniple. Every man remembered being young and inexperienced. It was that memory driving their emotions when Centurion Pashalis uncaged the infantry.

"Forward," he said.

"Rah!" the infantrymen bellowed in response.

Two ranks of shields with steel blades powered by muscle and pride stalked onto the battlefield.

***

The arrival of an intact Legion unit did not escape notice. Major Vinzenz waved at one of his Captains and indicated the Legionaries.

"The Republic is offering us more victims," the Captain boasted.

"Do not take them lightly," Vinzenz warned. "Assemble your Company and as many Iberians as you can. We need to delay that formation."

"We will cut through them like butter," the Captain stated. "And butcher them like we have the others."

"Half the others, as you call them, are very young," the Major pointed out. "Follow orders. Hold the formation until reinforcements arrive."

"Yes, sir," the Captain responded halfheartedly. "We will hold them."

In a shorter time than the mayhem would seem to allow, the Captain collected another hundred Iberians to fuse with the hundred soldiers of his Company.

"When you engage the Legionaries," the Captain instructed the Lieutenants after a furtive glance to be sure the Major was occupied, "carve holes in their lines. I want them broken."

217

The Empire mercenaries rushed to throw themselves on the front line of the Second Maniple's left side.

***

Good Noric steel, when used properly in a controlled formation, was a formidable tool. However, when swung wildly by warriors expecting to charge through shields and over Legionaries, the blades offered limited advantage.

"Brace," Pashalis instructed.

Locking the edges of their shields together, the double line of Legionaries tensed and leaned slightly forward. Moments later, the Noricum and Iberian mercenaries stacked up in front of the shields. Before they could disengage…

"Advance, advance, advance," Centurion Pashalis commanded.

Even as the first, short and brief shove of the shields barely moved the Empire soldiers, the officers and NCOs of the Centuries repeated the orders. "Advance, advance, advance!"

On the next thrust of the Legion shields, the wounded and shocked mercenaries fell away further reducing the mass of the attack.

"Advance, Advance, advance."

When the shields shot forward and bodily moved the remaining Iberians and Noricums, the gladii had room for full powered stabs.

"Forward stomp, forward stomp," Centurion Pashalis directed.

In unison, the left feet of the Legionaries lifted and were placed next to wounded mercenaries. The next step took their right feet high before the bottoms of their hobnailed boots stomped and crushed the Empire soldiers. Again, they repeated the pace forward, allowing another stomping by the second rank.

"Brush them off and give them a home," Pashalis encouraged.

As the Legion trained, isolated infantrymen were taught to migrate to a larger fighting group. Designed to rebuild a shield wall and create order out of chaos, the maneuver was drilled into every man. Soon, dispersed clusters of Legionaries began fighting their way towards Centurion Pashalis and the double row of shields.

One of the knots of Legionaries brought acting Tribune Siglum behind the Legion line.

"Orders, sir?" Pashalis asked.

"Centurion, we charged in and began defending the First Maniple," Siglum described. "Then the Noricums ran up our spine and kicked us in the head on the way by."

"I don't understand, acting Tribune?" Pashalis questioned.

"Centurion Pashalis, you are doing a stellar job," Siglum responded. "Keep doing it. Where do you want me?"

"We have wounded to collect before we can disengage," Pashalis directed. "Organize their withdrawal."

The almost complete maniple flexed and powered forward. With every foot taken, they pushed the Qart

Hadasht forces back and retrieved their injured and dead Legionaries.

Then the ground shook and rumbling echoed off the trees sending leaves to the ground. From the north, the leading units of General Hanno's three thousand mercenaries bore down on the Legionaries.

Chapter 28 – Let Momentum

Major Vinzenz lifted his helmet allowing air to flow around and cool his head. The brash Captain ruined a strong Company of Noricum warriors, and the senior officer was steamed. He might have punished the Company commander, but the Celtic warriors had already begun ignoring the man's orders. The Captain would be lucky to run a herd of goats when he returned to Noricum.

"Fall back and regroup," he ordered the second Company commander and several Iberian Lieutenants.

When the Celts stepped away from the fighting the Iberians followed.

"The Legionaries are exhausted," Vinzenz declared as he strolled to the front of the mixed unit. "And they are weighed down with dead and injured. One coordinated attack and their formation will break."

Helmets nodded in agreement, but no one cheered. The Major knew that without the heart, the head could go logical and cause hesitation.

"Is there a strong Iberian soldier who speaks my tongue?" Vinzenz asked.

An infantryman pushed his way to the front of his formation.

"I speak your language," he stated.

"Come out here and stand by my side," the Major offered. "We are going to destroy the Republic force. What do you Iberians want to help us?"

"We lead the assault," the infantryman bragged. "You Noricums are loud and arrogant. But Iberians are fighters."

Major Vinzenz grabbed the infantryman's arm and raised it into the air.

"Tell them, the Iberians will spearhead the assault," he ordered.

Then the rumbling reached them and Vinzenz dropped the arm. Once General Hanno arrived, he would decide on the order of the assault. With the unbalanced forces, momentum was not an issue.

***

Centurion Pashalis recognized the signs of a stampede. Knowing the marching sandals were not Legionaries coming to save them, he directed.

"Step back, step back to the tree line," he instructed.

They could not fight a superior force in the open and retreat. He hoped some of his men could escape the battle by dodging through the trees. And maybe, just maybe, a few would make it back to the warships.

Qart Hadasht mercenaries poured into the open field. Every time Centurion Pashalis faced off against them, he marveled at the different cultures, shapes, and colors of the Empire soldiers. And with three thousand plus warriors there was a great deal of diversity.

Exhaling, Pashalis prepared to order his formation to dissolve and make a disorganized dash for the ships. It was better to run before the enemy began their attack than afterward.

"Second Maniple," he began…

From behind Centurion Pashalis, a gruff voice, so ragged it almost hurt his ears, sang out.

"Legion, halt! Standby, steady the cavalry, bring up the bolt throwers," Tribune Sisera chanted while indicating areas with his arms. "Spare none of the Qart Hadasht cattle. And if they run, cut their legs, and watch them bleed. Legion, stand by."

The threat of a full Legion joining the battle was hard to imagine. Both Centurion Pashalis and General Hanno would not have believed it. Except for the voice and the Tribune standing boldly at the edge of the tree line.

Pashalis recognized an overdressed Tribune Sisera. The Empire General only saw a red cape blowing in the midday wind, ceremonial armor with silver trim, a helmet with a bright horsehair comb, and a Legion officer oozing confidence.

"Empire commander, do you surrender?" Alerio shouted the question across the field. "I will allow you a moment to reflect on your life and the lives of your men."

Shields became visible in the trees to either side of Tribune Sisera. It appeared as if sixteen ranks of Legionaries were shifting forward in anticipation of a fight.

"Step back," Pashalis instructed his formation. "Look sharp. The Legion is watching. Smartly, now."

"Which Legion is that sir?" a Tesserarius near the senior Centurion asked.

"The one keeping a horde of warriors off your neck," Pashalis replied. Then he called out. "Keep your spacing and adjust those lines."

The wounded and the dead were carried between the ghost Legion's shields. Once out of sight of the mercenaries, Centurion Siglum and his porters helped the wounded and carried the dead. They were pushed and encouraged by injured combat officers and NCOs. But soon, healthy Legionaries joined them in the flight through the trees.

Pashalis was the last to leave the field. He turned about and saluted Alerio.

"How long can you hold them, Tribune Sisera?" he asked.

"Hopefully long enough for you to reach and board the warships," Alerio replied.

"We will hold a ship for you," Pashalis offered.

"No, Centurion," Alerio instructed. "Get my Centuries off the beach, away from Sardinia, and take them home."

"Tribune Alerio Carvilius Sisera," Pashalis said while lifting an arm in salute. "It has been a pleasure, sir."

"Rah," Alerio replied as he returned the salute.

Pashalis marched into the woods and noticed the sixteen shields hanging from branches. Behind him, Tribune Sisera added to his one-man performance.

"Steady the ballistae," Alerio ordered over his shoulder. "I do not want any premature discharges."

To emphasize his warning, Alerio lowered his gladius and pointed at the mercenary line. As if they had been targeted by a bolt thrower, the Empire soldiers separated to create a lane for the bolt.

***

Centurion Pashalis caught up to a group stumbling under the weight of two injured Legionaries.

"Tribune Sisera has sacrificed himself so you could escape," Pashalis informed them. "Do not make his death meaningless. Move your feet, Legionaries."

He wanted to stay and shepherd them to the beach. But his responsibility was to Second Maniple, so he forged ahead of the stragglers.

Two of the five warships had loaded infantrymen, pushed off, and were rowing for the mouth of the bay. Another over filled its deck and oarsmen pushed the vessel into the water.

Files of Legionaries loaded the wounded as they arrived. Everyone was panicked and hustling to board the last two warships. Everyone except for sixteen men.

The two squads from the Fourteenth Century, the ones Alerio borrowed, rested on their shields behind Sors' Talisman.

It was not that they were leaning and motionless while other scurried around. The two squads had worked hard to hang the shields in the trees to fool the Qart Hadasht. Or them occupying a position behind the warship or even the four javelins each Legionary had stuck in the sand for easy access. What puzzled the Centurion? The sixteen men were naked.

The last of the stragglers appeared from the trees as the fourth warship launched. Behind the slower Legionaries, the trees shook from soldiers colliding with the trunks as they careened down to the beach.

"Sir, you should get on board," a Decanus suggested.

He also was nude and unarmored.

"What about your squads?" Pashalis inquired.

"Sir, our job is not done," the other squad leader told him.

"When will it be?" Pashalis questioned.

The wounded being carried groaned in pain and the Legionaries carrying them gasped for air. They jogged through the sand and behind them a line of mercenaries broke from the greenery.

"Just what is your job?" the senior Centurion demanded.

The two squad leaders pointed out the one hundred oarsmen standing on the beach waiting to launch Sors' Talisman.

"Tribune Sisera said if any of those oarsmen so much as gets a scratch," one Decanus answered. "He will find us in Hades and have us on latrine duty for eternity."

"Can he do that, sir?" the other squad leader asked.

"I just watched the Tribune stop an army," Pashalis stated. "I imagine there isn't much Death Caller can't accomplish. Carry on."

"Yes, sir," the Decani acknowledged. Then to their squads, they ordered. "Javelins. And make them count."

The sixteen picked up their shields but didn't strap them to their arms. Holding them loose, they snatched their first javelin from the sand.

***

Centurion Pashalis stood at the stern peaking between shields. He watched the last of the men from the battle at Tharros struggle to reach the ramp.

"Third Principale, hold," the first deck officer encouraged. "Hold."

His words were meant to calm the nervous deck officer standing on the beach. Stretched out around the keel, the launch crew of unarmed rowers vibrated with nervous energy. They were overly ready to push their warship into the surf, scamper aboard, and be gone.

"Hold, hold," the Third Principale repeated.

Screaming across the sand, mercenaries came, threatening to disrupt the launch process. Pashalis concentrated on the advancing Qart Hadasht soldiers and pondered if Sisera's ploy would work.

"Throw, throw one," came from the beach below.

Sixteen Legion javelins soared through the air. They impacted. Two landed in the sand. But fourteen javelins punched fourteen mercenaries out of the mad scramble to reach and capture a Republic warship.

"Throw, throw two," the naked squad leaders shouted.

Two more flights arched up and over. As men were swept off their feet by the sharp barbed points, the other flight of javelins dropped in creating more havoc. But there were additional mercenaries coming from the trees. The beach was filling with loud, vocal Qart Hadasht warriors.

"Third Principale, get us wet," the senior deck officer shouted to be heard over the screaming soldiers.

After giving the order, First Principale Dormivi ducked behind the infantry shields station at the stern of the warship.

"Push, push," the third deck officer yelled down the port side and again down the starboard side. "Push, push."

The last Legionary up dove onto the deck and the ramp was shoved away from the hull. As the vessel slid across the sand, spears arched, and arrows ran straight from the mass of Empire warriors.

The naked sixteen infantrymen stepped into ankle deep water and used their shields to protect the oarsmen. Then, Sors' Talisman dipped at the bow, leveled, and oars splashed into the water. The one hundred men of the launch crew scrambled up the sides and ran for their oar stations. Once his team was up, the Third Principale climbed to the top deck. That left sixteen unarmored Legionaries on the beach.

"Throw, throw one," the Decani ordered.

Sixteen iron tips found flesh and sixteen mercenaries fell to the beach.

"Swim," the sixteen naked Legionaries bellowed at the same time.

They shook the shields off their arms. But held on to them as they ran into the surf.

227

Flights of spears and arrows followed their progress. But as the Legionaries splashed into thigh high water, they released their Legion shields and hooked leather straps around their necks. Dragging the wooden scutums behind, they used the shields to protect their backs. All Legionaries were trained to swim. But not always while towing shields peppered with spears and arrows. Despite the drag, the sixteen stroked and kicked away from the beach.

Cheering broke out among the infantrymen, sailors, and oarsmen when the two squads climbed on board. Everyone celebrated the sixteen heroic men who defended the oarsmen. Everyone rejoiced except for Legion Centurion Pashalis and Ship's Centurion Naulum.

Silently, they watched the coast of Tharros as the warship rowed for the mouth of the bay. They were the only two searching the shoreline for signs of Tribune Alerio Sisera.

Act 8

Chapter 29 – Skills and Luck

As a weapon's instructor, Alerio prided himself on the ability to read his opponents. The skill served him well in training groups of Legionaries and in combat situations. At the present, he only needed to judge one man's attitude.

When the Qart Hadasht General rapped his knuckles on his chin, Alerio recognized it as a man attempting to knock doubt out of his mind. And that doubt would concern the imaginary Legion behind the staff officer.

"I said to hold," Alerio shouted to his right. Then he took a step in that direction and said. "I will not abide by disobedience."

In sham outrage, the Legion Tribune stalked into the woods. Behind him, the General made his decision.

"Attack, attack," he ordered. "Go, go."

Three thousand warriors surged across the field. The fastest and bravest threw themselves against the Legion shields at the edge of the tree line. To their surprise, the shields tumbled to the ground along with the first wave. The only danger to the first rank of warriors was getting kicked or stomped by the second wave.

While the mercenaries smiled at being alive, they cursed at being fooled. Not too far in front of them,

Alerio Sisera ran. His red cape flapping behind him and the comb on his helmet wobbling from side to side. The manner of dress and his rapid pace gave Alerio the appearance of a big red hawk.

He was halfway to the beach and escape when a group of Empire soldiers met him on the trail. Only two kinds of units would be out alone in the forest. A trusted team given the duty to flank the battle, or they were foul ups, hiding in the woods and avoiding the fight.

As a youth at his father's farm, Alerio spent his evenings training with a pair of practice gladii. Between sessions on the training post, he sat on a stone wall and watched the birds return to their nests at sunset. During those rest periods, Alerio learned a few things about the language of birds.

"Chirp, chirp," he made the sounds as sharp and piercing as possible.

Alerio knew it as an avian call of danger. The soldiers might not have recognized the meaning, but their nerves registered menace. They hesitated, gawked, and stared at the Legion staff officer.

Bent forward and flapping his arms, Alerio raced down a side trail.

"Chirp, chirp," he screamed again.

The stunned soldiers were too shocked to pursue, or they feared an encounter with a mad Legion officer. In either case, Alerio had the path to himself. Unfortunately, the trail took Alerio away from the beach and the Republic warships.

***

A long way down the path, Alerio stopped, checked to be sure he was alone, then stepped off the trail. He scooped leaves out of a hollow, slid off his helmet and dropped it into the depression. Following, he deposited his armor and armored skirt. Next, he cut slices from his bright red cape. Strips of material were useful as rope if he needed ties of some kind.

"I am sorry, Lady Carvilius," he stated before dropping the rest of the expensive gift from his adopted mother onto the discarded armor.

Then he kicked leaves over the decorative gear and jogged back to the trail.

"In hindsight," Alerio sighed. "Senior Tribune Vergilius was right. A staff officer must dress the part if he wants to get respect. Especially the respect of a Qart Hadasht General."

Once on the trail, he fell into the rhythm of a Legion jog. Although he traveled north, soon he needed to angle right and circle the bay before heading south towards the coast. But first, he had to steal a Qart Hadasht horse while avoiding enemy patrols.

***

There was no magic or special power or blessings from Prometheus. The idea of stealing from the staff, or even that the headquarters was close, had less to do with the God of Forethought and more to do with logic.

The Empire infantry came from an area north of the bay. As Alerio had not seen any quartermasters or servants at the battle site, they must be where the infantry staged before the attack.

Picking his way through the woods, then into a section of swamp, and back onto firm soil, Alerio reached the northern area of the bay. From there, the smell of smoke guided him to the supply camp.

The good news was all the horses were stabled in the same corral. The bad was the mounts were attended to by a handful of grooms. Realizing a daylight raid gave his presence away and assured a chase, he eased back into the woods to wait for nightfall.

***

The fires cooled and the night breezes blew away the final wisps of smoke. A few sentries sauntered between staff tents, but they seemed uninterested in exploring beyond the headquarters' sleeping area. It seemed as if the sentries belonged to a different military force.

Further emphasizing the disparity of the Empire army, just before nightfall, several infantry units returned from the fort. They spread out into isolated bivouac spaces. Between Companies of different origins, there seemed to be animosity which showed itself by the wide strips of land between the units.

Although all citizens of the Republic, theft in the Legion did occur. To prevent robbery between squads, posted guards at each tent stood vigil overnight. But during the daylight, Legionaries freely mixed with other Centuries. Regional pride led to competition but that was the extent of tension between Legion Centuries.

Observing the behavior of the Qart Hadasht units, Alerio could not imagine working through the cultural divisions and mistrust that created the camps sleeping arrangements. On the other hand, the lanes separating mercenary camps allowed him to stroll unchallenged to the backside of the corral.

***

The box frame fence with the crossed-pole filler came apart easily. A cut at the corners of the top log, a slice at each end of the cross poles and soon Alerio had a stack of fence rails set off to the side. He snuck through the hole in the fence and walked up to the horses. There he began eliminating possible mounts.

One shivered under his touch, another shied away, but one stood still while tossing its head in Alerio's direction. After tying three sections of robe material together, he dropped the makeshift rope over the horse's neck. Gently, Alerio led the mount out of the corral.

They walked the lane between mercenary units and out of the Qart Hadasht camp. Alerio did not stop until they were seventeen hundred and sixty steps, or about a mile away, and the backtrail had no sounds of pursuit.

Lack of a real bridle was the reason he selected the calmest horse. Now he practiced farm ingenuity. The art of making do with what you possessed to make what you needed.

A few wraps and knots later and he had fashioned a bitless bridle from strips of the cape.

"We have eighty miles to travel," Alerio informed the mare. "You take care of me, and I will see you go to a good home when I leave."

The horse bowed her head testing the extent of the bridle and reins. Satisfied that her rider had control, the mare stepped forward on the dark trail heading south.

Alerio was settling in on the uncomfortable bareback when the mare stopped. Sounds of running water alerted him to a hazard blocking the trail. After investigating, he walked the mare to the river's edge.

"If it gets deep, we'll swim," Alerio told the horse. Then he teased. "You can swim, can't you?"

With a nervous laugh, Alerio guided the mount into the chilly water. His unease came from wading into an unknown body of water in the middle of the night. If possible, he preferred to wait for daybreak. But dawn might bring a patrol and he needed to be long gone by then.

On the far side of the river, he stripped off his faded red under-armor tunic, wrung out excess water, and slipped it on again.

"That was fun," he lied to the horse while leaping onto her back. "No more rivers, okay?"

***

Early that afternoon, Alerio noted the coastal plain drifting inland. Between the flat land and the sea, hills rising to a thousand feet and down to rough mounds forced him and the mare to travel in a southeasterly direction. While skirting the heights, Alerio searched for a village or a town.

"I'm hungry and I need a saddle for your scrawny backside," he said to the horse. Then remembering the mare was doing the walking added. "I bet you could use some grain."

The beast did not reply, it simply continued putting one hoof in front of the other.

Much later, sandstone roofs appeared in the distance. At first Alerio assumed it was a rock formation based on the color. But as they drew closer, the shapes became regular, and the sandstone split to reveal separate structures.

"Food and vino for me," Alerio declared. "And a saddle and grain for you."

With no sign of understanding, the mare moved steadily forward.

Chapter 30 – Anxiety in a Small Town

The sun had almost dipped behind the hills when Alerio guided the horse into the town. Tired and irritable from the ride, he decided to walk for the last half mile. Three intersecting streets made up the road system and about thirty houses created the village. It only took a heartbeat to realize why the town even existed. A large grain storage building filled the view at the end of one street. But it was spring, and the village appeared to be empty.

"We are in luck," Alerio informed the horse. "A grain transfer station will have teamsters. And with teamsters you get leather workers. And those fine craftsmen make saddles. But first, feed for you and meat for me."

They strolled down the middle of a dusty street eyeing the signs on the buildings. He studied not the lettering, it was in Sardo and had not been part of Alerio's education. But each sign had pictures of the business' trade. Passing one with etchings of grapes and bread let him know his second stop.

At an intersection, Alerio spied a stable in the distance. That would be his first stop. Any Legion NCO will tell you to tend to your tools first before taking care of yourself. And the horse was an asset.

"I believe we have located…" Alerio started to say to the mare.

"I'll take the horse," a voice challenged. "You seem too ragged and shabby to be riding."

Peering back at the grape and bread sign, Alerio noted a young man. Built like an oarsman, he had a sneer on his face and held a Noric sword in his hand.

"Do you know how to use that?" Alerio inquired. "Because if you don't, you should not…"

"Shouldn't what?" the youth interrupted. "Bother a rider in pink night clothing holding my horse by a red cloth rope. The inn is one block over. Go ahead and get back to your nap. But first, leave the horse."

Big, strong, and fast has been the downfall of many a young swordsman. They assumed their natural abilities would grant them victory. When they matured, if they lived that long, the juvenile sword swingers would learn. Learn that experience and skill made up for the three attributes of youth.

"That's a nice sword," Alerio complimented, "and an exquisitely crafted belt and sheath. I don't suppose you purchased the weapon."

"I took them off a dead Qart Hadasht Admiral," the youth bragged. He stepped away from the inn and moved onto the street. "Just like my brothers and I are going to take the horse from you. And that gladius. And the dagger. And your coin purse."

Four other young men, each resembling the swordsman, stepped out of the restaurant and onto the street.

"Well, if you must," Alerio said while drooping his shoulders in defeat. "Can I at least get her fed and watered? It's been a long day and we've come a long way."

"No. I want to go riding, like the fine folks at home," one of the brothers announced.

He swayed from too much vino and his eyes were unfocused. Alerio checked him off as the one least dangerous to him. For the horse, the intoxicated one meant the already exhausted mount would be ridden to death. It was not what Alerio promised the mare when he took her.

"You forgot one," Alerio announced as he pulled the horse's head around until the mare faced the stable.

"Forgot what, ragged rider?" the swordsman demanded.

Alerio swatted the mare hard on her haunches. The usually calm horse bolted forward, ran for three paces, then slowed, and finally stopped.

"Not what I wanted," Alerio said in exacerbation.

He meant to put distance between the horse and the brothers. But her relaxed nature and fatigue were the undoing of Alerio's plan.

All five brothers laughed.

"What did I forget, pink tunic rider?" the swordsman questioned.

The phrase brought another round of chuckles for the siblings.

Suddenly, the mare raised her head. Catching a scent of either the water trough or a feed bin, she trotted away.

"I have another dagger," Alerio informed the brothers. "And there is a question for you. What type of man carries two visible and one concealed blade?"

The door to the restaurant opened and a young lady slipped out and shuffled sideways while keeping her eyes on the brothers.

"Whoa there," one of them instructed.

He leaped to the girl, wrapped her hair in his fist and twisted.

"I said to wait for me," he screamed at her. "Get back in there and pour a glass for when I finish my business."

The woman slinked back to the doorway and vanished inside. Alerio was beginning to dislike the brash and cruel brothers.

"Give me one," Alerio offered. "Give me one excuse not to hurt you."

"If anyone is going to get hurt, it's you, rider in the pink tunic," the swordsman spit out.

"Not funny the first time, and tedious the second," Alerio told him. Shifting to his right, the Tribune moved forcing the brothers further into the street. "Do you have a God? If so, now would be a good time to pray. I plan to."

Chapter 31 – Ragged Rider

"Nenia Dea, these young men do not deserve to die," Alerio prayed. "Show me a way to avoid this fight. Or come and take their souls. And if it is my end, take me quickly."

The five brothers exchanged glances then puffed up their chests. They did not fear a single ragged rider or his dumb prayer to a foreign deity.

"We were just going to beat you and take your horse," another of the brothers boasted. "But now, you are going to die."

By his speech, the sibling identified himself as the leader. Now that the rider, who warned about toting three blades, knew where to start, he closed the distance to the youths.

"By the way, I am a Legion weapon's instructor," Tribune Sisera warned. "Get on your knees or die."

With his right hand, he pulled a dagger from the small of his back. The long doubled edged blade flashed in the waning light of the day.

The brothers watched as the rider pointed to the dagger, and told them, "It is a wicked instrument."

The siblings shifted apart to give each of them room to slash. In their careers as oarsmen for the Qart Hadasht Navy, they had not lost a fight. Whether it was armed or bare-knuckled, five siblings brawling together presented a formidable force. They took on other rowers, sailors, and warriors. They saw no reason the shabby rider could stand against them.

With his left hand, the rider drew a gladius. Most swordsmen when holding a weapon in their weaker hand, seemed awkward. Their victim flipped the Legion sword in the air. It rose high, spinning rapidly.

Then the rider began to chant. So badly did he sing, the brothers felt it was their public duty to silence the man.

> *"These men are taken with sadness, Goddess Nenia*
> *For every life is sacred and every soul unique*
> *This fight, this day, I did not seek*
> *Not lightly do I call upon you*
> *For one day is the day I rue*
> *With care I ask for intervention*
> *Judge me and my intention*
> *And if you select me*
> *I agree*
> *But take me quickly please."*

All five brothers were watching the heavy blade spin in the air. None noticed the long dagger as it flipped forward. The leader of the five siblings grabbed his neck and fell to his knees. Both hands wrapped around the dagger in his throat.

> *"Nenia Dea, come take this gift*
> *Seize his soul and make it swift*
> *End his misery, stop the pain*
> *Hades waits on a different plane*
> *Life is sacred and every soul unique*
> *This fight, this day, I did not seek."*

The chanting rider easily snagged the hilt of the gladius out of the air. Racing forward, he moved in behind the thrown dagger and kicked the brother with the Noric sword in the hand. Bones shattered under the hobnails of his Legion boots.

The drunk brother swung, but only hit empty air. He twisted himself sideways and stumbled away.

The two uninjured brothers backed up.

"Too late, lads," Alerio growled.

He ran at them and sang while pulling his Legion dagger.

"Nenia Dea, come take this present
Their blood with shame I vent
End the notions, stop the grief
I never planned to be a soul thief
Not lightly do I call upon you
For one day is the day I rue."

They turned preparing to run when the dagger and the gladius stabbed the siblings in their backs. Pulling the weapons, the shabby rider walked to the choking brother and snatched his long dagger from the neck.

Alerio had tears in his eyes as he carried the bloody blades back to the swordsman.

"Who are you?' the brother with the shattered hand asked.

"I've been called many things," Alerio Sisera replied.

The intoxicated sibling pulled a knife, screamed, and ran at the man's back. Spinning, the rider whipped the gladius around and sliced the drunk's neck. At the end of the rotation, he again faced the swordsman.

"Legionary, heavy infantryman, Raider, weapon's instructor, Corporal," the rider listed. "Centurion, and Tribune. But the one title I reject, keeps coming back in my actions and my deeds. I am a disciple of the Goddess Nenia. I am Death Caller."

With those words, he stabbed the swordsman in the eye. The dagger drove through the socket and pierced the brain of the last brother.

"These men are taken with sadness Goddess Nenia
For every life is sacred and every soul unique
This fight, this day, I did not seek
Not lightly do I call upon you
For one day is the day I rue
With care I ask for intervention
Judge me and my intention
And if you select me
I agree
But take me quickly please."

The town's residents appeared in the doorways of shops. From the inn, a fat man and the young, abused girl stepped onto the street. While the fat man glared hard at the brothers, the girl screamed and ran to one. Taking the brother in her arms, she cooed to him as Nenia Dea lifted his soul from the wounded body.

The shabby rider reached down and picked up the Noric sword from beside the failed swordsman. Then he took the coin pouches from each brother. Lately, he strolled down the street in the direction of the stables.

***

It was almost dark when Alerio wandered from the barn. Brushing the mare had given him time to sort out his feelings. After examining the confrontation, he realized the brothers did not have to die. But once he started slaying, it felt as if he was another person. And that person offered no mercy or sanctuary. As he neared the sign with grapes and bread etchings, Alerio promised himself that the butcher in him would never be released again.

"I hope you have beef, or lamb, or goat," he called out as he entered the restaurant.

"The brothers killed my milking goat," the fat proprietor replied. "So, I have roasted goat meat, cheese, and bread, but no goat's milk."

"Speaking of the brothers," Alerio mentioned while sitting at a table. "Who will bury them?"

"We have good topsoil but below the planting level it's rock," the fat owner informed him. "No graves. We'll pile the bodies onto a cart and haul them to the sea."

"Is that how you bury your dead?" Alerio asked.

"Locals are cremated on funeral fires," the proprietor explained. "Wine, beer, or spring water?"

Alerio needed his coins to get home if he missed the fleet. Then he recalled his emotional response to killing the youths.

"Is this enough to build five funeral pyres?" he asked. Between his finger, Alerio displayed a silver coin.

"That will cover it," the fat man agreed. "I'll have some boys stack the wood and the bodies while you eat."

Alerio took his time dining. Although it had been a long day and he was exhausted, he purchased a wineskin before leaving the restaurant. He had one more task to perform before sleeping.

***

In the distance, a single flame glowed in the dark. As Alerio approached, he found a campfire blazing and

243

five unlit wooden structures holding the bodies of the brothers. He pulled a burning stick from the campfire and walked to the first body.

Deep shadows hid the features, but Alerio was able to locate the face. After placing coins over the eyes, he moved to the next sibling. At the third one, he placed the coins in the mouth as one eye was shredded. When each brother had coins for passage across the river Styx, Alerio lit the funeral pyres.

"To untamed youth," Alerio announced. He took a stream of vino. "If you only had guidance in your lives we would not have fought. And you would not have died."

The fires roared and flames shot high into the night sky. Alerio sat alone drinking and watching the flames consume the wood and the bodies.

***

Early the next morning, Alerio and the mare left the town behind. He never looked back at the five piles of still smoking ash.

The saddle was old and the frame creaky. But the double layer of horse blankets helped cushion both man and beast. With better seating, the mare moved quicker with an easier gait.

By the next afternoon, they made the farming and trading town of Musei. Just three miles from high hills on both sides, the town rested in the center of freshly planted fields.

They found a large stable run by two men. Showing their passion for animals, the men made a fuss about the condition of the mare.

"I don't know how she was treated before I acquired her," Alerio informed them. "She's carried me a long way."

"A little feed and a few days of rest and she'll be ready to take you across Sardinia," one exclaimed.

"I'm heading for the coast," Alerio told them. "I need to catch a ship heading east."

"Wrong time of year, friend," the other stable owner added. "Spring is slow. Come harvest time, Portoscuso will have two or more merchant ships a day."

"Portoscuso?" Alerio asked. "I met a fisherman from there once. He has a big fishing boat."

"That's Gavia the Fisherman," the two handlers said at the same time.

"How far is Portoscuso?" Alerio asked.

"About seventeen miles," the other stableman replied.

"I'll need a ride in the morning," Alerio remarked. Then he patted the mare's neck and instructed. "She took care of me. I ask that you take care of her."

"We will," the stable owners assured him.

***

The next day, a wagon rolled into the small port town of Portoscuso. From the bed of the transport, Alerio had an excellent view of the sea. And as they neared a small beach, he saw the large fishing boat.

"Take care of the mare," Alerio reminded the driver.

"That we will do," the stable owner confirmed.

Alerio jump from the wagon, picked up his bundle, and marched to the fishing boat where a group of men were unloading the catch.

"Gavia the Fisherman, how much can you make in a day?" Alerio asked.

Gavia looked up from where he was inspecting a net.

"Why?" the fisherman asked.

"I'll pay it for a ride," Alerio informed him. "And more if you will cross the Tyrrhenian Sea and deliver me to the shoreline of the Republic."

"I will not cross the sea," Gavia informed Alerio. "But I can sail you to the port at Cagliari on the east coast. There you will find merchants ships aplenty. Some will be heading eastward, I'm sure."

Chapter 32 – Funeral Announcement

Thank you for your understanding at this time. The loss of a son, even an adopted one, is hard on everyone in the Carvilius Maximus households. The lady Aquila, the staff, and I beg your indulgence as we seek solitude to heal.

To quell errant rumors of his demise, Tribune Sisera went missing during a Legion campaign on Sardinia. Through a selfless act, he saved the men of Second Maniple, Paterculus Legion West. For his sacrifice, the Senate of the Republic has awarded my son a posthumous accommodation for bravery.

We do request that you pray for our son, Alerio Carvilius. Meeting his demise alone on a battlefield, there were no companions to place coins on his eyes or in his mouth. Without coins to pay Charon, the ferryman, the river Styx is closed to our son. Alerio was resourceful in life and we take solace in knowing he will find a way to be judged. And that the Judges will find him worthy and grant him access to Elysium.

A funeral procession through the Capital will take place on the Ides of May. The planned route includes courtesy stops at temples adjacent to the forum before ending at the Temple of Nenia, our son's personal Goddess. Vocal mourning during the procession is appreciated.

Feasting will follow at the Maximus Villa, attendance by invitation only.

The Carvilius Maximus family wishes you good health and a long life.

General Spurius Carvilius Maximus, Citizen, and Senator of the Republic

***

Former Centurion Accantus trotted to a group of farmhands working on a drainage ditch. This was his fifth stop, and he was running out of daylight.

"Let's be sure the sides are tamped down hard," he instructed. "The last big rain washed two miles of dirt into our irrigation pond."

"We are, supervisor," an old worker assured him.

Accantus straightened his back and gritted his teeth. His bad hip was reminding him that he had been pushing hard. But he had no choice. The funeral was in three days. The Maximus Farm needed to be running perfectly before he left for the Capital.

Glancing up at the hills to the east, he saw a hooded man sitting on the crest of the hill.

"I don't have time for this," Accantus complained as he kneed his horse in the man's direction.

If highwaymen were planning to attack the farm, he would have to hire a few infantrymen to defend it. The horse made the climb with power and grace. The former

Centurion barely held back a yelp of pain as the mount topped the rise.

"Down there is the Maximus Farm. If you are looking for somewhere to rob?" Accantus threatened while placing a hand on the hilt of his gladius. "You will not enjoy the visit."

The sitting man shifted before turning his head.

"That is not a nice way to speak to a dead man," Alerio teased. He tossed back the hood and stood. "But I thought up here was part of the farm."

"Tribune Sisera, I didn't mean to be disrespectful," the farm manager apologized. "The report said..."

"I can guess what the report states. But it is mistaken, at least as far as the conclusion," Alerio described. Then he asked. "These hills. Before I left, I had Belen buy the land. This is supposed to be for the Lady Aquila's vineyard. Imagine my surprise when I found it untouched."

"That's the odd part, Tribune," Accantus responded by sweeping an arm around to take in the landscape. "I began to clear away the brush and trees when Lady Carvilius came by and ordered me to stop. It seems she sold the land, and we would not be planting grape vines."

"She sold the land. Why?" Alerio questioned.

"Sir, I have no idea," Accantus admitted. "I was as disappointed as you seem to be. But speaking of disappointed, have you seen the Senator or the Lady. I am sure they will be overjoyed to see that you are alive."

"I was headed to the villa at Tusculum," Alerio replied. He lowered his eyes, dropped his chin, and paused. "But I wanted to feel fresh dirt between my toes and run my hands through it."

"Things get rough in Sardinia?" the former combat officer asked. He slid from the saddle and groaned as his feet hit the ground, jarring his bad hip. "Sorry, dumb question. You are presumed killed by a Qart Hadasht army."

"There aren't many individuals killed by an entire army, are there?" Alerio teased.

"I talked to Gaius Claudius about you, Tribune," Accantus informed Alerio. "You were in Messina when he crossed over with the advanced Centuries. That was eight years ago. And you have been in the merda ever since. It's a wonder you don't want to crawl under the dirt and pull it up over your head."

"I've watched a lot of good men die," Alerio replied.

"Plus, your responsibilities have expanded," Accantus observed. "Most Legionaries who advance through the ranks to become combat officers do it slowly. Over years. With time to adjust at every level. Not you. You reached Centurion quickly. I am not saying you didn't deserve it. But from there, you leaped, not just to a staff officer's commission, you shot up to another level of society. I am surprised you haven't broken apart like pieces of pottery, Tribune Sisera."

"Maybe, I have. Maybe that's why I haven't reported to a Legion yet," Alerio remarked. "I told myself that telling my parents I was alive in person was better than them hearing it from a courier."

"It is, but you are justifying the delay," Accantus pointed out. "That tells me you aren't really sure of the reason for holding off on telling your parents. Or for reporting to a Legion, for that matter."

"Do me a favor," Alerio begged, "keep this meeting between us a secret."

"Of course, Tribune," Accantus agreed. "But let me ask, will I have to go to the Capital, put on a wax mask of your face, and limp through the streets crying and agonizing about your death?"

"It'll get you off the farm for a day or two," Alerio reminded the supervisor.

"Tribune Sisera, I've been in a lot of situations including places with pig slop up to my chin," the former Centurion responded. "And, sir, working the Carvilius Maximus farm is among the best of the lot."

"I'll let you know about the parade," Alerio promised. He took a step towards the hills. "Before you ask, I do not need your horse."

"You are a lot like General Maximus," Accantus offered while rubbing his hip. "You care about your men and pay attention to their needs."

Feeling a sense of pride at the comparison, Alerio hiked away heading in a northwest direction.

***

The Carvilius country estate occupied the far side of a hill near the village of Tusculum. To the north, the land fell away in waves of green trees and grazing sheep. Alerio topped the rise and stopped on the road.

'How exactly,' he thought, 'does one politely return from the dead?'

Other large estates bracketed the Carvilius property but compared to the crowding in the Capital, properties at Tusculum provided privacy. It was why when Alerio approached the main gate, no one in the villa saw him.

"Who is in charge of the guard?" Alerio asked the armed sentry.

He kept his head down and the hood dangling over his face.

"Who wants to know?" the former Legionary responded.

Alerio knew he was former infantry. All his adopted father's household men-at-arms had served in the Legion.

"Let me guess," Alerio offered by rubbing his chin as if thinking. "You served in the east. I'd say Brindisi."

"How would you know that?" the sentry asked.

"You hold your spear at shoulder height," Alerio said. "It's the way Greek hoplites do because their spears are so long. Legion spears are shorter, so we hold them just above the hip. In the east, we adopted a lot of their habits."

"Optio Affatus is in command," the sentry told Alerio.

"I'd like to speak to him, but no, I will not give you a name," Alerio told the man. "Just tell Civi he is a one note musician."

"Runner to the front gate," the sentry bellowed. "Visitor for Sergeant Affatus."

A voice from the side of the villa responded, "His lordship is not receiving."

"Go ahead, interrupt Civi's dinner," Alerio laughed.

"Inform the Optio that the visitor said he is a one note musician," the guard bellowed.

Alerio stepped back from the gate and waited.

The horse came at a full gallop and was just slowing when Affatus leaped from its back. Athletic landings are a young man's trick and certainly not for an old Legion NCO with two bad knees.

"Who dares use that expression" an enraged Civi demanded as he limped to the gate.

"He is right outside," the guard said deflecting the ire.

"Well, open the gate so I can get my hands on him," Civi ordered.

The Optio rushed up to the stranger, grabbed his shoulder and spun him around.

"Number one do not say anything," Alerio warned from under the hood. "I am not dead. Second, I want to see Lady Carvilius before she hears about me second hand."

"Yes, sir," Civi acknowledged. "The General is out inspecting the herds this afternoon. He does that a lot lately. He misses you, Tribune..."

"Number one," Alerio reminded the NCO.

They walked through the gate and stopped at the Optio's mount.

"Take my horse," Civi offered.

"At this point it's probably best," Alerio said as he vaulted up into the saddle. "Where can I find the Lady Carvilius?"

"At this time of day, sir, she'll be on the patio waiting for the stars to rise," Civi informed him.

Alerio kneed the mount and rode for the corner of the villa.

Aquila Carvilius sat perfectly in the chair. Her back rigid, feet together on the floor, and her head held high. The only thing revealing her emotional state were the red rims around her eyes.

To her credit as a lady, when the strange horse rode from around the villa and trampled the flower bed, she simply raised a hand and extended a finger. Then her pose to deliver a lecture about invading her evening meditation dissolved and she collapsed.

Alerio slid off the horse and ran to her side. Gently, he wrapped an arm protectively around her shoulders.

"I was afraid of something like this," he mumbled.

"Since when do apparitions speak?" Aquila questioned.

"Since when do mothers of Tribunes faint at homecomings," Alerio teased.

She touched his face and scowled.

"You require grooming, young man," Aquila remarked. "But later. After we have talked, and you explain your absence. And we have a meal together so I can look at you."

"All that sounds wonderful," Alerio admitted. "But I'd rather talk about me with the General present. It'll save me a long recitation."

"That is wise," Aquila admitted. "But what will we talk about until Spurius returns?"

"Your vineyard for one," Alerio questioned. "Why did you sell the land?"

He expected the astute Lady Carvilius to have a snappy answer. Maybe she wanted to buy a matched team of horses. Or she found an opportunity to purchase another property. He didn't expect the bone rattling shiver that racked her body. Or the sobs and tears when he lifted her chin.

"Please tell me what happened?" he inquired.

"You tell me why you had to face an army by yourself," Aquila ordered between sniffles.

"The First Maniple walked into a trap and parts of the Second Maniple went in to pull the youngsters out," Alerio described. "I saw the enemy reinforcements coming. After setting guards on the beach, I put on my finest staff officer armor and the red cape you sent me. It was beautiful."

"Was beautiful?" Aquila asked.

"I had to cut it up during my escape…"

"I don't care about material," she said. "Tell me. Tell me. Why you were there?"

"Because I believed I could make a difference to my men," Alerio informed her. "And I did. I stood shouting orders to an imaginary Legion until my Maniple, and what was left of the First, got off the battlefield. After that, it got messy."

"No one ordered you to attack an army alone?" Aquila demanded. She pushed away his arm, stood, and began to pace. "No Priest of Jupiter instructed you to, to perform that dangerous and insane action?"

"No, Aquila. It was all my idea," Alerio assured her. "Now. It's your turn to tell me, just what is going on?"

The Lady Carvilius squared her shoulders and looked into Alerio's eyes.

"After you left for Sardinia, a Fetial Priest visited me," she explained. "He said you stole something valuable from him and that I owed him three hundred gold coins to replace the coins you took."

"I can assure you, Lady Carvilius, I did not rob a temple or a priest especially a Fetial Priest," Alerio said defending himself. "Is that why you sold the land?"

"Fetial Priest Mattia said if I did not pay, he would see that your Maniple would be sent into the most dangerous situations. And that you," she couldn't finish as tears filled her eyes and clogged her throat.

"And you thought I was killed because of something you did?" Alerio questioned her, keeping his voice calm.

While his voice soothed, at his sides his hands squeezed into fists, and inside he seethed with rage. This grand lady had suffered nights and days of guilt believing she had caused her adopted son's death.

"What else did this Priest of Jupiter have to say?" he asked in the same deadly quiet manner.

"He warned that with a few whispers he could ruin Spurius' businesses and end his political career," Aquila reported. "And that with words to the proper buyers, the farm would fail."

"Did he threaten your social standing?" Alerio asked.

"I am so unimportant," she suggested. "You and Spurius are the important things in my life."

"Fetial Priest Mattia of the Jupiter's Temple," Alerio mouthed the words as if he was a wolf gnashing his teeth at smelling prey. "But you have one thing wrong, Lady Carvilius."

"What is it, Alerio?" she inquired.

"It's you that I consider important," Alerio informed her. "And I will take care of this issue."

From inside the villa, Spurius Carvilius Maximus called softly as if he were afraid of what he would find or not find on the patio.

"Alerio?" the Senator queried.

"Spurius, get out here," Aquila Carvilius commanded. "And see who finally found his way home."

Spurius Maximus rushed through the door and stopped.

"I guess the funeral feast is off," he commented. "But what do I tell Isos Monos? The artist has spent two days creating wax masks of your likeness for the sorrow parade."

Then his professional demeanor snapped, and he went to Alerio, and the men embraced.

"General Maximus, this may seem an odd request," Alerio advised. "But you need to go ahead with the funeral."

"I need to do what?" Maximus growled.

Aquila stepped forward and rested a hand on the Senator's arm.

"Spurius, let Alerio explain," she encouraged.

Act 9

Chapter 33 – Wax Masks

Isos Monos dribbled a bead of wax from the beeswax candle onto the coated cloth. Then, while it was warm and pliable, he smoothed the wax into a ridge with his thumb and forefinger.

"The hands of an artist," he declared after lifting his fingers at just the perfect angle, "are his greatest asset."

Another bead of wax and he finished shaping the nose of the death mask.

"How goes the creations?" Optio Civi Affatus inquired.

He marched onto the patio and examined the rows of masks. They resembled Alerio Sisera, down to the scar above his left eye and the one below the eyebrow on his right eye. But the facial lines formed from a veteran's hard experiences were missing. Without those details, the masks made Alerio seem to be a nobleman's son without a worry in the world.

"You do know Tribune Sisera was a Legionary," Affatus remarked while running a finger across a forehead of wax and paint, "a fighting man."

"I am aware of Tribune Sisera's martial skills," the Greek artist replied. "But I choose to see beauty where others remember brutal details."

"This mask," Affatus inquired, "is it finished?"

"Yes. It was the first one. I used the mask as a model," Isos responded. "Please don't touch the masks."

Ignoring the artist, Civi picked up the mask and held it behind his back. With the other hand, he counted the rows.

"You are two masks short," Civi offered.

"No, just one more. There are eleven finished," Isos explained.

"No, Greek, I count ten on the table," Civi insisted.

"What about the one behind your back?" Isos exclaimed. "You..."

He stopped talking when Civi drew a Legion dagger.

"How many masks are on the table?" the Optio inquired while indicating the masks with the steel tip.

"Ten but..." Isos started to protest.

"There you go. You are two masks short," Civi Affatus directed as he backed off the patio and vanished into the villa.

"The poor man," Isos pondered while pulling two pieces of cloth off a pile. "He misses Master Sisera so much, he needs a mask of the young man. I can't fault him that remembrance."

The Greek artist dipped one of the pieces into a bowl of warm wax. During the afternoon, he would repeat the process of building up layers until the death mask could be shaped into the likeness of the deceased, Alerio Carvilius Sisera.

***

Civi Affatus rode his mount hard once he left the crowded streets behind and passed through the southern

258

gate. The stone surface gave him a smooth track for the first mile. Then he guided the beast off the paved road and went overland. Three miles southeast of the Capital, he slowed and walked the mount into a clump of trees.

"Camp stew?" Alerio asked.

Civi reined in, slid off the saddle, and slowly dropped to the ground.

"Food? I can take it or leave it," he answered. Bending down, Civi rubbed his legs. "But if you have a pair of young knees around, I'll take those."

"Are you going to be able to complete the funeral procession?" Alerio questioned while handing the former Optio a bowl of stew.

There were three things you could count on when dealing with a long-time infantryman. Complaints about his knees or hips, his gracious acceptance of any offer of food, and his sense of duty that will drive him to complete any task required of him.

For those reasons, Alerio Sisera did not asked about the mask or permission to fill the bowl. Both actions were guaranteed by the Legion NCO's personality.

"I will not miss sending the son of my General off with the proper portion of tears and wailing," Civi declared. "Or the proper helping of vino and beef when he returns from the dead."

"Let's not get ahead of my rebirth," Alerio warned. "The funeral procession might not turn out to be as premature as you think."

"You could be more confident of your success, if you would let me in on your plan," Civi complained. "I can't help you, sir, if I don't know your tactics."

"For your own safety," Alerio assured him, "it is best if you don't know."

"I got the mask for you," Civi pointed out.

"The what?" Alerio questioned. He walked to the horse and lifted a bag from a rear horn on the saddle. The outline of a death mask was pressed against the material. "Optio Affatus, I have no idea what you are talking about."

***

A group of drunk, loud guests staggered down the steps. A carriage rolled up in front of the Chronicles Humanum Inn and the intoxicated men weaved a path to it.

"Thank you. Thank you for coming," Thomasious Harricus called from the porch. "And please, come again."

Once the party made it into the carriage, the driver snapped his whip and the horses stepped off. Before the lantern hanging from the rear of the transport was fully visible, a man standing in shadows spoke.

"They must have had some juicy gossip for you to allow them to stay so late," the veiled man observed.

Thomasious grabbed his chest in fright and stumbled back. Then he bent forward attempting to see into the shadows.

"Say that again," the proprietor of the inn demanded. "Or begone with you, specter."

"You could offer a ghoul a drink," Alerio teased. He stepped out of the darkness. "I need a favor innkeeper."

When Thomasious did not reply, Alerio took his arm and walked him off the porch and into the great room.

"Now I know you aren't a spirit," the innkeeper declared.

"Because you can see me clearly?" Alerio inquired.

"No. Because you asked for a favor," Thomasious explained. "I can't imagine, even you, would make the long journey from Hades just to pester me with a request."

"It's good to see you too, Master Harricus," Alerio stated.

"How is it that you are alive?" Thomasious asked.

"The Qart Hadasht General only brought one army," Alerio remarked. "Plus, I am fast when I am scared."

"But you arrived almost two weeks after the fleet," the innkeeper pointed out. "Obviously, you are not that fast. But you did return home, and I can't wait for the Clay Ear to announce it."

"That is why I came to see you," Alerio disclosed. "Things are going to happen in the next two days, and it would be best for me, and the Carvilius Maximus households, if I was still dead."

"Can I surmise, if a rumor got out that you survived Sardinia," Thomasious projected, "you could be implicated in some nefarious actions?"

"To be blunt, yes," Alerio confirmed. "But there is something else, Master Harricus."

"You have cut the legs out from under the best story I've had in years," Thomasious complained. "Why not ask for another favor?"

"This one is easier," Alerio promised. "I need a horse."

***

On the streets, the city guardsmen passed and Alerio slipped from the shadows. To be questioned by the guard at this point would get him recognized, ruin his plans, and spoil the purpose of the funeral feast. For his ploy to succeed, he needed everyone associated with his adopted parent's household to be seen at the event by important citizens.

Several blocks and dark alleys later, Alerio scurried across one of the main boulevards. Once out of sight from the throughfare, he jogged along a stone wall until reaching a gate. From behind his back, Alerio pulled the ally of the Golden Valley dagger and pounded on the gate's door.

"We open at daybreak," a voice whispered from inside.

Alerio chuckled. Most managers and owners of businesses, if disturbed in the middle of the night, would raise a fuss. Not so the Golden Valley Trading House. They believed in low tones and privacy, especially in the quiet stillness before dawn.

"Have you no hospitality for an ally?" Alerio inquired.

The gate opened and he slipped through and into a lantern's light. Then he stopped. The tip of a sword floated a hand's width from his nose.

"That's new," Alerio observed while extending a hand with the ally dagger.

"We are practicing long blades this week," Favus explained. The manager of the Golden Valley Trading House used an arm to push aside the blade and take the dagger. "I had thought to hire a weapon's instructor for my apprentices. But the best sword teacher in the Republic died. Would you know anything about that?"

"I know he needs to remain dead," Alerio stated. "And he needs a place to stay, and information."

"Maybe a shave and your hair trimmed?" Favus inquired while directing Alerio towards the building.

"The unkept traveler look, unfortunately, remains for now," Alerio replied

"If you stay here," Favus informed him. "I require your services."

"Odd that you phrased it that way," Alerio countered. "I was thinking the same thing."

***

Late the next morning, steel clashed, and feet shuffled on gravel. Hidden from curious eyes behind the walls of the Golden Valley Trading House, Alerio and an apprentice assassin sparred.

"If you stop there," Alerio instructed. He rested the tip of the sword on a young girl's collar bone. "Your opponent simply leans forward, and in a flick of the wrist, you are mortally wounded."

"But that is wasted energy and additional movement," Ephyra suggested.

"I know they teach short blade work and stealth at the Golden Valley," Alerio began to explain.

The apprentice's eyes flickered to the manager.

"It is allowed, Ephyra," Favus relayed to his student. "Tribune Sisera is the only person who, during the testing, stopped to instruct the younger students. It would be wise to heed his words."

She bowed her head and waited for Alerio to continue.

"A sword's blade is an extension of your fingers," he described. "Unlike your fist which mimics the close in fighting of a dagger. You can duck a hammer fist or lean away from a jab with a short blade. But for long blades, if you retreat just to arm's length, you are still within range of a sword."

Ephyra made a fist with her left hand and performed quick cuts in the air. Then she opened her right hand and did the same drill.

"I can feel the length," she conveyed. "And I can imagine the distance. Thank you, Master."

Favus strolled over from where he had watched his two students learn tips on sword work from Tribune Sisera.

"Run along and do your chores," he ordered the youths. Then to Alerio, he said. "I know you are not hiding here because you have no place to go."

"You are correct," Alerio said as he handed the sword to the manager. "I need information on the Fetial Priest's quarters at the Temple of Jupiter. And a way into Fetial Mattia's apartment."

"Do you want to fulfill the rumor of your death?" Favus questioned. "Because you did not ask about a way out."

"I do have an escape route in mind," Alerio responded. "But I am open to suggestions."

"How much time do I have to think on it?" Favus asked.

"The funeral procession is tomorrow," Alerio responded, "on the Ides of May."

***

Deep in the night, a wagon rolled slowly up Capitoline Hill. The driver urged the horses to keep moving on the steepest part of the road and the passenger held on as the angle changed. At the crest, the road leveled, and the transport rolled easily between the platform at the top of Tarpeian Rock and the driveway to the Temple of Juno. A short way down the road, the wagon passed the Shrine of Minerva. Near the middle of the mount, it rolled to a stop at the entrance to the Temple of Jupiter.

"What have you got?" the sentry asked.

A Temple Guard leaped into the bed and threw back the cover. Then he moved between the cargo items rocking barrels, pushing on amphorae, and tipping boxes.

"Who ordered this?" the sentry inquired.

"A donor and admirer of Jupiter," the driver replied. "It is cargo from the Golden Valley Trading House for the clerics."

"Lucky priests," the Temple Guard remarked. Then to the driver before stepping down, he instructed. "The load is fine. Take it to the refectory."

As the wagon pulled away from the gate, the guard commented to the sentry, "everything from the Golden

265

Valley Trading House is exquisite. But way too expensive for me."

"You could always become a priest," the sentry teased.

"Not me," the Temple Guard pushed back. "I'm happy carrying a spear for a living."

"Still," the sentry countered, "some good cheese and expensive vino sound good."

The wagon rolled through the complex until reaching the dining hall. At an attached building, the driver eased the transport to a stop.

"Help me unload first," the driver said to the passenger.

He took a lantern from the rear of the wagon leaving the cargo bed in moon shadows. Once the lantern was placed over the doorway to the storage building, the two men met at the back of the wagon and started to remove items.

"Are you going to be long?" a Temple Guard asked as he walked out of the night.

"Just a few more items," the driver assured him.

"We want delivery vehicles to be gone before early risers come to worship," the guard warned. "Hurry it up."

"Certainly," the driver acknowledged as he slid a crate to the tailgate.

The men lifted the container. While they carried it to the storeroom, the guard continued his rounds.

Only half the cargo had been stacked in the storage building when the moonlight that guided them across the city faded with the setting of Luna. On his way to the rear of the wagon, the driver leaned over the sideboard and rapped on a box.

In the dark of the night, the top of the box opened, and two youths climbed out. One lifted a section of rope from the floor while the other dropped the sides and flattened the box until it blended with the bed of the wagon.

"Go now. I'll take care of the rest," the driver whispered. "Success on your mission, Tribune Sisera."

"I will take care of Ephyra," Alerio promised.

"My apprentice is a master at stealth," Favus told him. "It is not her I am worried about."

Alerio followed the young girl into a row of hedges. Once they vanished, Favus and his male apprentice finished unloading.

Empty, the wagon rolled from the refectory to the gate of the Jupiter complex.

"Looks good," the guard announced from the back of the wagon. "Move along."

Two men rode the wagon onto the Temple grounds, and two rode it out. In the dark, neither the sentry nor the Temple Guard noticed the size difference. Favus' other apprentice matched Alerio's height by sitting on boards and that was enough to fool Temple security.

The freight wagon would be back at the Golden Valley Trading House before dawn. Favus hoped Ephyra had Tribune Sisera sequestered long before sunrise.

To Alerio's displeasure and discomfort, she had.

Chapter 34 – Funeral Procession

The sun climbed into the sky and the shadows from the temples shrunk. Senator Maximus' social standing required the funeral of his son to be a spectacle. To that end, twelve men clustered at the bottom of the travertine steps. When Senator Spurius Maximus emerged from the Senate Building, the twelve men wailed and extended their arms overhead. Flexing their fingers while waving their limbs as if they were in pain, they gave the impression of the damned rising from the depths of Tartarus.

"I feel the anguish of each of you," Maximus exclaimed, his voice breaking with emotion. He stopped, glanced back, and watched the doors of the Senate Building.

Senators, wealthy solicitors, and secretaries filed out of the building and onto the porch. They wanted to witness the start of the funeral procession. After the initial speech, most would head home to their villas. But a few would tag along with the procession to hear the elegies and lend emotional support to the grieving father.

"My son is gone," Maximus stated. Moaning from the twelve men of the procession accompanied the statement. "He died on a foreign shore, far from those who loved him. Separated even from his beloved Legion comrades. Alone, save for the enemy and their blades that attacked in unfathomable numbers. Although no one witnessed his final battle, anyone familiar with my son knows he fought until the end."

The dozen men cried out in pain as if they were suffering death by a thousand cuts. Maximus paused to allow the emotional tide to wash over him. Once he gathered his composure, he continued.

"My son passed from earth with no coins for the ferryman," the Senator declared. "Today, I will walk the forum and beseech the Gods to aid my son in crossing the river Styx. And plead for their help in guiding him to the Elysian Fields."

The twelve screamed in frustration as if they were the ones denied access to a hero's paradise. The clamor faded and Spurius Maximus raised his face and hands to the sky.

"I will not allow my son to become a homeless spirit, spreading illness and bad luck among the citizens," he promised. "Instead, by every way possible, I will see him in Hades as a benefactor to all who call his name."

The dozen cried out as if entreating the dead son to come to their aid.

"My son was a hero in life as he will be in death," Maximus swore. Muffled cheers rose from the twelve. Almost as if they felt grateful but were too heartbroken to be joyous. The Senator lowered his arms and pointed at the dozen men of the chorus. Then he looked down and acknowledged them. "I require voices to chant to the Gods about my son and let them know of his value."

The dozen men groaned in sadness.

"And who can I count on to represent a hero?" the Senator questioned.

The men in the procession bowed their heads and lowered one of their arms. Twelve hands remained in the air, undoubtably volunteering for the challenge.

Spurius Maximus accepted the help by saying "It is right and just that the best person to speak on my son's behalf is himself. And, praise be, I see Alerio Carvilius Sisera in each of your faces."

Twelve wax masks with the likeness of Alerio elevated to peer at the grieving father. Behind the masks, the men wailed in grief for the dead man whose face they wore.

Maximus marched down the steps and his strides were matched by the dozen mask wearers as he headed towards the forum. Falling in behind the funeral procession, friends of the Senator and curiosity seekers followed. To the rear of them, Belen, the Senator's secretary, and an animal handler with a donkey, brought up the rear. A wooden structure rested on the animal's back and from it hung dozens of wineskins. The vino was a prerequisite as participating in a funeral procession was thirsty work.

***

Alerio shivered. Not because the weather was unnecessarily cold, but the enclosure held dampness. And no warmth from sunlight reached the inside of the cistern.

A splash in the reservoir water alerted him to movement.

"Tribune, are you ready?" Ephyra inquired.

Her voice pitched low. The tone prevented echoes in the enclosed space.

"I'm ready to get out of the water," he whispered in the dark.

"Then I am sorry to disappoint you," the apprentice assassin apologized.

A pluck of water sounded which confused Alerio. Following the noise, the cistern grew quiet until Ephyra resurfaced. He recognized the noise of water running off her.

"Follow me," she instructed. "It's a tight fit but I think you will fit."

"Not to be ungrateful," Alerio remarked. "But you aren't the one who will get stuck under the water and drown. Can't we leave the way we came in?"

"You can," the young assassin agreed. "The exit is just above the courtyard of the Temple Guard's barracks. The choice is yours, Tribune."

"I get your point," Alerio caved. "How small is the pipe?"

"Keep your arms extended and you should be fine," she described. "I've removed the screen to the channel. Are you ready?"

"Yes," he said without enthusiasm.

They ducked underwater and followed the sloping bottom of the tank. At the wall, Alerio located a circular opening in time to feel Ephyra vanish into the tube. With his hands, he measured the gap.

'I always assumed my end would be from a well-placed blade, Goddess Nenia,' Alerio prayed. 'If this is my end, please, oh please, come for me quickly.'

Then he put his palms together, pushed off the bottom, kicked, and squeezed his way into the water pipe.

***

The funeral procession gathered around the Comitium. One of the masked men climbed to the podium, crossed it, and stopped beside a decorative column with bronze fins jutting from the pillar.

"I stood with Consul Gaius Duilius on the decks of warships at the Battle of Mylae," the masked figure boomed as if he was Alerio Sisera. "On the day he won the battle and removed these bronze fins from a Qart Hadasht ram, the General awarded me two Naval Crowns for bravery."

The man masked in the Alerio Sisera facsimile rapped on the fins with his knuckles. And the eleven masks on the street wept in loud sobs at the loss of such a stalwart fellow.

"A brave man who holds the Republic dear is lost in Hades," the man boomed while raising a fist in victory. "Gods, show a hero the way to the Elysian Fields."

Sobbing and shoulder shaking racked the eleven men on the ground. Their suffering mimicked an honorable man who was lost in the wilderness.

The speaker climbed down and joined the other masked men. After everyone consumed a quantity of vino, Senator Maximus marched to the left heading for the Temple of Vesta. The funeral procession trailed out behind him as they followed.

***

Almost as if his hands were millipedes, Alerio used his fingers to walk the sides, propelling himself along the pipe. Moving slowly, he held his breath. But with each passing moment, he became more aware of the tight space, the darkness, and the lack of anywhere to get air.

272

Spots appeared in his vision despite the fact his eyelids were clamped shut. Crawling and resisting the urge to inhale, Alerio fought the panic and continued to wiggle-walk with his fingers while kicking with his legs.

Then two small hands gripped his wrists and yanked him free of the suffocating tube. He popped out but got confused. Thrashing around wildly, Alerio searched for relief.

A hand grabbed the growth on his chin and jerked his head up. His face felt warmth and his lungs filled with air.

"Well, that was entertaining," he gasped.

"Keep your voice down, Tribune," Ephyra warned. "We are in the aeration channel."

Alerio opened his eyes to see the tops of an artificial trench. Not only was the opening wide enough to allow sunlight to reach the water, but he could hear voices.

"Where are we?" he asked.

"Above the second floor of the apartment building for the Priests of Jupiter," Ephyra informed him. "The voices you hear are coming from the rear suite."

"Mattia?" he asked.

"No, sir. Your target lives in the front of the building," she told him.

"How do I get there?" Alerio questioned.

"When I get back, you'll walk," Ephyra stated.

"Just like that? I'll walk?" Alerio asked. "How?"

"I won't know until I get back," the young assassin stated.

Then she climbed to the top of the trench. After pausing for a moment, she vanished over the side.

Alerio could face down an army or fight multiple enemies. In both cases, he had a semblance of control. Laying in a wide-open channel, waiting for a future killer to return, placed him at the mercy of the fates. And to add to his problem, Alerio was hungry.

***

The funeral procession formed a half circle at the steps to the Temple of Vesta. Waiting at the top, a Vestal Virgin stood holding a tray.

"As you do with the eternal flame, I defended the Republic with my gladius," a masked figure informed the Priestess. He talked as he climbed. "My family I held close to my heart. And just as resolutely, I held my blade near my enemy's throat. But now I am tired and need the help of the Goddess of the Hearth."

"Take this cake as a remembrance of the homes and hearths that you defended," the Priestess called to the procession. But she held the tray just out of his reach. Only when the man in the Alerio mask passed her a coin did she hand him the cake. "Know, your life of defending our city is recognized. The Goddess Vesta will help you in the afterlife."

The eleven masked men on the ground wept and called blessings to Vesta. When the man with the cake descended the steps, wineskins were passed around.

Spurius Maximus walked the forum in a northern direction heading to the center of Rome. The funeral procession fell into his wake.

***

274

Ephyra's face appeared over the lip of the rim, and she smiled. Alerio glared at her from the bottom of the pond.

"What is so funny?" he demanded.

"I was beginning to believe, Master, that escorting was harder than a simple kill," she replied.

The easy talk of taking a life from a young person troubled Alerio. Then he thought of his own life and realized the only difference between a swordsman and an assassin was the beginning of the fight. In the end, both freed souls and left bodies to rot.

"Was beginning to believe?" he questioned after shaking off the morose comparison of murderers. "What changed?"

"Follow me," she instructed.

Ephyra disappeared and Alerio climbed to the top of the open tank. He caught sight of her as she vanished into a square access hatch in the building. Below him, a gravel path meandered through hedgerows and grassy expanses with tables. At the tables sat Priests of Jupiter talking or studying scrolls. If any glanced up, he would be discovered. Quickly, Alerio crawled through the opening and fell five feet to the tile floor.

"Ummah," he coughed as the air was driven from his lungs.

"I take it back," Ephyra complained. "Killing is easier than escorting a great lumbering beast."

"That's not very respectful," Alerio pointed out as he scrambled to his feet.

She laughed and for a moment, Ephyra appeared to be just a young girl enjoying a joke.

"If you think that is disrespectful," she cautioned. "Wait until you see the disguise, I found for you."

***

The funeral processions circled a granite mushroom cap. Set in the center of the forum, the marker stood out among the surrounding clay brick pavers.

"I have traveled far in the service of the Republic," a masked man declared as he leaped to the top of the cap. "From here, the navel of the Capital, my journeys have taken me to Greece, Etruria, Sicilia, and Sardinia. Plus, duty has directed me to the north, south, east, and west of our Republic."

Groans of pain, as if the Alerio stand-ins were exhausted and disheartened, carried to the people near the monument. Citizens and slaves traveling by the Umbilicus Urbis paid little attention to the funeral parade. It was an almost everyday occurrence at the zero-mile marker for all roads leading to Rome.

"But in the end, at the terminus of my life's journey," the masked man shouted, "I return to the Capital, to the marker, only in spirit. Terminus, God of Boundaries, guide me in the afterlife."

Calls begging the God to assist Alerio arose from the twelve. The speaker dropped to the pavers, and everyone drank vino. Finally, Spurius Maximus steered the procession to the Temple of Concordia.

***

Bent forward as if ashamed and forbidden to make eye contact, Alerio wheeled the small cart down the hallway. No one he passed looked at the slave in the smock or at the contents of the buckets in the cart.

"I'll meet you downstairs, if you live that long," Ephyra had said before vanishing into an empty apartment. Then from the doorway, the young assassin advised. "Oh no, it stinks. You need to start in here."

And Alerio did. The chamber pot with the Priest's issuing's from last night sat just inside the apartment. Tribune Sisera had been around Legionaries and latrines since he was a young teen. And he recognized that the priest who lived here had stomach and bowel troubles.

'At this rate,' Alerio pondered, 'by the time I reach Mattia's apartment, I'll have a bucket full of merda. Its watery enough, if we can't reach an agreement, I could drown the Fetial Priest in it.'

Finished in that apartment, he rolled the buckets to the hallways, moved to the next suite, and knocked.

***

In the garden of Concordia's Temple, a fountain splashed water onto rocks. The musical sound added to the peaceful environment. And rather than the loud expressions of grief, the twelve mourners of the procession kept their outbursts at a respectful level.

"Goddess of Social Agreement, in all my days, I kept my word and honored all contracts," the masked man explained while passing a priest some coins. "But now I am lost with no direction. I seek only to reach my final place. A location where I can once again fit into a culture and be a good citizen."

"The Goddess Concordia hears your pleas," the priest announced. "She offers her hand and will walk with you for a distance."

Soft sobs accompanied the announcement. The masked men strolled from the garden, left the temple grounds, and headed uphill to the Temple of Saturn.

Masks were lifted and streams of vino flowed as they walked. Honoring the dead as a participant in a funeral procession, required a lot of vino to keep the throats of the mourners from going dry.

***

Alerio rapped on yet another door. It opened and the priest using his foot pushed the pot to the doorway. After dumping the content in one bucket, Alerio used a brush and rinsed the chamber pot before placing it over the threshold. As he wheeled the cart away, a vision of the worst depth of Hades flashed through his mind. What if the terror in the pits of Tartarus was an endless row of night soil pots that required emptying? He shivered at the thought.

As he moved to the next door, Alerio noted two things. A stairwell to the ground floor in the middle of the building, and at the far end of the corridor, a guard. He now had a location for Fetial Mattia. But that presented its own problems. How to get into the apartment unobserved? And out undetected?

At the next residence where someone did not answer, Alerio opened the door and entered the suite. The building served as housing for Priests of Jupiter, and no locks were required. Obviously, for important Priests such as Mattia, a guard fulfilled the duty.

Inside, Alerio searched the walls looking to see if there was a connection between apartments. While he looked for a way into the adjoining unit, he began to the process of emptying and washing the pot. The last thing he wanted was a returning priest challenging him for skipping a residence.

He picked up the pot and an insufferable stink assaulted his nose. In a reflex action, he tossed his head back and squeezed his eyes shut. This priest needed to eat more fruits and vegetables. Then he opened his eyes and saw the means to complete his stealth insertion.

***

The Priests of Saturn came out in twos to greet the funeral procession.

"I plowed, sowed, and reaped so citizens could eat," another of the masked procession declared. "As any good farmer does, I turned the land green under my tillage, and the land gave us back nourishment. Saturn, God of Agriculture, place my feet on the fertile path to my destination."

Spurius Maximus walked down the line of Priests handing each a coin.

"Great Saturn hears you," a cleric assured the speaker. "The path will reveal itself to your spirit to hasten your journey."

The twelve men bellowed their pain so everyone within hearing range could feel the anguish. Then, led by the Senator, the funeral procession left the Temple of Saturn, crossed the toe of Capitoline Hill, and started up the winding road.

Spurius Maximus took an extra long stream of vino. So far, the smaller temples had been cheap. But Saturn was a major God. With Saturnalia a massive winter celebration, the Priest of Saturn knew their importance. It was why they came out in force looking for offerings.

"Alerio, my son," Maximus mumbled so no one could hear, "I hope you know what you are doing. Because this funeral procession is getting expensive."

Act 10

Chapter 35 - The Capitoline Triad

Once beyond the stairwell, Alerio rolled the cart carefully down the hallway. Sticking close to the wall, he remained out of sight from the guard at Mattia's apartment. Two units away from the residence, Alerio rapped on the door and waited for a response. When none came, he opened the door and wheeled his slop and rinse buckets into the apartment.

Just as the others he investigated, the suite consisted of a large outer room with couches and tables. Off a short hallway, an office took up one side and a changing room occupied the other. In the back of the apartment, a large room had a seating area for relaxed reading and a bed.

Not bad living accommodations but not villa nice or near as spacious. After seeing the apartments, Alerio knew why Mattia wanted a country estate at Malagrotta. The last thought brought up a puzzle.

Why did Fetial Priest Mattia think Alerio had stolen from him? If anyone damaged the country estate, it was an angry Colonel Claudius and the Legion. Alerio was nowhere in the vicinity of the fake armory when the Centuries arrived.

***

The climb up Capitoline Hill made the funeral procession thirsty. In front of the gates to the Temple of

Juno, they paused to catch their breath and sip vino. Several took the opportunity to nurse sore knees or hips.

"Love is what I felt when I defended women and children," another imitation Alerio Sisera professed. "And it is what I held in my heart for my Legionaries in the last moments of my life."

He handed the Priest of Juno an offering.

"The Goddess of Love and Marriage recognizes the heart of this man," the cleric declared as he placed the coins in a pouch. "His spirit will travel surrounded by a cloud of love as he journeys through Hades."

The Priest's words brought howling and sobbing from the twelve masked men. After another round of vino, the procession pushed the Senator in the direction of the Shrine of Minerva.

***

Five hundred feet away from the funeral procession, the real Alerio Sisera pulled a table under the access hatch. He mounted the tabletop, reached up, and shoved aside a piece of board. The cover moved easily.

"How convenient the Temple can afford the best construction," Alerio said. "If this was a farmhouse there wouldn't be any crawl space."

Alerio pulled himself up through the hole and onto the ceiling joists. After replacing the cover, the Tribune got on his hands and knees and edged towards Mattia's apartment.

Tedious and slow, he ducked under roof rafters while carefully placing his hands and knees on the ceiling boards. If he misstepped or placed his hand incorrectly, he would fall through the ceiling. Ending up on the floor of the apartment below was not part of the plan.

Alerio reached the next access hole, discounted it, and moved forward. The hatch led to the neighboring unit and not to Alerio's target.

Near the end of the building, he located the last hatch. Shifting to the least uncomfortable position, Alerio slid the cover two fingers off center. Bending down, he put an eye to the opening and studied the room below.

Rather than a bedroom, it was an office and, luckily, an empty workspace. Did the last suite in the building have an entirely different configuration? The thought forced Alerio to hesitate.

Although he was making up the mission as he went, knowledge of the layout gave him confidence. With a different floor plan for Mattia's unit, he needed to think for a moment.

It would do no good dropping in on a conference or a luncheon engagement if there was a separate dining room. But he had come so far and allowed his adopted father to carry out the sham funeral procession, Alerio had no choice. He slid the cover all the way over, dropped his legs through the opening, and lowered himself to the desktop.

"How thoughtful," Alerio offered as his feet touched the desk.

Then from another area, he heard a man chuckle. Except, the voice echoed. None of the apartments Alerio visited were large enough to create an echo. Sneaking to the doorway, he chanced a glance down a hallway.

After double checking, Alerio left the cover of the doorframe and ran down a hallway towards the other room.

***

Possibly due to the emotional overload and aided by the vino, the dozen men wearing Alerio masks were getting sloppier at every stop. By the time they staggered to the Shrine of Minerva, the twelve were howling in full voice.

"Hush," the one selected to speak for Alerio's spirit at the shrine yelled. "I said, shut your stew holes!"

As the speaker was a former Legion NCO with two bad knees and a temper, the other eleven mourners went silent. Then the speaker straightened his shoulders and gazed at the statue of the Goddess who Protects Defenses during War and Promotes Art and Wisdom

"That's better. Now, where was I?" Civi asked.

"You are Alerio Sisera," one of the other mask wearers directed the former Optio. He indicated the other masks looking up at him. "Now say something profound."

"What in Hades name does that mean?" Civi barked. "I've stood on walls defending my men and the Republic. Good men fell and good men took their place. As long as there are brave men, the Republic will survive."

Another man from the procession stepped up and dropped a coin into the hand of the Priest.

"No evil will reach you as you travel the underworld," the cleric stated. "For the Goddess

Minerva will defend her brave Legionary on every step of your journey."

Civi stumbled off the steps and fell into the arms of the other eleven.

"Onward to the Temple of Jupiter," someone bellowed. Then, remembering the reason they were parading around in masks, he called out. "Everybody, cry!"

The twelve wept and sobbed as they migrated to the gate at the Temple of Jupiter.

***

Alerio Sisera sprinted several steps to cover the distance quickly. Then had to shuffle his feet to keep from running by his target. Leaning to the side, he hooked the man sitting on the blanket to slow down. Even with the weight of the priest acting as an anchor, he moved a couple of steps beyond the blanket. Once stationary, Alerio lifted Mattia off the floor.

If the man had been napping or reading it might have been normal. But Fetial Priest Mattia sat on the blanket running his fingers through coins. Almost as if bathing in the gold and silver metal discs.

"What are you doing?" Mattia screeched as coins scattered across the floor.

Unlike the other apartments, the Fetial Priest had expanded his suite to include the neighboring unit. The cavernous space echoed with anything above a whisper.

Alerio held the priest off the ground then dropped him straight to the floor.

Mattia landed hard between Alerio sandals and grunted.

Alerio knew about intimidation and dropping a man from chest height usually elicited a fear response. In that case, they could negotiate. Or the drop got you a fight. And that was fine as well.

"Who are you? What do you want?" Mattia demanded as he raked in coins with an arm. "Surely you don't think you can rob a Fetial Priest at the Temple of Jupiter."

"I am Alerio Carvilius Sisera," Alerio told him. "And we need to talk."

"No. You need to leave and get me the rest of my gold," Mattia ordered. Cocking his head to the side, he mentioned. "I thought you were dead."

"Not yet," Alerio replied while stepping back half a step.

The intimidation had not generated a reaction. And practically straddling an enemy left too many vulnerable spots exposed.

"It doesn't matter," the priest scowled. "As long as that old crow pays up, she can adopt as many dirt diggers as she wants."

"Please do not refer to Lady Carvilius as an old crow," Alerio suggested.

"You cost me a profitable enterprise and three hundred gold coins with your meddling. Because of you the Legion demolished my country estate, dismantled my organization, and took my gold," Mattia accused. "I was only looking to get my coins back. But now that you have invaded my sanctuary, I'll squeeze the crone for another three hundred gold."

"She won't pay you," Alerio informed the Priest.

"Oh, she will pay. Or I will ruin her social standing," he threatened. "And bring down the Senator. And you. I will see you back in the dirt. You crossed the wrong man. I am a Fetial Priest of Jupiter."

"You don't know me," Alerio advised the Fetial Priest. "You claim to speak for the Sky Father. That must give you an amazing feeling of power. But Mattia, the Goddess Nenia speaks through me. And it is not a feeling of power. In fact, the voice of death creates a sensation of hopelessness."

Most people never survived the fang strike. Untrained and unaware, the average person missed the thin tight set of his lips and the tip of his tongue when it flicked as if tasting his victim. Or the hooded eyes and the tension running through the muscles as Mattia's limbs prepared to strike.

As quick as a snake, the priest drew a thin dagger from a wrist sheath. Faster than the blink of an eye, the blade snapped around and stabbed at the inside of Alerio's thigh.

But the thigh shifted. And Alerio's hand shot downward to trap the priest's fist. His other hand captured Mattia's left arm.

"I am known as Death Caller," Alerio exclaimed. The priest looked up in horror at a man who moved quicker than the fang could strike. "A servant of the Goddess of Death, and often her instrument."

Muscling the arms together, Alerio guided the dagger until the blade pointed at Mattia's opposite arm.

"I assume the blade is poisoned," Alerio remarked. Then his eyes became unfocused as if he had drifted off.

When he refocused, Alerio said the most frightening thing the priest had ever heard. "Nenia Dea is looking over my shoulder. I wanted to spare your life and reason with you. But she demands a soul."

The dagger known as the fang stabbed Mattia in the left wrist. The cleric rolled over and foamed at the mouth while his eyes turned red.

"Nasty stuff, priest," Alerio remarked while raking in handfuls of gold coins.

Alerio's coin purse could not hold enough. In a frenzy, he searched and located a larger pouch. Although uncounted, to Alerio it felt like three hundred gold coins. Leaving the rest of the silver and gold strewn on the floor, he tied the bag around his hips, shifted it under the smock, and jogged to the office.

***

At the gate to the complex, a sentry braced for the funeral procession. A couple of times a day some noble died and a procession of death masks staggered from the Shrine of Minerva to the Temple of Jupiter.

"Who seeks to consult with the God of Good Faith?" the sentry demanded.

"I, Alerio Carvilius Sisera, need the guidance of the Sky Father," a mourner replied.

"Then pass through, Alerio Carvilius Sisera," the sentry stated. "The Temple of Jupiter awaits you."

Spurius Maximus led the way into the complex. Behind him, the swaying mass of moaning masks followed. Next came citizens who were just as inebriated as the procession. Belen and the beverage donkey were the last to pass through the gate.

"You deliver the line well," a guard complimented the gate sentry.

"Practice," he disclosed. "I get lots of chances to practice."

"Do you ever count the members in the funeral processions?" the guard inquired.

"By the time the mask wearers reach the last temple of the Capitoline Triad, they are so unsteady, it's almost impossible to get a proper count," the sentry informed the guard. "The Sisera group was more stable than most. Not by much, but none fell or puked. That is a testament to the respect they have for the deceased."

As the procession moved from the gate, the columns on Jupiter's Temple seemed to grow taller. Almost as if when they reached the façade, the pillars would touch the sky and be within arms reach of the Sky Father.

A priest appeared on the steps of the Temple and held out his arms in greeting.

***

The very much alive Alerio Sisera dropped from the hole in the ceiling onto the tabletop. After replacing the cover to the access hatch, he slid the table back to its original place. Then, he emptied the chamber pot, rinsed the container, and wheeled the cart to the doorway.

"You," the guard at Mattia's door shouted.

Alerio froze, thought for a moment, then turned preparing to defend himself. But the man-at-arms had not moved.

"Stay right there," the guard ordered.

When he vanished into the apartment, Alerio picked up the merda bucket and the one with the dirty rinse water and rushed to the steps. At the first floor, he located the exit, and scurried out of the building. Several priests saw him, but no one paid attention to a slave charged with collecting night soil.

Outside, Alerio walked the buckets to a row of bushes. In his haste, the rinse bucket splashed over the rim.

"That stinks," Ephyra offered. Several feet away, her arm waved from a bush, and she invited. "Step into my place of business."

Alerio ducked through the branches and found himself in a hollow cut in the back of the greenery.

"Change into your shirt and trousers," she instructed. After he dressed, the assassin buried the chamber pot smock before handing Alerio a death mask. "Hurry. You don't want to be late for your own funeral."

When they emerged from the bushes, Ephyra slipped her hand into Alerio's and skipped along beside him. They appeared to be an older brother with his younger sister. Together, they turned the corner of the temple and headed for the funeral procession.

Moments later, Mattia's guard charged down the steps.

"Fetial Priest Mattia has been murdered," he declared.

A Sergeant of the Temple Guards ran up and asked, "What happened?"

"I saw the chamber pot slave and told him to wait. He had missed the Priest's apartment," the guard reported. "I went in to get the pot and found Mattia dead."

"What did he look like?" the NCO demanded.

"He is a night soil slave," the guard confessed. "Who remembers them. But I would recognize him if I saw him again."

"Then come on, we'll search the complex."

A handful of Temple Guards burst through the exit. Jogging alongside the temple, they peered into the bushes and stopped when two of them located the slop buckets.

"There's your proof the slave isn't what he seems," the Sergeant announced. "Let's move, he could not have gotten far."

Led by the NCO and Mattia's man-at-arms, the guards ran to the corner of the temple and sprinted around the building.

"What is it?" the Sergeant demanded. His progress had been halted by the arm of Mattia's guard.

"You asked me what the slave looked like," the guard remarked. He pointed at the funeral procession gathered at the steps of the temple. "He resembled them, only unshaven."

"Alright, we have a description," the NCO declared. "Spread out and search every building. I want to question that slave."

The Temple Guards broke into pairs and ran off in different directions. Their search for a slave matching the description of a man's death mask would prove fruitless.

***

"I, Alerio Carvilius Sisera, implore the Sky Father for intervention," a masked man explained as he mounted the steps. He favored his hip which made him limp from riser to riser. "As a Tribune, I died in combat on foreign soil. Alas, I am lost in the underworld with no coins for the ferryman."

"Jupiter, the God of our Republic, knows of your sacrifice," the priest proclaimed after receiving several coins. "Thunder will guide his faithful Legionary through the wilderness to the Elysian Fields."

Howling and sniveling followed the promise of aid from the foremost God. But one masked man did not express his grief. Another interceded by poking him in the ribs.

"Get with the program," he insisted. "We are here to honor Master Sisera."

Then the man staggered away uttering his expression of grief.

"What is the matter?" Ephyra asked while yanking on Alerio's arm. "Don't you feel remorse for the loss of Alerio Sisera?"

Alerio heard her question. But it struck a deeper note than merely a performance. Had he lost Alerio Sisera? Was he doomed to always be Death Caller? A man who preferred to take up a blade and take a life instead of assuming responsibility and solving problems? Although he had no answer, he added sobbing to the sounds of the funeral procession as it felt appropriate.

"Much better," the assassin complimented him.

Senator Maximus waved the masks away and the procession drank and staggered back to the gate. Feeling magnanimous, Spurius pressed a coin into the sentry's hand.

"My son favors infantrymen," he clarified.

"Thank you, Master," the sentry said.

Maximus snorted and scolded himself.

'I must be drunk,' he thought. 'Passing out coins as if there was no tomorrow.'

The funeral procession trekked back by the Shrine of Minerva and passed the Temple of Juno before starting the hike down from Capitoline Hill. As the mourners neared the Temple of Vulcan, a masked man bumped into the Senator.

"Out of respect for my son, I'll forgive you," Spurius Maximus stated. Then he warned. "However, going forward, keep a respectful distance."

The masked mourner took the Senators hands as if pleading for his forgiveness. Then a heavy weight dropped into Maximus' hands causing Spurius to glance down. When he looked up, the masked man had faded back into the crowd.

Drifting to the rear of the procession, Maximus was surprised to find a young girl walking besides the donkey.

"Who is that?" Maximus questioned his secretary.

"I am not sure, Senator," Belen admitted. "She attached herself to our group at the temple. Do you need a beverage?"

"No. I need you to take care of this," Maximus responded.

He walked close to the Greek and handed off a large sack of coins.

"Stash that and don't ask any questions," the Senator ordered. "I need to go and give another priest an offering."

Spurius Maximus fought the urge to smile. His son was safe and somewhere in the procession. It was a good thing he did not recognize Alerio as he might have embraced his adopted son at his own funeral.

The Shrine of Vulcan rested at the bottom of Capitoline Hill. With cries of misery, the procession entered the gates. As was fitting, Vulcan's gates were constructed of iron.

"God of Metalworking, and The Forge, I am Alerio Carvilius Sisera," a mourner exclaimed. "I carried the yield from your forge into battle…"

Chapter 36 – Homecoming

From the Temple of Vulcon, the procession strolled the length of the forum crying and wailing. They reached the Shrine at the Spring of Juturna, and a speaker mounted the steps.

"No longer do I need the health of a living man," he stated. "It is useless for me to partake of the healing powers of the waters. Here, where Castor and Pollux stopped to water their horses after the victory at Lake Regillus, the water is wasted on me. But to honor Alerio Carvilius Sisera, we will each drink of the nymph's water."

Weeping, thirteen masked men dipped cups and drank to the health of the living. After the ceremony, the funeral procession turned towards the Temple of Castor and Pollux. But when they walked from the shrine, only twelve masked mourners approached the temple. One missed the pleas to the Twin Gods of Seamanship and Horsemanship for speed through Hades.

***

Alerio slipped behind the shrine. Once out of sight from the funeral procession, he escaped down an alley.

"Nice mask," Erebus remarked.

The yardman from the Chronicles Humanum Inn offered the reins for a horse as well as his opinion.

"I am a handsome man," Alerio teased, "even in death."

He pulled a hooded cape from the saddle and tied it around his neck. After flipping the cowl over his head, he pulled the mask off and crushed the wax.

"Melt this down for me?" Alerio requested.

"The Clay Ear said every service will cost you," Erebus told him.

"I know," Alerio acknowledged as he leaped onto the horse. "Tell him, he will get the news of my amazing arrival, first."

"I am looking forward to when you get home. And I am glad you survived Sardinia," the yardman said. Then, he swatted the horse's rump.

***

Three miles southeast of the Capital, Alerio guided the horse into a grove of trees. He rode under a limb, reached up, and untied a bundle that hung from a branch.

On the ground, he stripped off the cape, his shirt, trousers, and sandals. They were buried and he dressed in the fisherman's clothing he wore from Sardinia. After tying on his hobnailed boots, he hung the gladius, the

Legion dagger, and a small bundle from his shoulders. Once satisfied he appeared just as he did when he arrived from the island, he took the saddle off the horse.

Moments later, the mount trotted to the northwest in the direction of the Capital while Alerio jogged to the south. It was early afternoon and Tribune Sisera had to cover twelve miles to reach the Legion Camp at Ariccia. Colonel Gaius Claudius would not be there and that was for the best.

***

The sun hovered over the horizon and the Legionary on gate duty watched the approaching figure. From a spec in the distance, the man became clearer until, the sentry could make out a fisherman.

"You are a long way from the sea," the sentry offered.

"I realize that Private, it's eleven miles that way. Good to know you understand direction," Alerio acknowledged. "Now if you will kindly get your Sergeant of The Guard, please."

"What do...?" the Legionary started to challenge.

"I am Tribune Sisera," Alerio barked. "I am tired, foot sore, and hungry. Get your S.O.G., now."

"Yes, sir," the Legionary replied. Then over his shoulder, he shouted. "Optio to the gate."

Heartbeats later, an NCO and five infantrymen raced to the gate.

"Good response time," Alerio observed. "Take me to Colonel Claudius."

"And you are?" the Optio asked.

"Tribune Alerio Sisera," Alerio responded.

"Tribune Sisera?" the NCO gushed. "You are dead, sir."

"That's news to me," Alerio remarked. "But I am hungry and dirty. And I need to report to the Battle Commander."

The sentry and the five-man response team stood open mouthed with their eyes bulging. Here was the staff officer who stood against a Qart Hadasht army and died on Sardinia.

"Sir, the Colonel is in Rome," the Optio explained. "He is attending your funeral feast. We should get you to the city, Tribune."

"I have been traveling for weeks," Alerio pushed back. "I need food, a bath, a shave, a haircut, and proper clothing before I go anywhere. Let alone to a feast. Even if I am the guest of honor."

"Sir, if you'll follow me," the NCO requested. "We'll get the Senior Centurion involved."

"An excellent idea, Optio," Alerio told him. "And I must confess, it's good to be home."

Before moonrise, the entire camp would hear about Tribune Sisera's miraculous return. Having two thousand witnesses to his homecoming, gave credibility to the date. In a Legion camp, if six men witnessed an event, the other two thousand would claim to have seen it as well. Should Alerio need an alibi, they would swear to his state when he arrived.

***

Much later during the evening of the Ides of May, six horses pranced through the streets of the Capital. Although dark, there was enough lantern light to identify five of the riders as Legion cavalry. The sixth rider wore a white tunic with silver Tribune ribbons.

"Was it bad, sir?" the junior cavalry officer asked.

"Not once I escaped," Alerio told him. "Before then, it was as ugly a fight as you can imagine."

"We all heard about you and the ghost Legion," the Centurion stated. "Sir, that took guts and a cool head. I want you to know we are honored to escort you home."

"Thank you," Alerio accepted the compliment. "I need a favor."

"Anything," the Centurion replied.

"My friend runs the Chronicles Humanum Inn," Alerio explained. "Can you go there, have a meal, and tell him about my arrival?"

"Yes, sir, it will be my pleasure," the junior officer agreed.

The riders turned off the boulevard, trotted up a driveway, and reined in at the front door of a city villa.

"Tribune Alerio Sisera," the Centurion announced while saluting. "The forty-fifth Cavalry Century of the Central Legion is honored to have escorted you home."

Alerio returned the salute and responded, "Centurion, it is good to be home. Thank you."

Five figures marched from the Maximus Villa. Two flanked each side of the front door while Civi Affatus marched to Alerio.

"Welcome home, Tribune Sisera," the former NCO greeted him.

"Optio, are you drunk?" Alerio question as he slid off the horse.

"Sir, I was part of your funeral procession," Civi informed him. "It is expected."

"Where are my parents?" Alerio asked while passing the NCO a bundle.

"With the guests at your funeral feast," Civi replied. "Do you want me to announce you?"

"No, no, I'll handle that chore," Alerio informed him. "Put the bundle in the Senator's office for me."

"Yes, sir," Civi declared. Then he saluted and exclaimed. "It's good to have you home, Tribune Sisera."

Alerio marched between the men-at-arms standing at the front door and entered the villa.

***

Servants scurried between attendees. Moving in controlled chaos, they refilled mugs of vino and replaced empty platters of food. The funeral feast sprawled from where the overflow of lesser guests reclined in an adjoining room, all the way into the great room where Spurius Carvilius Maximus and Aquila Carvilius held court.

As with all funeral feasts, the talk earlier had been of the deceased with much expression of sorrow. But the dead can not help a business deal, assist in one's social standing, collect coins for a temple, or create a political faction. By the time Alerio entered the villa, the conversations had moved far afield of the guest of honor. In small groups, people talked of their own needs.

"Hello, Cleric Evandrus," Alerio greeted the Priest of Jupiter from Alban Hills. "Did you get that letter off praising the generosity of Senator Maximus?"

Seeing who was speaking, Evandrus spit a mouthful of vino across a platter of food. An older priest, dressed in a much better robe, noticed the provincial cleric's distress, and looked up.

"What seems to be the problem, Tribune?" Rastellus inquired.

"There is no problem," Alerio replied. "I was just asking about a letter Evandrus was going to send about a gift to the temple from the Senator."

"Oh, that has been handled," Rastellus said dismissively. Obviously, the Priest of Jupiter failed to recognize Alerio from Colonel Claudius' dinner party. "Fetial Priest Mattia is taking a personal interest in the matter. He asked us to distance ourselves from the Carvilius Maximus household."

"Yet here you are eating the Senator's food and spitting out his vino," Alerio remarked. "I guess I'll have to have a talk with this Fetial Priest."

"You, a Tribune, will have a talk with a Fetial Priest?" Rastellus questioned. "I do not believe you have the authority. However, based on your attitude, I am considering a report to your Colonel about your impudence."

"You are in luck, priest," Alerio told him. "I believe Gaius Claudius is in the main room."

"Such audacity and disrespect," Rastellus blustered. As the priest from Jupiter's Temple in Rome spoke, he ignored Evandrus' tugging on his sleeve to get the priest's attention. Finally, a fuming Rastellus demanded. "I will have your name, Tribune."

"Alerio Carvilius Sisera," Alerio stated.

The heads of people in the smaller room jerked in his direction. Before Alerio left to make his entrance into the main feasting room, he placed a hand on Evandrus' shoulder and squeezed.

"I expect another letter thanking the Senator," Alerio instructed. "Maybe, you should note an additional donation of five gold coins from him. Do not disappoint me, again, priest."

Then, Alerio straightened his back and marched into the great room.

***

After the tears, hugs, and greetings, Alerio was given a couch near his adopted parents. He ate while regaling the attendees with the story of the ghost Legion and his daring escape.

He neglected mentioning the five brothers and his regret at their deaths. In the back of his mind, Alerio realized he could no longer be just a swordsman and the instrument of death for the Goddess. He needed to grow into a proper leader.

Early in the morning the last guest left. Aquila gave Alerio a peck and a pat on the cheek before hugging him hard and going off to bed.

"I have something for you, General," Alerio offered. "It's in your office."

They strolled arm in arm down the hallway. Spurius leaned into the younger man as if to assure himself that Alerio was actually present.

"I will tell you, son," Spurius Maximus admitted. "My greatest gift is you being here."

"Beyond what's on your desk," Alerio submitted. "Our issue with Mattia is resolved."

Maximus unrolled the bundle and exposed a sword.

"I carried that all the way from Sardinia for you," Alerio told him.

 Spurius Maximus picked up the Noricum sword, examined it, and tested the balance with several swings.

"A little long for shield work," Maximus observed. Then he changed subjects. "What happened with Mattia?"

"Did you know the Fetial Priest carried a poisoned dagger?" Alerio commented. "He did. And managed to stab himself with it."

"One must be careful with blades," Maximus remarked. "I'll put the pair of swords on the wall with my weapons display."

"What pair of swords?" Alerio questioned.

"While you were missing, a Centurion showed up with another of these," Maximus related. He held up the sword. "After hearing about your last actions, I wasn't in the mood for admiring foreign weapons."

"Centurion Pashalis is a good man," Alerio stated. "Where is the sword he brought you?"

"Behind my door," Maximus told him.

Alerio located the weapon, walked to the center of the room, and motioned for the Senator to join him.

"Strike my sword," Alerio directed. "Hard, make it count."

The Senator as a young man had fought in many battles. At the insistence of his adopted son, he struck with authority. Almost as clear as a bell, the steel blades rang.

"There isn't a notch or a curling of the edges on either blade," Maximus professed after inspecting both swords. "What manner of steel is this?"

"It's made from iron ore mined in a region to the northeast of the Adriatic Sea," Alerio reported. "According to the fisherman who sailed me to a major port, the Noricums are warriors and traders. They live about sixty miles from the sea."

"What does that have to do with these swords?" Maximus inquired.

"We need a boat load of that ore," Alerio advised. "We'll smelt it down, make steel, and forge test swords."

"And if the gladii are this hard," Maximus exclaimed while slashing the sword through the air. "Everyone will want a gladius made from Noric steel."

"Yes, sir," Alerio acknowledged.

"I'll get a merchant ship and an expedition headed that way tomorrow," the Senator promised. Then he got quiet and studied his adopted son. "I am glad you are home."

"It is good to be home," Alerio agreed.

Chapter 37 – Dirt and Identity

The team of stallions blew hard, dropped low, and strained. Above their heads a whip cracked and from behind a harsh voice bellowed.

"Pull, pull," Alerio screamed.

Sweat glistened on his naked torso and his own muscles flexed under the tension. As if his strength could enhance the power of a team of plow horses, Alerio pulled to the limit of his endurance.

Then cracks reverberated in the air as the tree stump's deep root system snapped. Freed from the underground anchors, the stump bumped out of its bed, flew into the air, and cut a furrow in the earth before Alerio could rein in the pair of excited horses.

After unhooking the stump, he walked the stallions to a trough of water.

"A Legionary always takes care of his equipment," former Centurion Accantus observed as he rode up the slope. "Speaking of taking care, you've been at this for a week without a day off."

Alerio looked around, studying the hilly landscape. Fallen trees and stumps lay as if deposited by a flood. Bending down, he scooped up a handful of rich topsoil.

"Aquila Carvilius wants a vineyard," Alerio offered. He allowed the soil to run through his fingers. "The project has been delayed too long."

"You do realize sir, we have crews who can clear and prepare the land," Accantus informed him. "Unless you are doing something else?"

"What do you mean?" Alerio challenged.

"I mean sometimes a man needs hard work to reach a conclusion," Accantus theorized. "Or a good sweat to make a decision."

"And what decision would that be?" Alerio asked.

"If I knew that Master Sisera," Accantus admitted. "I wouldn't be me. I'd be you."

"And who am I?" Alerio inquired, allowing a little of his thinking to drift into the conversation.

"We know who you are," Accantus informed him. "Maybe the proper question is what are you?"

From down on the flat of the farm, a Legion carrier galloped between green fields. He reached the toe of the slope, kneed the horse, and rode effortless up to the pair of men.

"Tribune Sisera?" he asked.

"I'm Sisera," Alerio identified himself.

"Sir, compliments of Colonel Bonum Digessi, Battle Commander for Calatinus Legion South," the messenger announced as he handed Alerio a sealed message. "I am ordered to await your reply."

Alerio scanned the letter then peered up at the mounted courier.

"Please inform Colonel Digessi that I will report to the Legion within the week," Alerio told him. As the courier rode down the hill, Alerio shifted his attention to the farm manager and admitted. "At least I know what I am for the rest of the year."

"And what is that sir?" Accantus inquired.

"A Tribune of the Legion. I've been ordered back to Sicilia," Alerio replied. He folded the letter and shoved it into a pouch. Then almost sadly, he relinquished his part in preparing the land for Aquila's vineyard. "Now Accantus, you can bring up your crews."

The End

A note from J. Clifton Slater

Congratulations, you have read through 13 books in the Clay Warrior Stories series. We have taken Alerio from an undersized lad to the son of a wealthy and powerful man and a confident staff officer of the Legion. Some may not realize it, but those who sent me ideas about Tribune Sisera's life will recognize their input in his development. While the historical events are set in a timeline, comments in your e-mails help shape Alerio's personal story.

In case you were wondering, the sausage quote that Alerio utters in the café was from book 18 of 'Homer's the Odyssey'. And the Latin word for sausage was botulus. As in botulism, which tells us that not all butchers in ancient Rome were proficient in the making of cured meat products.

Coins varied in value, and I used the 25 Silver equals one Gold with 10 Bronze coins for one Silver exchange rate. The names of the coins and exchange value varied over the centuries. As I did with military ranks, the monetary names were simplified.

The marshes at Ostia, on both sides of the Tiber River, were salt producing areas. From roughly 450 B.C. through the 19th Century, the drying ponds supplied sea salt to the population of Rome. An important mineral, salt preserved meats, was used in offerings to the deities, in the leather tanning process, in preparations of medicine, and for flavoring food.

Around 658 B.C., the Kingdom of Rome and the city of Alba Longa were preparing to go to war. Rather than armies fighting, which would weaken both cities, the third King of Rome, Tullus Hostilius, and the King of Alba Longa decided to have champions fight and settle the dispute. Rome's fighters were the Horatii triplets, and their adversaries were the three Curiatii brothers.

It was such a good story, I had to use parts of it in *Death Caller*. May the ancient historian, Livy, forgive me.

The location where I placed Mattia's fake armory was chosen for its modern history. For 30 years Malagrotta, Italy was the trash dump for Rome. In 2013, the dump at Malagrotta failed to meet European Union Standards and was closed. But in 2020, the overflowing trash from the eternal city forced politicians to talk about opening another rubbish dump in the same area.

Fantasy writers love to make up rare steels to use for their edged weapons. Thankfully for me, as a historical adventure writer, I did not have to invent a unique steel. Noricum was a region defined by modern Austria and part of Slovenia. Celtic Tribes settled the area and by the 2nd Century B.C. the area was known for iron ore that created Noric Steel. By the 1st Century B.C., the steel was coveted by the Legions for its hardness and quality. Beyond iron ore rich in natural magnesium (the secret ingredient), Noricum provided a plant called Saliunca, meaning the Wild. A relative to lavender it grew in abundance and was used as a perfume according to Historian Pliny the Elder.

I found the dichotomy of steel versus flowers to be a fun contrast. Thus, I used Noricum mercenaries as bodyguards for the return of Admiral Hannibal Gisco to introduce Noric steel. After surviving his court martial, the government of Carthage assigned Gisco to Sardinia where he met his fate. The historical details are few, leaving the scenes of his end to my imagination. Which is pure joy for a historical fiction writer.

Later, after the victory at Sulci, General/Consul Sulpicius Paterculus Legion was defeated by General Hanno. Although Rome failed to remove Carthage from Sardinia, the loss of ships-of-war ended the immediate threat from the island.

And a final note. In ancient Rome to lament the dead of a wealthy or famous person, a funeral procession was organized. Either paid performers or household personnel were given wax masks and instructed to march through Rome crying and wailing about the loss. I found few specifics about the processions in my research. But as the ancient Romans were religious and drank vino, I imagined the funeral processions drank, visited temples, and asked the Gods and Goddesses for blessings for the deceased.

Alerio's funeral procession touched on all the temples that existed around the forum. Later years would see more temples added to the location. And during the Imperial era, the forum was moved to make room for even more temples and buildings. But for Alerio's funeral, the procession stopped at all the temples that were available between Velian Ridge to the southeast and the top of Capitoline Hill to the northwest in 258 B.C.

If you have comments or thoughts, please email me: **GalacticCouncilRealm@gmail.com**

Sign up for my newsletter and read blogs about ancient Rome on my website.

www.JCliftonSlater.com

Until we meet again, Alerio Carvilius Sisera and I wish you good health and offer you a hardy, Rah!

I write military adventure both future and ancient.
Books by J. Clifton Slater

Historical Adventure – *Clay Warrior Stories series*

#1 Clay Legionary   #2 Spilled Blood

#3 Bloody Water   #4 Reluctant Siege

#5 Brutal Diplomacy   #6 Fortune Reigns

#7 Fatal Obligation   #8 Infinite Courage

#9 Deceptive Valor   #10 Neptune's Fury

#11 Unjust Sacrifice   #12 Muted Implications

#13 Death Caller   #14 Rome's Tribune

#15 Deranged Sovereignty

#16 Uncertain Honor   #17 Tribune's Oath

#18 Savage Birthright   #19 Abject Authority

Novels of the 2nd Punic War – A Legion Archer series

#1 Journey from Exile   #2 Pity the Rebellious

#3 Heritage of Threat   #4 A Legion Legacy

Military Science Fiction – *Call Sign Warlock series*

#1 Op File Revenge   #2 Op File Treason

#3 Op File Sanction

Military Science Fiction – *Galactic Council Realm series*

#1 On Station   #2 On Duty

#3 On Guard   #4 On Point